Dead or Alive

ALSO BY BILL KITSON

DEAD OR ALIVE

BILL KITSON

DI Mike Nash Book 18

JOFFE BOOKS

Joffe Books, London
www.joffebooks.com

First published in Great Britain in 2025

Cover art by Nick Castle

ISBN: 978-1-80573-096-5

For Wen and Dave,

with grateful thanks for a wonderful birthday in Athens.

PROLOGUE

Late 1990s — Spain

The weather was hot, more so than usual, even for one of Europe's favourite suntraps. The couple, who had taken advantage of a rare chance to be alone together, were lying on a king-sized bed, gasping and sweating, not only from the high temperature, but also the intense and prolonged physical activity they had just been enjoying.

Once she had recovered her breath sufficiently to speak, the young woman asked her companion, 'How can we change this situation? We've waited for so long, and I want us to be together.'

'I've been thinking about that, and I've come up with an idea. It needs to be planned with extreme care, right down to the last, most minute detail. It could take a long time to achieve but if my idea works, we'll be free and then we can make a fresh start. In order to achieve that, two people will have to die. Not only that, but the manner of their deaths must be made to look completely accidental, so there's no chance of anyone asking awkward questions. It also needs to be done with extreme violence, so there is no possibility of the victims of the "accident"' — he made an apostrophe air sign with his fingers — 'being identified.'

She was mystified, not for the first time, by the way his mind worked, which was part of what had attracted her to him — that and his undoubted prowess as a lover. Her inability to follow his thought processes was emphasized by his answer to her next question.

'So, who must die?'

'I thought you'd have already guessed.' He smiled. 'The two people who must die are you and me.' He grinned.

She sat up in the bed and stared at him, her mouth open wide with astonishment. Eventually, when she had recovered from the shock, she asked, 'Is this some form of suicide pact you're proposing? If so, you can count me out. Or have you joined some weird religious cult where only true believers can go to heaven by taking their own lives?'

He laughed so much it was a long time before he could speak. 'Let me explain what I have in mind . . .'

CHAPTER ONE

Present day

The room, a large oblong space, was cold and uninviting, sterile almost. This was by no means accidental, although nobody in their right mind would wish to enter such a place voluntarily. What little illumination there was came from two opaque windows set high in the wall with bars to the outside.

There were three occupants within the cheerless room. Two of them were seated against the wall, their hands tied, cowering together in terror at the lethal weapon the third person was pointing at them.

He spoke, delivering what they knew was the death sentence he had been instructed to repeat. 'You have wilfully disobeyed your employer, the person who provided you with an affluent lifestyle. Now you must pay for your misbehaviour.'

By way of punctuation, he fired the handgun twice. Then he watched dispassionately as his victims slid sideways onto the floor, bleeding copiously from the head wounds he had inflicted.

Having checked they were dead, the killer smiled as he manhandled the corpses, ensuring they were as far apart as possible. The stench of decaying flesh, intensified by close proximity, could trigger alarm and premature discovery from someone entering the chamber. Such an event was now unlikely to happen, but he wasn't prepared to take the chance. His client was paying a large sum for him to carry out the execution, and demanded a flawless job.

Normally, his only other concern would have been someone hearing the sound of the gunshots. If what he had been told about this place was accurate, there was no chance of that occurring. As he headed for the door, he removed the silencer from his pistol. He exited, locking the heavy door behind him.

Vincent smiled. He would be well rewarded for what had been a simple task, and he knew his client had further work for him. Setting up a minor celebrity for attempted murder would be even easier. He turned to walk away, reflecting that there could be few more appropriate places to leave bodies than within the cabinets of a disused mortuary.

* * *

Several months later, two teenagers met up outside a large abandoned building. Earlier that day at school, Charlie had met his girlfriend and asked, 'You busy tonight?'

'Not 'specially. Why?'

'I've got some weed.'

Kaz looked surprised. 'You come into money without letting on?'

'Nah, I nicked it from my brother's stash. He's that wasted he'll never notice. I'll bring a blanket so we can make a night of it.'

His accompanying gesture had made her smile. She'd already guessed what he had in mind. The cannabis would be good, but the sex would be even better.

Now, as she stared at the old building, she was wondering how they would get inside.

'I don't reckon anyone will worry if another window gets put in, do you?' He grinned, before adding, 'Once it's broken, I'll get my leg over, hop inside and help you. Then I'll get my leg over again.'

She smiled, the darkness masking her excitement.

Across the ring road, a young mother was nursing her son, trying to comfort him, as she stared out of the window. A slight movement in her peripheral vision caught her attention. She spotted the teenagers, and heard the sound of breaking glass. Was this vandalism, or something more serious? She waited a few seconds then picked up her mobile.

* * *

When Charlie heard the approaching siren, he tried to reassure Kaz. 'It'll be nowt to do with us, probably some drunks having a set-to at one of the pubs.' The volume began to increase dramatically as the emergency vehicle drew near.

Kaz was panicking. 'It's coming here. We'd better scarper. Ditch the weed — we don't want to get caught in possession.'

Charlie tossed the cannabis wrap into the far corner of the room, flinging the roll-up they had been sharing after it. Neither of them noticed the stack of papers and cardboard boxes. As they vanished into the night, several pieces of paper, disturbed by the draught, slid from the pile and came to rest on top of the burning spliff.

The patrol car drew to a halt and an officer approached the broken window. He smelled smoke and seconds later saw the flicker of flames. He retreated, summoning assistance from the fire service.

By the time the first tender arrived, the whole of the ground floor was ablaze. The roaring sound of the flames was accompanied by loud splintering crashes from falling timber and breaking glass. Minutes later, the first-floor windows were brightly illuminated, as if someone had switched on a bank of lights.

* * *

As the fire crew directed their jets of water towards the inferno, a second and third engine arrived. The chief fire officer, Doug Curran, pulled up in his gaudily decorated car and began assessing the situation. He approached the police officers and issued instructions. 'We need backup. The ring road and market place must be sealed off to both vehicular and pedestrian traffic. The cordon will probably have to stay in place until tomorrow.' He didn't add 'at the earliest', but they had already guessed that.

'What about the building?' one of the policemen asked.

'I'm afraid that's already gone beyond the point of no return. The fire has got too strong a hold, and the roof's about to give way. The structure will soon be unsafe. This is an old building, and there's a lot of dried-out timber, which is why the fire has spread so rapidly. I just hope whoever was inside managed to escape — otherwise they'll have been cremated by now.

'One good thing,' Curran added, 'if the building had still been in its original use, the number of potential casualties would have been horrendous. It doesn't even bear thinking about. Evacuating dozens of bed-ridden patients from hospital wards in the middle of a blazing inferno would have been a nightmare.' He shook his head. 'I'm so glad the new hospital was built.'

* * *

The following morning, DI Mike Nash was driving to work in Helmsdale, his car radio tuned to the local station. He whistled with surprise as he listened to the news bulletin, the presenter's tone grave as he imparted what little detail had emerged so far about the shocking fire.

'Netherdale town centre remains sealed off to both vehicular and pedestrian traffic this morning, as the fire which destroyed the disused cottage hospital continues to rage, despite the efforts of the local brigade, backed up by units from other areas. The building has been used by several tenants since it was decommissioned, but we believe the property was vacant before the fire broke out.'

The presenter's tone became even more sombre as he added the grim footnote, '*Fears are growing for the safety of two young people who were seen entering the premises shortly before the fire started. Eyewitness accounts said the flames engulfed the building within minutes.*'

Nash reached the police station, noticing the empty bays where fire engines were normally parked in the multi-purpose building which housed all three emergency services. He paused at reception for a word with their uniform sergeant, Steve Meadows, before heading upstairs to the CID suite. He entered the room to find DC Adil Hassan staring at papers on his desk, trying to hide his smile, as DC Viv Pearce was receiving a dressing-down from Nash's second in command, DS Clara Mironova.

'Sometimes you're a really sick bastard, Viv,' Clara told the tall Antiguan.

'We all know that,' Nash commented. 'So what's provoked your outburst?'

'We were discussing the fire at the old infirmary,' Clara explained, 'and this twisted son of a bitch said something totally inappropriate.'

'And that was?'

'He said if the people that broke in were still inside' — she glared at Viv — 'they'd have gone straight down to the mortuary without need of a lift.'

'Definitely twisted,' Nash agreed. 'But I fail to see the relevance.'

'Apparently, Tom Pratt told Viv that the basement of the cottage hospital was the original mortuary.'

'That must have been a while ago. I don't remember that building being in use as a medical facility.'

'Tom says the new hospital was opened around twenty years ago,' Pearce said.

'Well, Tom would know better than anyone.'

Tom Pratt, formerly a detective superintendent within the force, now acted as a civilian support officer, a role he had taken up after his retirement from active duty. Having lived and worked in the area all his life, Tom was a fount of local knowledge.

Whatever had happened inside the disused building, Nash couldn't see any way it might involve him and his team in a professional capacity. It wasn't long before he was compelled to revise that opinion — and to do so drastically.

CHAPTER TWO

Immediate demolition work and site clearance at the ruined hospital building was a necessity as it was declared a danger to the public. Work had been in process for almost a fortnight. During that time, what remained of the building's outer shell had been crushed. The ring road had been closed, to give access for the plant and equipment and the constant stream of wagons needed for removal. The market place was accessible only by a one-way system controlled by temporary traffic lights. This had caused considerable inconvenience to vehicles, plus shoppers, retail outlets and the stallholders who displayed their wares during market day. Despite their many vocal complaints, the work of making the ruin safe was deemed to be a greater priority.

The operator manoeuvring the JCB excavator was concentrating his machine's efforts on removing rubble from the basement. He had been at work for several hours and was about to knock off for lunch. The excavator inched closer — one more load and he would switch the engine off. He began scooping up the debris, the bucket crashing into the metal cabinets along one wall, causing the doors to swing open. He raised the boom to load the waiting truck. He had reached the halfway stage when he killed the engine, staring in horror at the contents of the bucket.

* * *

In Helmsdale, Nash was reading reports of the weekend's incidents, none of which were particularly serious, and somewhat less than enthralling: a couple of drink-fuelled fights, plus one failed shoplifting were hardly likely to appear on *Crimewatch*. The traffic division had stopped a drunk driver, and later followed a stolen car and successfully arrested the thief. He had just finished reading when his internal phone rang. Nash listened to the news imparted by Sergeant Meadows and then replied, 'OK, Steve, we're on our way. Will you inform Mexican Pete? At least this time he'll be on home ground.' Nash grinned as he envisaged the reaction from their Spanish pathologist, Professor Ramirez, known throughout the force as Mexican Pete — an insider joke, based on the *Ballard of Eskimo Nell*.

Nash wandered into the main office, glanced at Viv Pearce, and asked DS Mironova, 'Do you remember his bad mortuary gag?'

Clara blinked with surprise. She nodded.

'Maybe this will teach him to keep those remarks to himself. One of the crew demolishing the old hospital in Netherdale has just unearthed human remains with his JCB. Better tell Viv that JCB doesn't stand for Just Contains Body.'

'Now I'm not sure who has the sicker sense of humour, you or Viv,' Clara retorted as she picked her jacket up.

'Adil,' Nash said, 'ring down to reception and ask Steve to arrange a pool car, will you? I'm not taking mine near a building site.' Nash's Range Rover was his pride and joy.

* * *

It took a while for Nash and Clara to penetrate the cordon placed around the building. Having donned protective suits

10

and headgear, they approached the inner line, marked by blue-and-white incident tape. A uniformed officer, wearing a hard hat in place of a helmet, greeted them. Nash asked the man to point out the person who had found the body.

After listening to the JCB operator's short account, which revealed little they didn't already know, the detectives headed into the no-go area to view the corpse. The sound of approaching vehicles caused Clara to glance back.

'Mexican Pete and his crew have arrived,' she told Nash.

Professor Ramirez had been their pathologist for many years, and was wont to tease Nash by pointing out the number of bodies he'd been called on to inspect, and the remote locations where some of those corpses had been found. On this occasion, however, he was in strictly business mode.

As they watched the pathologist conduct a preliminary examination of the remains, Mironova speculated as to the identity of the victim. 'I guess this is one of the people seen entering the building shortly before the fire broke out.'

'I'm not prepared to jump to any conclusions,' Nash replied. 'Let's leave it to the experts.'

'It can't be anyone else, surely?' Mironova protested. 'This place has been empty for ages. If that person was trapped by the fire, the body would have fallen into the basement once the floor had been destroyed.'

'It seems a rational theory, but it could equally be someone who was homeless and had bedded down there for the night. However, it looks as if we're about to get a professional opinion.' Nash gestured towards Ramirez, who was striding towards them.

As he got nearer, Clara noticed the pathologist's puzzled expression. She got no enlightenment from what little he told them. 'The only thing I can tell you at this stage is the corpse is definitely that of a male. Further than that, I'm not prepared to say until I have conducted a post-mortem. That will be tomorrow morning at eight thirty.' He nodded farewell and went across to his assistants, instructing them to continue the forensic examination of the body and the scene.

'What's up with him?' Clara asked. 'No caustic comments, no insults. Have you upset him?'

'Maybe he's having an off day.' Nash shrugged.

* * *

It was lunchtime when Nash arrived at Helmsdale, having been the attending officer at the post-mortem. On entering the CID suite he went straight through to his office, signalling Mironova to follow him. Once inside, he closed the door and pressed a short code on his mobile. 'Good morning, Jackie,' he began, which told Clara he was speaking to Detective Superintendent Fleming, his immediate superior. 'I'm calling about the body recovered from the old cottage hospital building. One thing for certain, this wasn't one of the people seen entering the premises just before the fire. Mexican Pete reckons this man's been dead for several months. He's also established cause of death, which was certainly not what we expected. There was no sign of burns and no evidence of smoke inhalation, having being concealed inside the steel mortuary cabinet. Plus, the body was in an early stage of decomposition. He did comment that had the cabinet been switched on, decomposition would have been much less.'

'I take it the professor was in good humour?'

'Almost,' Nash replied. 'The victim had suffered a single gunshot wound to the head, execution style. Because of the extensive damage it caused to the skull, Mexican Pete believes he was shot at close range. That makes it murder.'

'So, where do we go from here?' Fleming asked.

'I've absolutely no idea.'

* * *

The hiatus following the grim discovery was extended by the knowledge that the corpse was that of a murder victim. This was to allow a CSI team to extend the search area immediately surrounding the place where the JCB had unearthed the body. Only when they had finished work was the incident tape removed and the demolition crew given the all-clear to resume operations, by which time it was the weekend, so work began on the following Monday.

The JCB operator was instructed by the site manager, a man you didn't argue with, to make up for lost time. After an hour he had made significant inroads into clearing the jumbled mess of concrete, wood and steel in the basement. The task was overseen by his foreman, who was standing alongside to supervise. He instructed the operator to get the rest of the mortuary cabinets removed. As the driver raised the JCB boom containing a mass of broken steel, his boss was signalling furiously for him to stop.

Once he had killed the engine, the driver climbed out of the cab in response to the foreman's gesture. 'What's wrong?'

The foreman didn't reply, merely waving his hand for his colleague to join him as he stared into the trench. The digger driver walked carefully across the rubble-strewn ground to where his superior was standing. He glanced down into the jumble of masonry, concrete, metal and charred timber, before taking an involuntary step back. 'I don't fucking believe it,' he muttered.

* * *

Nash, usually the first to arrive, was late, one of the penalties of recent parenthood — his infant daughter, Lucy, having had a restless night. He had overslept, and by the time he had breakfasted and walked the dog, he was later than expected. This usually caused him no concern; his team of detectives could manage without him under Clara's direction. He was surprised, therefore, to find his DS and DC Adil Hassan standing in reception talking to Steve Meadows. Obviously, Nash thought, something had happened. And to judge by their expressions, it wasn't going to be good news.

Clara stepped forward and told him, 'We were just about to phone you. We have to go back to the cottage hospital.

13

The demolition crew resumed work there this morning and they've unearthed another body.'

Nash stared at his deputy in disbelief. 'Another body in the same location? Please tell me you're joking.'

'No, Mike. This is certainly no laughing matter.'

Five minutes later, the trio of detectives set off, but by the time they arrived at the demolition site, their pathologist was already at the scene. 'You're late,' he told Nash with mock severity. 'I hope you have a good excuse.'

'I do apologise, Professor, but the blame rests squarely with my daughter — teething. I didn't appreciate how much you valued my presence on these occasions. Have you inspected the body?'

'I have conducted a preliminary examination, and I can tell you the cause of death appears to be identical to the previous victim. This time it's female.' Ramirez gestured to the half-completed demolition work. 'I'm of the opinion that both bodies were in the storage cabinets. It might be worth getting some cadaver dogs in to check the rest of this site over before work resumes. It would appear the CSI team have lost their sense of smell,' he added caustically. 'And an excavator isn't exactly the most delicate of instruments when it comes to dealing with corpses.'

'I'll ensure it's dealt with, Professor.'

As a parting shot, Ramirez told Nash, 'It was a good idea closing this place down. The mortuary here would have been unable to cope with the number of bodies you collect.'

'He's feeling better,' Clara commented as he walked away.

CHAPTER THREE

The news of the fresh discovery shocked Superintendent Fleming, who was in charge of the area's detective force while Chief Constable Ruth Edwards was on annual leave. Fleming agreed with their pathologist's suggestion and promised to update Nash once arrangements had been made. 'I can't think of anything else we should do at this juncture,' she said.

'Neither can I,' Nash replied. 'At some point we ought to get the media involved, but I think that should wait until we're certain this place has yielded all its secrets. Only then will we know exactly what we're up against and we can provide the press with a complete picture, not merely half a tale. Happily, they're only aware two bodies have been discovered at present.'

When Nash had attended the second post-mortem, Professor Ramirez told him, 'I can give you very little information because of the condition of the remains. What I am able to tell you is that the bodies are of one male and one female, somewhere in their late thirties or early forties. Both were killed by a single gunshot to the head. I have retrieved the bullets, and sent them for ballistic testing. I have also taken DNA samples — hopefully they will provide us with identification.'

With that, and knowing the cadaver dogs had found nothing more, Nash had to be content.

The knowledge there were no further corpses in the rest of the ruined building enabled Ruth Edwards, now back from holiday, to call a media conference, which she insisted Jackie Fleming and Mike Nash should attend. The resulting headlines, as Nash told Clara after returning to Helmsdale, would cause a sensation locally and nationally, possibly even further. He couldn't have guessed how far the repercussions of the announcement would reach.

* * *

Ten days before the discovery of the bodies, Nash and Clara had walked into CID and asked Viv where Adil was.

'Sergeant Meadows got a phone call from a Mrs Burrows, who lives on Fairway Drive alongside Netherdale Golf Course. He's gone to speak to her.'

'I'd say Fairway Drive was a very appropriate name for a road near a golf course. What's her problem, somebody's bad driving?' Clara asked.

Nash shook his head at Clara's dreadful joke, but any semblance of humour soon vanished when Viv revealed more. 'The lady in question, a woman in her seventies, was persuaded to phone us by her niece. The old lady got a cold-caller knocking on her door a few weeks ago, a man purporting to be a builder. He asked if she needed any work doing, and as it happened, Mrs B had been planning to have a conservatory built. She'd received a quote for the building itself, but needed a concrete base laying. The guy seemed genuine enough and promised he could start work as soon as the weather was warmer. He supplied a written estimate and told her that because he was self-employed and hadn't been in business long, he'd need the money for the materials up front. She handed over three thousand pounds. That was the last she saw of him. The mobile number he gave her was out of service. Adil's gone to take a statement.'

'I was thinking about the address where Mrs Burrows lives. From what I can recall, it's known locally as "bungalow land", which probably means there will be quite a number of elderly or retired residents. People who would be vulnerable to scams such as this,' Clara said.

'Wait until Adil's back,' Nash had told her. 'See what you think and ask the *Netherdale Gazette* to run a piece with a warning, if necessary.'

Within days of the newspaper being issued, reports came in of two further incidents. The first was from a gentleman living on the outskirts of Bishopton, and it referred to some roofing work. Once again, he had been asked to pay up front for the building materials. Proof this was the same offender came via the mobile number he'd provided. The company name "Andy Mann, Your Handyman" gave an address on an industrial estate in York.

'There is no business with that name,' Hassan told his colleagues.

'It looks as if we've hit a brick wall,' Pearce suggested.

'Viv, I've told you before, Mike's in charge of the bad puns round here,' Clara told him.

Nash snorted. 'May I remind you, Clara, that it was only recently you were joking about fairways and driving?'

* * *

The next complaint was even closer, being on the outskirts of Helmsdale. On this occasion, the victims had been considering having their driveway replaced with block paving.

Within minutes of arriving, as Adil listened to the elderly couple's tale of woe, he spotted something on the wall of a house directly opposite. Once he had their statement, he asked, 'Do you know the people who live across the road?' He pointed to the house in question.

'Yes, Fred and I are both members of Netherdale Horticultural Society. The missus and Fred's wife also go to bingo once a week, although they never win much. They've just got back from a fortnight in France, so I've been tending his plants for him. Why are you asking about him?'

'I wondered if the CCTV camera he's got mounted on his house wall is operational.'

'I'm sure it will be. They were burgled while they were abroad the year before last. That's why he had it installed.'

'In that case, I must have a word with Fred and see what it reveals.'

When Adil called Nash, his excitement was obvious. 'I've got an excellent image of the vehicle, including the reg number. The man is in profile. He had one hand raised, shielding his face as if he was aware of the camera. I think the other victims would be able to confirm it's the same person, if only by the pickup he was driving.'

Adil set off back to the office to be met with disappointing news. 'It's a cloned vehicle. The genuine article belongs to a construction company in Bristol,' Viv paused to let this information sink in. Of course it changed things, knowing that the registration plate had been forged. 'Their pickup never travels outside the West Country. However,' he added on a more optimistic note, 'I've loaded it onto the ANPR. As soon as it hits one of our cameras, we'll be in business.'

However, the DCs reckoned without the offender's determination to avoid capture by using multiple registration numbers cloned from other vehicles.

* * *

As more cases came to light, sparked by the press coverage, Nash suggested they should broaden the scope of their enquiries by contacting neighbouring forces. 'The way he went about defrauding his victims suggests he has previous experience. I think it's highly unlikely he's suddenly decided on this scheme. I'll have a word with Jackie — she carries more weight than me.'

It didn't take long for Jackie's email canvassing to provoke positive responses. A week after they initiated the strategy, she arrived in Helmsdale bearing a large box.

'These are the case files for offences committed outside our area. There are nineteen in total over a period of twelve months, prior to him starting work around here. Assuming these were committed by the same person, he has reaped a reward totalling somewhere in the region of over a hundred thousand pounds. In view of what we have learned so far, the chief has asked me to widen the scope of our enquiries. I'll keep you up to date with any further developments.'

Once Fleming had left, Nash and his colleagues began studying this new information. 'I'm willing to bet there will be further instances in the extended areas Jackie's contacting, with the exception of inner cities,' Nash commented.

'What leads you to that line of thinking, Mike?' Clara asked.

'I've noticed a distinct similarity in the addresses where the victims live. From my knowledge of the various regions, I'm fairly certain they are all in semi-rural locations, villages and market towns. Again, the victims' details all seem to be similar. In other words, this criminal has targeted areas with a large percentage of elderly or retired people.'

'It's all very well knowing we're only chasing one criminal, but apart from a photo that could be a match to thousands of men, we know nothing more about him than we did on day one,' Hassan commented.

'That's true, and it's extremely frustrating,' Nash agreed. 'What we really need is a stroke of luck, or for this perpetrator to make a mistake. Without that, it's difficult to see a way forward.'

He could tell how depressed the team members were by their inability to make progress. All that was to change rapidly, however, and in this instance it owed nothing to skilled detective work, nor was it down to the criminal making an elementary mistake. It was purely down to the actions of someone with an axe to grind.

CHAPTER FOUR

Jolene Fraser was serving ten years' imprisonment for attempted murder. The pop group she fronted, known as Jo-Jo and the Tykes, were on the road to stardom. Much of their success was down to the young guitarist, lead singer and composer. Her name, Jolene — given as homage to the renowned country singer, Dolly Parton — plus the band's origins in Yorkshire gave rise to the band's unusual name.

Jolene, or Jo-Jo, was twenty-eight years old when her world, and that of the group came crashing down. Accused of a major crime, she had already been tried and convicted by the media before she appeared in court — a day she would always remember.

'How do you find the defendant, guilty or not guilty?'
'Guilty, your honour.'
'And is that the verdict of you all?'
'It is indeed.'

After the judge delivered his sentence, the courtroom had begun to empty. As she was being led away by prison officers, she had glanced towards the public gallery. A man was standing at the end of the row of seats, staring fixedly in her direction. Jolene had become used to admiring glances from men, both on stage and off, but somehow his expression seemed different. In other circumstances she'd have been attracted by his good looks, his dark hair, blue eyes and neatly trimmed beard, but by the time she'd entered the cell that was to be her home for the foreseeable future, she had forgotten all about him.

In Blackwell Women's Prison, Jolene made few friends. For some reason she soon became unpopular with several of the other inmates. At first, she put their spite down to envy of her fame and success. Several attempts were made to harm her, but Jolene Fraser knew how to stand up for herself. The martial arts course her stepfather had insisted she attend proved useful on three separate occasions. Her assailants ended up in the prison hospital, with severe injuries they refused to explain. After that, Jolene was given a wide berth, which suited her fine.

Jolene did make one friend, the woman who shared the same cell, albeit briefly. After the woman was released, Jolene thought that would be the last she saw or heard of her. She was surprised when she received a letter from the woman which contained an introduction to someone who might have an interesting proposal to put to her. *He came to see me, and asked me to write. He's certain you're innocent,* she wrote.

After considerable thought, and with a degree of reluctance, Jolene wrote back, agreeing to arrange a visiting order and meet the person her friend had warmly recommended. She was puzzled as to the reason for the request, though, because his name meant absolutely nothing to her.

* * *

A week later, she entered the visiting room and saw the man she had agreed to talk with. It was several seconds before she recognized the good-looking stranger as the person who had been watching her so intently in the courtroom at the end of her trial.

He introduced himself.

He was surprised when Jolene said, 'I remember you now. You were at my trial. What do you want?'

'I have a proposition for you. Once you're released from here, I want to join forces, with you making use of your special talent.' He smiled before adding, 'And I'm not referring to your singing voice.'

'Hah, you'll have a long wait! And what do you mean, "join forces"? Or "special talent" for that matter?'

His explanation appalled her.

'Are you mad?' she demanded. 'Do you think I like it so much in here I'd be prepared to risk another term of imprisonment because someone I've never met wants me to do something so outrageous?'

'That won't happen. I promise you will not have to face trial for what I have planned. Let me explain . . .'

He told her what he had in mind, before adding, 'If you pair up with me, it will benefit both of us. You can help me get revenge, which is something I guess you also want, and together we will try to bring justice to a lot of people. Apart from that, I can provide you with protection. I'm fairly certain someone out there has it in for you, and once you're out of here, you'll be alone — and therefore vulnerable.'

'And why would I be vulnerable?'

'A couple of reasons spring to mind. For one thing, someone went to great lengths to have you framed for attempted murder. I believe that was designed to have you imprisoned. I understand there have been a few attempts on you in here, and I certainly don't believe they were random assaults — probably paid for. That's happened before, in connection with another matter, one I think might have a bearing on your situation, but that's only speculation. If I'm correct, without protection, you won't survive long after you leave here, because outside, you would be at the mercy of professional assassins. Bear that in mind, because I feel sure it would be in your best interests to team up with me.'

Jolene was appalled by the revelation that she was being targeted, but the man's next claim left her totally confused. 'Apart from all that, you owe me,' he said.

'What makes you think I owe you anything?'

'Who do you think found the evidence that will help overturn your conviction? And who has persuaded your solicitor to lodge an appeal? One, which I understand, the Crown Prosecution Service will not contest.'

Jolene stared at him for a long moment, unsure whether to believe his claim. 'Prove it,' she challenged him. 'Tell me how you got hold of that evidence, and if I believe you, I might be convinced.'

He explained, and she did believe him. Nobody else could have known what he told her. The evidence, together with the way he'd acquired it, was highly appropriate, in an ironic sort of way.

'OK, I accept that. How do you plan to set about this, and how can you protect me?' She studied him carefully. 'Above all, why are you doing this?'

If Jolene had been startled by what she'd heard so far, what followed left her speechless. Eventually, as the visiting time was almost over, she conceded, accepting his proposal. One thing puzzled her, though. 'How did you know about my "special talent", as you called it?'

His reply amazed her, because she believed nobody knew what he disclosed. If he was aware of it, this might explain the attacks on her. If his plan worked, she thought, a lot of people were in for some huge shocks.

At the Appeal Court, exactly as Jolene's visitor, Graham Lawson, had predicted, the fresh evidence he had provided was accepted. With the prosecution offering no new evidence, the conviction was overturned, and Jolene was completely exonerated.

CHAPTER FIVE

While the detectives were becoming concerned about the building scam, Julie Finch was more concerned about the state of her marriage. She had become suspicious of her husband Barry's activities on two fronts. The first of these regarded the source of his money, which seemed rather too much for someone supposedly having to scrape by on benefits alone. This was compounded by his frequent absences from home, which he claimed were purely down to his search for a job. As a nurse in Netherdale General Hospital's ICU, Julie was far too busy to keep track of Barry's movements, but an isolated incident caused her to question his account of how he spent his time while she was at work.

It was Julie's day off, and she was doing some housework. Part of this included loading the washing machine, a task she had overlooked the previous week. As she removed one of Barry's T-shirts from the laundry basket, she noticed a faint but distinctive aroma. It was women's perfume, but definitely not the one she used.

She examined the T-shirt closely and noticed a faint smudge on the rounded collar, a pale pink colour, definitely not part of the garment's pattern. Barry had obviously been in close proximity to another woman. But as he had no female relatives, there was no possibility of an innocent explanation. She drew a clear and unsavoury conclusion from the evidence.

Julie sat in their kitchen pondering her next move. She needed confirmation her suspicions were well-founded, but how? She discounted the option of confronting Barry directly, knowing he would deny her accusation, dismissing it as a flight of fancy. He might even take umbrage and express his displeasure physically, something he had done before on more than one occasion.

Julie was an avid reader. She had also watched many movies where aggrieved wives had hired private investigators to check out their errant husbands. Such work wouldn't come cheap, and Julie didn't have that sort of money to spare.

Eventually, a plan began to form. If she couldn't afford to hire an enquiry agent, she would do the job herself. Before that, she would need to consider how to tackle the task, and do so covertly.

* * *

A week later, with her preparations in place, Julie knew she would be able to commence her espionage activities. Aware that Barry would recognize her distinctly coloured Renault Clio, she had rented a grey Audi saloon, one with tinted windows, which would be far less noticeable. Her other disguise involved concealing her short blonde hair beneath a black wig she had acquired, in addition to purchasing garments more in keeping with a middle-aged woman than someone in their early thirties.

Bright and early on Monday, Julie left home at the time she normally did to report for her day shift. Having driven to the hospital car park, she parked alongside the Audi she had left there. She headed for the toilets, changed her outer garments and donned the wig. Once inside her decoy vehicle, she commenced the return journey home.

As she drove away from the hospital, Julie remembered the conversation with her superior when she had requested

25

a week's holiday. Julie had told her she intended to spend her leisure time redecorating the house. That had sounded plausible, and the real reason was definitely not for public knowledge. Fifteen minutes later, Julie was parked a discreet distance away from her house, ready to commence surveillance.

Two long, boring, fruitless days passed. It was reaching the point where Julie was beginning to wonder if she had made a dreadful mistake. But then, on Wednesday, everything changed. In what she privately acknowledged to be a last desperate measure to provoke some activity, Julie had told Barry she would be absent until the following day. 'We're understaffed already, and a couple of the other nurses have gone down with cold or flu, so I've volunteered to do a double shift. It'll be the early hours of the morning when I finish, and as I'm on duty again a few hours later, there's little point in coming home. I'll kip down at the hospital, providing I can find a bed. If not, I'll use a stretcher.'

Her ruse worked a treat, although, as Julie followed her errant husband at a discreet distance, she was puzzled by his first port of call, and even more perplexed by his second one. Barry left the house an hour after she had departed and walked a short distance to a piece of spare ground to the rear of their estate, where he opened one of the lock-up garages. Julie was surprised when he emerged behind the wheel of a slightly battered-looking pickup truck.

* * *

She followed the vehicle until it pulled up midway down a side road, where the buildings consisted mainly of bungalows. Julie waited a couple of hundred yards away and watched as her husband greeted the woman who opened the door and then clearly invited him inside. Although she suspected Barry of being unfaithful, she was fairly sure this wasn't his *inamorata*. Of course, it was entirely possible that he had suddenly developed a fetish for a woman who appeared to be over the age of seventy, but somehow Julie doubted it.

After driving to a point further along the road where she could turn the Audi round, Julie waited for almost half an hour until Barry emerged, then maintained a safe distance behind him as he returned towards Netherdale town centre. They had only been travelling for twenty minutes when she saw the pickup signalling a right turn, into the car park of an apartment block.

She waited on the main road until she saw Barry walk towards the entrance. From her vantage point, she saw him go inside, and a few seconds later watched as he came into view once more, his face clearly visible through the window of a ground-floor flat. She also saw the woman who embraced him passionately, and Julie gasped with surprise as she recognized her.

The woman in the flat was a barmaid at the Horse and Jockey, the pub which had long been one of Barry's favourite watering holes. Julie swung the Audi into a convenient parking place and waited a few minutes as she pondered her next move. The apartment block was set well back from the main road, which made a covert approach difficult, but as she watched, Julie saw the woman draw the curtains across the window. Fortunately for Julie, but not those inside the flat, the woman had left the window open a couple of inches.

Although Julie wouldn't be able to see what the couple inside were doing — and to be fair, she didn't want to — at least she might be able to hear what they were saying, providing they had sufficient breath left to talk. She walked confidently towards the apartment block, mimicking the actions of someone with every right to be there. Minutes later, as she took up position outside the open window, Julie began her eavesdropping.

Although there was ample evidence of the nature of their relationship, what was being discussed seemed, for the most part, like a business meeting.

Shock followed shock, and after hearing a few details, Julie reached into her pocket, took out her mobile phone and switched on the recording app. It was almost an hour later when she drove away. By that time, she had photographic evidence of her husband's infidelity, via the picture she had taken of him embracing the woman. Even more devastating was the revelation of what he and his mistress had been doing, and what they were planning as their next move. Now, all she had to do was decide how to use this information.

As she returned to where she had parked her own car, Julie saw a woman dressed in a nurse's uniform. The uniform reminded her, not only of work, but of a friend and colleague, Lianne Pearce, who was married to a detective. Now Julie knew exactly what her next move would be.

* * *

Having phoned the ICU to ascertain when Lianne would be on duty, the following morning Julie drove to the hospital. As soon as she saw Lianne emerge from her car, Julie strode across the car park and hailed her.

Lianne stared at her colleague, her expression one of puzzlement. 'I thought you were on holiday this week?'

'I am, but something unexpected cropped up. It's all to do with that scam builder, the one who preys on old and vulnerable houseowners. I feel certain your husband would be interested in what I've discovered.'

'Normally, Viv would be more than happy to listen, but he's at Netherdale Crown Court today. He's not sure when he'll be giving evidence, and there's always the possibility of a witness recall, so he's pretty much unavailable.'

Lianne thought for a moment. 'If it's important, why not talk to Viv's boss, Mike Nash? He's the detective inspector in charge of the area's CID unit. He's a nice bloke and very easy to talk to. Or, if Mike isn't available, you could ask for his second in command, Detective Sergeant Mironova. They're all based in Helmsdale. Why don't I give you the phone number and you can take it from there?'

'Actually, I'd much rather discuss this face to face than over the phone.'

Lianne thought for a couple of seconds. 'In that case, give me a moment and I'll phone Mike or Clara, then I can set up an appointment for you. How does that suit?'

'That would be really helpful, but who's Clara?'

Lianne laughed. 'Sorry, I should have explained. Clara is DS Mironova.'

CHAPTER SIX

Steve Meadows rang through to tell Nash there was a phone call. 'It's Lianne, Viv's wife. She's got someone with her who's very keen to speak to you.'

'OK, put her through.'

Having greeted Lianne, Nash asked her if everything was OK, and enquired about her son Brian. Once the pleasantries had been dealt with, he listened with growing interest to what Lianne had to tell him. 'That's OK, both Clara and I will be here all day, unless there's an emergency call out. I assume your friend would prefer meeting somewhere in private. As soon as she arrives, we'll bring her straight up to the CID suite, where she'll be less visible than in reception.'

Lianne told Julie what Nash had said, which Julie thought demonstrated a level of consideration she hadn't expected. This gave her more confidence to face the upcoming encounter.

Nash wandered into the general office, where Clara had just arrived and was in the process of removing her coat.

'Follow me to the coffee machine,' he instructed her. 'I've just had a phone call I think you'll be interested in. Lianne Pearce has just phoned.'

'Is Viv ill?'

'No, nothing like that. She was waylaid on her way to work by one of her colleagues, a lady by the name of Julie Finch. Apparently, she has some information about the scam builder and didn't know who to tell about it. Then she remembered that Viv is a detective, so she tried asking Lianne. As he's unavailable, Lianne persuaded her to talk to us. For some reason or other she doesn't want to discuss the matter over the phone, so she's coming here to meet us later this morning. Reading between the lines, I think this might just be the lucky break we've been waiting for.'

* * *

An hour and a half later, Nash ushered their visitor upstairs and into his office, where Clara was already seated. He made the introductions, which gave Clara chance to assess the visitor. Julie, she guessed, was in her early thirties, quite attractive and smart in her nurse's uniform. As Julie was explaining she was on leave that week, Clara wondered why she was dressed for work. The reason for this soon became apparent.

'I've found out who the person stealing money from people by pretending to be a builder is, and I wish I hadn't. Actually, there are two people involved — the man who does the doorstepping, and the woman in charge of handling the money side of things. It's a very sordid tale, I'm sorry to say.'

'Why not tell us what you've discovered, then we can make a judgement?' Nash suggested. 'Do you have solid evidence that this couple is the one scamming victims?'

'I certainly do, although I wish it wasn't so. Let me explain how I found this out.' She took a deep breath and began, 'I've suspected for some time that my husband was up to something. He was made redundant over a year ago when the building company he worked for went bust, but he never seems short of money. Then I came across something that suggested he was also being unfaithful. That was when I decided to find out what he was up to and who with.' Surprisingly, given the subject of her narrative, Julie smiled.

31

'I didn't have the money to hire a private detective, so I decided to follow him myself.'

She went on to describe the measures she'd taken to ensure her surveillance activities went undetected.

This caused Nash to smile as he told her, 'If you ever want to change your line of work, you'd make an excellent undercover police officer. Alternatively, I believe MI5 are also keen to hire top-class recruits.'

Julie then told Nash and Clara about the lock-up garage, and her surprise when she saw her husband driving a pickup truck she wasn't aware he owned. She went on to tell them how puzzled she'd been when she saw him call on an elderly woman in Netherdale, and was about to reveal what she'd learned during her surveillance at the apartment, when Clara interrupted.

'Can you give us the address of the old lady he called on? She might be a victim we're unaware of.'

Julie repeated the details, and Clara went into the general office. 'Adil, here's another possible address to add to your scammed people list. Check it out now, will you?'

* * *

Clara returned and Julie continued her account, telling the detectives what she had overheard when she'd listened outside the woman's flat. 'Apparently, their plan is to get enough money together so they can live abroad. Quite honestly, I'd be glad to see the back of him, but I wouldn't want him to profit at the expense of other people's misery. Knowing he's a lying, cheating, dirty bastard is bad enough, but now I've also found out the tart he's been shagging has been up to her neck in this rotten swindle right from the start. My only ambition is to see the pair of them where they belong, behind bars.' Julie paused before adding, 'And I don't mean behind a bar in Benidorm. That slag is as bad as Barry, because she's been dealing with the money. Don't they call that laundering?'

'That's correct, Julie,' Clara answered. As she spoke, she glanced across at Nash, noticing the serious expression on his face, and wondered what the reason for it was. That soon became apparent, as he responded to Julie's account.

'There's one big difficulty with all this, as I see it. Don't for one minute think that I disbelieve anything and everything you've told us, but all we have is purely circumstantial. In order to make a case like this stick, we need solid evidence, and that might mean getting the victims to carry out identification, which would probably cause them further distress. At present, even obtaining arrest and search warrants would be tricky with the few details we'd be able to present.'

He and Clara were surprised when Julie smiled. That surprise turned to outright amazement as she told them, 'You want proof? How about this for solid evidence?'

She removed her mobile phone from her pocket and directed their attention to the images in the photo gallery, identifying the people as her husband Barry, together with his mistress and partner-in-crime, Kelly Ford. 'These show the date and time they were together in her apartment. The recording app also shows the corresponding date and time when I overheard them discussing what they were doing.'

Nash and Mironova listened closely, and both were soon aware the evidence provided by the recording was definitive proof of the couple's guilt. When Julie switched the recording app off, Nash told her, 'If you do get seconded to MI5, you'll probably end up running the outfit.'

At this point, he summoned Viv into his office and instructed him to copy the images and recorded evidence onto their computer. As this was being done, Clara made arrangements with Netherdale for Julie to visit their headquarters the following day to give her witness statement.

'As soon as we've got that in place, we can make our next move,' Nash told Julie. 'And with luck, that means you won't have to stand the sight of your husband for a long time, possibly as much as five years.'

'That's fine by me. The longer the better,' Julie replied. 'By the time he comes out of prison, I'll probably have moved away.' She paused and smiled. 'Anywhere except Spain, I guess.'

Once she had left, Nash turned to Clara and said, 'That's an exceedingly good result, and I think it demonstrates the accuracy of the old saying.'

'What old saying is that?

'The one that says, "Hell hath no fury like a woman scorned".'

* * *

The delighted reaction from Superintendent Fleming to the news was all very well, but as Nash reminded her during the arrest strategy meeting, 'We still have two unsolved murders to contend with. I agree the fraud is an extremely serious crime, but for us it has been an unwelcome distraction. I want this out of our hair and on the way to the Crown Prosecution Service as quickly as possible. Only then can we return to what I consider to be our main priority.'

With that sobering reminder to prompt them, the team pulled out all the stops to expedite the closure of the fraud case. Their civilian support officers were already busy transcribing Julie Finch's recording, and two days later, early morning arrests were made of the two suspects.

Nash, who had supervised the detention of Barry Finch, received two enlightening phone calls as he followed the van containing the arrested man to Helmsdale. The first of these came from Viv Pearce. He and Adil had been charged with the task of going to the lock-up garage indicated in Julie's witness statement. Having gained entry using the key found in Barry Finch's possession, they then supervised the removal of the pickup truck believed to have been used as part of the scam.

'The vehicle is still bearing the plates cloned from that truck in Bristol,' Pearce began, 'but we've also seized five more pairs of number plates. Adil's checked them out, and they all refer to similar vehicles. We also found bags of sand and cement, plus a wheelbarrow and shovel in the back of the pickup, which I guess were there to make Finch's story more credible.'

The other phone call came from DS Mironova, who had been responsible for the arrest of Finch's alleged mistress, Kelly Ford, plus the search of the apartment in Netherdale. Having overseen the woman's detention, Clara had remained on site, checking the contents of the flat as the CSI team set to work.

'We've got a great find here,' Clara told Nash, 'I've discovered a pad of A4 notepaper. The first few pages bear a list of names and addresses, with the monetary amounts each one yielded alongside. All the victims we know about are on that list, plus a lot more, both within our area and further afield. I reckon that has to be game, set and match, don't you? Especially when you tie it in to the other piece of evidence CSI have just shown me.'

'What's that?'

'A bank paying-in book. The account is in joint names, those being Barry Finch and Kelly Ford. I've only had a couple of minutes to glance at it, but I did notice several entries showing deposits made, and the amounts and dates tally closely to some of the offences on our list.'

'I agree that all sounds extremely damaging. Let's see what the suspects have to say for themselves when they're faced with the weight of the evidence against them.'

* * *

Nash told his colleagues he had decided to take DC Hassan along with him to question Barry Finch. 'Adil took this on in the beginning, and I think he should have the pleasure. Clara, I'd like you and Viv to conduct a simultaneous session with Finch's mistress, Kelly Ford. Before we start, however, both suspects have requested legal representation, so we'll wait for their solicitors to arrive, following which we'll go through the disclosure process, which again, I want everyone to attend. I don't want the legal eagles to get their claws into any break in operational procedure.'

Although both suspects had protested their innocence as they were being arrested, once their legal representatives were aware of the strength of the case against their clients, any resistance to the charges vanished. Having outlined the concrete evidence supporting the allegations, Nash told the solicitors, 'In addition to what we are already in possession of, I'm quite prepared to arrange for each and every one of their victims to be brought here to attend an identity parade. I am absolutely certain they will pick out Barry Finch. The CPS will, I'm sure, bring as many victims as necessary to give evidence at the subsequent trial. I think it would be prudent for you to advise your clients that, given the age and vulnerability of the people they ruthlessly cheated, a full and frank admission of guilt would be advisable. Otherwise, we will be seeking the maximum penalty for each and every one of the offences. Given the number involved, that will result in hefty prison sentences. I certainly do not want to hear a string of "no comment" answers to our questions, because that would be most unsatisfactory, so please do not advise them to go down that route.'

Clara, who had been present at many of Nash's previous disclosure meetings, reckoned this had to be the most detailed instruction he had given during the time they had worked together. It was hardly surprising, given this stringent directive, allied to the weight of evidence on hand, that when the detectives compared notes later that day, they were in position to send the files they had compiled to their civilian support officers, ready for transcription to present to the CPS. Among these were the full confessions of both defendants to all the offences listed.

'Apart from attending the trial, which in view of the confessions will be pretty much a formality, that's our work on this case closed,' Nash told the team.

CHAPTER SEVEN

Jolene Fraser, wearing the same clothing as on the day she entered and carrying two black bin bags, walked out of Blackwell Prison and looked cautiously around. She was hugely relieved to see there were no reporters or TV cameramen lurking nearby.

The railway station was half a mile away, and she had only taken a few steps when a large black SUV, its windows heavily tinted, pulled to a halt alongside her. The passenger window opened and the driver hailed her. 'Care for a lift?'

She glanced inside, her initial suspicion turning to fear until she recognized the driver. She put the bags she was carrying in the back and climbed into the passenger seat.

'What is this car? Is it a hearse?'

The vehicle swerved slightly as the driver laughed. 'I'll have you know this is a top-of-the-range BMW.'

'I'm glad of the ride. I was worried the press jackals would be waiting. I'm surprised they missed the chance.'

The driver chuckled. 'They were clustered around the gates en masse until I told them you were being smuggled out of the delivery entrance. I said I needed to find a parking space for the Beamer before joining them there. They set off like a herd of sheep being rounded up by a Border collie.'

'How did you convince them?'

He turned slightly and flashed a press card hanging from a lanyard around his neck. Had she the leisure to examine it, Jolene would have spotted that it was many years out of date and bore a different name to the one he'd given her. This she would have found puzzling and more than a little disturbing.

'Thank you for doing that. So where are we going?'

'I'm taking you to a secluded place where we can be alone, and then we can have a bit of fun.'

For a moment, Jolene wondered if she had made a dreadful mistake, and that he had designs on her, until her companion explained what he had in mind.

'I think your idea of fun and mine are completely different,' she told him severely.

'Tell me your idea of fun and we could try that too, if you wish.'

Jolene's suspicion returned, until she saw the smile and realized he was teasing her. 'Is the place you're taking me to safe?'

'Certainly not, that's why I chose it. We're going there to put ourselves in danger, and if my plan provokes the reaction I suspect, it will prove to you the threat I mentioned wasn't a figment of my imagination. Added to that, if my stage management works, it will lead the enemy to believe they've eliminated you. I'm convinced that desire is behind everything you've endured. Of course, we could simply stay hidden and hope it will all blow over, but where's the fun in that?'

Jolene noticed her companion repeatedly glancing into the rear-view mirror. 'Is there a problem?'

'Not really. I'm just checking the Porsche 911 that's been following us is still behind us. We don't want to lose him.'

On reaching their destination, he stopped the car and told her, 'Right, into the bedroom and get your kit off. We might not have much time.'

Normally she would have been horrified by this statement, but following his earlier explanation, she knew exactly what he meant. This was yet another example of his wicked sense of humour.

* * *

How much further? Vincent wondered. As he stared towards the horizon, he saw the outline of the cottage roof silhouetted by the strong afternoon sun and realized he was almost at his destination. After walking for a few more minutes he could see the whole of the building's facade. Vincent paused, both to recover from the long walk and to reconnoitre the ground ahead.

After focusing his binoculars, he scanned the building that housed his target. 'This will be dead easy,' he muttered. The woman he'd been hired to kill was sitting with her back to an open window. There was no chance of mistaken identity. The brightly coloured floral print blouse she'd been wearing when she walked out of Blackwell Prison earlier that day, plus the long, flowing mane of blonde hair, convinced him it was his target. He wondered briefly why his client now wanted this minor celebrity dead having paid for her to be framed, but then discarded the idea. It wasn't up to him to ask questions. As long as he got paid, that was all he cared about. He just wished she hadn't come to such an outlandish place.

After a further scan of the area in front of the cottage, he checked the car parked alongside the building. It was the car she'd got into outside the prison — the registration number confirmed it. That made his decision easy. He would shoot her from outside, through the window, and if the bloke got in the way, he'd do him as well.

'The quicker I get this over with the better,' Vincent muttered. 'This wasteland spooks me. Give me a city centre any day.'

Conscious that sound would travel, he elected to walk the short remaining distance on the grass. He got to within a couple of yards of the open window before lifting his automatic pistol.

* * *

A split second later, a covey of grouse, dining on some tasty young heather shoots, took off in alarm at the sudden volley of gunshots. Their angry cries unnerved the killer. Before the echoes died away, Vincent had turned and was going back along the track to the main road, his gait almost a gallop. As he vanished out of sight, Jolene and her companion emerged from their hiding place. 'That was the most fun I've had in a bedroom for ages,' he told her.

'What should we do with the corpse?' Jolene was anxious to change the subject.

'We'd better dispose of it outside. We don't want to give the next occupant a heart attack.'

Jolene smiled. 'It's a shame about the blouse, though, I really liked it.'

'That's OK. If we get through all this safely, I'll happily buy you another one. If you ditch the body, I'll retrieve the video camera and check the footage contains the vital evidence.'

'Now I see why you opened the window,' Jolene said, as she made to close it.

'I didn't want any damage. The couple I leased this place from wouldn't be happy.'

As Jolene moved to pick up the dummy, she told him, 'That wig is very convincing. You did well to get such a close match to my hair.'

He chuckled. 'I think the ladies in the shop where I bought it believed I was entering some sort of drag competition, because I was so particular.'

As they approached his BMW, Jolene was surprised and somewhat afraid by his instructions. 'Why do you want me to lie down in the back of the car?' she demanded angrily.

He grinned. 'If the man who was paid to kill you is a professional, which seems most likely, he'll be waiting and watching for me to leave. If I go hurtling along the road, driving like Lewis Hamilton on Class A drugs and apparently alone, it might convince him the job's been done. If they believe you're dead, they'll cease coming after you.'

This made perfect sense, but Jolene felt every bump and twist as the BMW careered along the track. She braced her legs against the rear panels of the front seats as her companion flung the car round the last bend, then, as the front wheels hit the tarmac, he gunned the accelerator, causing the vehicle to swerve first one way then the other, the actions of a man apparently in a blind panic.

'Is he following us?' she called out. 'I can't see anything from down here.'

'He is, but with a bit of luck I'll be able to lose him before we get to where we're heading.'

'Where are we going?'

'I've a hiding place where we can hole up until we decide on our next move. As long as they believe you're dead, they won't come after you. That means you must continue to keep out of sight, so none of your adoring fans recognize you. If somebody posted a photo on social media, it would give the game away.'

'When are you going to explain why you're doing all this? Don't think I'm not grateful. You've saved me from years of imprisonment and just prevented someone from killing me, but that's made me even more curious. All you told me was you wanted to avenge the death of someone close to you.'

Jolene noticed his tone of voice change dramatically, to one far grimmer than previously. 'I'll tell you later,' he replied curtly.

* * *

As they were leaving the cottage, Vincent was reporting to his client. 'The job's done. She won't trouble you any longer.'

'What did you do with the body?'

'Left it in the shack out in the wilds where she went with the bloke who picked her up from Blackwell. They were

41

probably hoping for a spot of leg over, but I spoiled the plan with three bullets.'

'What bloke are you talking about?'

'The guy in the fancy Beamer who collected Fraser from prison.'

'Did you do him as well?'

'No, there was no sign of him. The poor bugger was probably waiting in the bedroom with a hard-on.'

'Do you know his name?'

'No, but the BMW will have cost a bomb, so he must be loaded.'

'I don't like the sound of that. Why didn't you dispose of him too?'

'It's a bit difficult to kill someone you can't see,' Vincent told his client, aware that he wasn't being exactly truthful. Admitting he'd been spooked by a few squawking birds would hardly be good for his hard-man image. 'I'm waiting at the end of the lane, so I can follow him when he leaves and find out who he is.'

'Do that. As soon as the opportunity arrives, waste him as well. I don't want any loose ends. If you can make it look like an accident, that would be a bonus.'

'He's here now. I'll chase him down and finish him off.' Vincent ended the call and edged the Porsche forward.

* * *

'Damn!'

'What's wrong?'

The hiker ceased rummaging through his backpack and looked up at his companion. 'I used up the water in my bottle yesterday and forgot to refill it before we left the guesthouse.'

He shook the empty container to prove his point. The second walker glanced at her map. 'There isn't a village for miles.'

It was a warm day for the time of year, although the long-range forecast was for storms, with heavy rain and gales. The route they had set themselves was a long and arduous one. No way could they manage without refreshment. She checked her own bottle. There was barely enough in it for one — certainly insufficient for two. She examined the map again, this time checking the area more closely.

'According to this map, there's a building of some description a mile or so up that path.' She gestured to her right.

He looked at the track without enthusiasm. 'It's probably nothing more than a barn, and most likely a ruined one at that. I can't imagine anyone actually wanting to live out here full-time, can you?'

'You can't be sure of that. Let's face it, the views are magnificent. It could be a holiday cottage. We might get lucky, and it's not far out of our way.'

She had a point. He slung the rucksack over his shoulder. 'Might as well give it a try, I guess.' He didn't sound overly optimistic. Twenty minutes or so later, they got their first glimpse of a building. 'Look,' she pointed, 'it's a cottage, and hopefully there'll be somebody at home.'

'I still can't believe that someone would live this far from civilization from choice,' he muttered.

When they reached the building, he knocked on the front door. There was no response from within. 'Maybe they've gone out for the day. Nobody in their right mind would live here without a car to get around in.'

'Are you determined to be this negative all the time? Knock again while I go round the back. There might be a car parked there out of sight, or even an outside tap.'

He banged again, but with no better luck. He had just raised his fist to try one last time when she screamed. The strident, high-pitched shriek disturbed the grouse that had returned to attacking the nearby heather. Their angry calls at having their dining interrupted a second time completed the shattering of the silence.

He abandoned the tattoo he'd been beating on the door and ran round the end of the small building to where she was standing. 'Whatever's wrong?'

She pointed, her finger shaking. 'Look there, behind the wall.'

He walked across to where a small piece of red cloth was just visible above the stone capping the wall. He leaned over and stared at the corpse for a few seconds, before turning to his companion, his face a mask of horror.

'Let's get out of here.'

'Shouldn't we call the police?'

'Fat chance of that — there's no mobile signal. I checked to see if we'd any messages half an hour ago. We'll call them as soon as we can.'

CHAPTER EIGHT

It was almost an hour after leaving the cottage when Jolene and her rescuer pulled up in a small parking area in the countryside. Apart from one or two farms, there was little sign of habitation. During the earlier part of their journey the driver had made one phone call, and his request to the person he spoke to puzzled her initially. After he ended the call, she asked, 'Why did you ask that person to do such a weird thing?'

His explanation resolved her last remaining doubt as to his motive and provided a degree of comfort. Everything he had done, and was intending to do, was carefully designed to protect her.

'It's taken a while, but I think with my pal's help I've managed to lose the guy following us.'

'That's a relief. So where are we going now?'

'We're going for a bit of a walk before we get to our new residence. Do you like boats?'

'Er . . . yes, I think so. I've never had much to do with them, though.'

'I own a canal boat. I thought we could stay there for the time being. I've bought some supplies in, so we won't need to venture out and risk getting spotted by the enemy.'

'What made you decide to buy a canal boat?'

For the second time that day, Jolene heard his voice change, and saw his expression become one of deep sadness. 'I wanted somewhere I could be alone and safe, but that's all part of the story. I'll tell you later. I'm not ready to talk about it yet.'

'I can hardly believe I'm going along with everything you suggest, when I know absolutely nothing about you. I'm not even certain the name you gave me is correct, or simply an alias.'

'I'll tell you everything you need to know in due course, but rest assured my main priority at present is to keep you safe.'

'Why are you going to so much trouble for someone you've only met once?'

'I'll explain later.'

Jolene wondered how many times he would repeat that phrase, but was slightly encouraged when he added, 'I could give you all sorts of answers, but not today. One thing I will never do is lie to you, that I promise.'

Jolene had one reservation about spending time alone in a constricted space with a man she barely knew. Almost as if he'd read her mind, he told her, 'Don't worry — I haven't brought you here for any reason but your safety. I'm not that sort of person. You are extremely attractive, but that part of my life is over with.' There it was again, that note of sorrow in his voice.

As they left the small parking area at the end of a dirt track, Jolene read the sign, with an arrow pointing along the canal bank to their right. The name, Mile Marina, seemed an odd one. She asked her companion about this.

'Possibly the bloke who set it up thought "marina" sounded fancier than "moorings", and it's about a mile from Bishopton. It's a quiet spot, seldom used. Boaters prefer moorings with facilities, usually a pub alongside.' He laughed. 'Sometimes a shower block entices them, but don't worry, I have a shower.'

* * *

Once they reached the boat, he examined the outer door before unlocking it. When they were inside, he showed her round, pointing to a cabin at the stern. 'That'll be yours. I've allocated it specifically, because it's the only one with a lock, so you won't have to worry about me behaving improperly.'

'How long are you suggesting we stay here?'

'I thought it would be a good place to remain hidden, and while you're here, you can start planning how to find out exactly who the opposition are, and what they're up to.'

'I'll need a laptop.'

'Don't worry. It's over there.'

'When are you going to tell me why you're doing all this?'

'I will soon, but not today. Of all days, this is the worst.'

She changed the subject to one less uncomfortable for him. 'I also wanted to know why at the exact moment I was allegedly trying to murder a woman — who was actually forty miles away from me — you were filming me. That video got me out of prison, for which I'm really grateful, but I need you to tell me why you shot it.'

His reply only went halfway towards providing an explanation, but Jolene realized that as things stood it was the best she could get. His final statement was an apology, which she was happy to accept. 'I'm only sorry I didn't find out you'd been arrested before the end of your trial. If I'd heard the date and time the supposed attack took place, I could have stopped that pantomime in its tracks. It was only later, when I read the transcript, that I knew the whole thing was a trumped-up charge designed to place you in a vulnerable position. Your death in prison could not be blamed on the people who wanted rid of you. It's a device they've used before, if it's the people I believe are behind it all.'

As Jolene and her companion were settling into the canal boat, Vincent was pondering whether to phone his client with an update. He decided against it, because the man paying him a huge sum for his services wouldn't be happy to learn Vincent had lost sight of the bloke who picked up the pop singer from clink. He'd been behind the BMW most of the way, but then he'd got held up out in the wilds by some stupid yokel who made a complete balls-up of reversing his tractor out of a field and blocked the road for five minutes. With no other alternative, Vincent decided to return home. From there, he could use the vehicle registration number to locate his target. Only when the mission had been accomplished would he contact his client.

* * *

It was Sunday afternoon, the traditional point in the week for British people who are so inclined to take a pleasure drive. The car travelling in leisurely fashion along the narrow, twisting country lanes seemed to be of that sort. There was no conversation inside, as the driver and front-seat passenger were keen not to disturb the other occupants, an infant enclosed in a car seat secured in the rear, and the black Labrador in the luggage compartment, both of whom were fast asleep. It was a pleasurable silence, representing a contented family unit. In between checking on her daughter, the passenger stared about her from time to time, taking in the scenery. As an artist, the dramatic changes of the seasons intrigued her.

Despite her examination of the passing terrain, her gaze inevitably returned to the driver, and if anything, this made her happiness even more complete. Moments like these were few. Alondra Nash smiled. 'How long before we're home?'

'Not long now. I want to get home before Lucy wakes up and starts singing for her supper, and Teal will need a walk.'

'Teal misses Daniel and all the long walks during the school holidays. He looked well today, though, don't you think?'

'Yes, apart from the bruises.' Nash laughed. 'But he opted to play rugby. I bet he's wishing the cricket season would come sooner now.'

'It will be half-term soon, then he can recover at home.'

'Yes, then you can smother him. Sorry — I should have said mother him.' Nash laughed. He knew Alondra's acceptance of his son worked both ways. Daniel now called his stepmother 'Mum', a situation satisfactory to all.

* * *

In Nash's office the following morning, he'd taken a call from Superintendent Jackie Fleming demanding a meeting, and now Clara was intent on making the most of the chance to wind Nash up and delay him.

'I'm willing to bet you can't guess where I was standing yesterday, can you?' she asked.

'I have absolutely no idea. To be honest, I left my crystal ball at home because I didn't think I'd need it. And don't make any snide comments about balls,' he added hastily.

'Would I do that? Anyway, the answer is, I was standing on the grass verge alongside a cottage on the road over Stark Ghyll, close to the summit on the Black Fell side. I could see your house from that point, although not from the building. You weren't at home, though.'

'No, we went to see Daniel. There was a rugby tournament between schools, and he was playing.'

'How did he do?'

'Black eye and a bruised shin — otherwise OK. His team is through to the knockout final after the half-term break. Alondra won't go to that, though — too tough for her delicate nature.' He grinned. 'Actually, to be truthful, it was just far too rowdy for Lucy. And Teal had to stay in the car and sulked when we got home.'

'Ah, family life.' Clara smiled as she remembered how nine years ago, six-year-old Daniel — the son Mike didn't know he had — had been brought to England by his French aunt after his mother, an earlier girlfriend of Mike's, had died. Now he had a beautiful, talented wife and an infant daughter as well.

She was brought back from her reverie when Nash said, 'So, you might care to explain what you were doing up there. I haven't got all day. I've got to go to a meeting at HQ.'

Despite the gravity of the situation, there was laughter in Clara's voice. 'Oh yes, sir.'

It didn't diminish, even when Nash told her, in a severe tone of voice, 'Clara, stop taking the piss — it's insubordinate. Instead, would you care to tell me what you're so desperate to reveal, or are you planning to keep that secret?'

She grinned. 'Sorry, I think the expression is "chasing wild geese".'

'As an explanation, that's a bit short on detail.'

'I got called out because uniform branch was busy with some soccer match or other, and the control room took a call from a pair of hikers who thought they'd found a body near a cottage up there. When I arrived, the cottage was secure, and I found the so-called corpse behind the building. There were three bullet holes in the back of her blouse and what looked like a load of bloodstains.'

'Any idea who the victim is?'

'Yes, I think it's Worzel Gummidge's pal, Aunt Sally.'

'Would you mind explaining your references to scarecrows, because you don't seem to be making any sense at the moment? Been at the gin again, have you?'

Clara grinned at the testy edge to Nash's voice. Ignoring the insult, she began to tell him what she'd found. 'The corpse the hikers saw is actually a set of women's clothes — namely, a vivid floral blouse and a pair of deep red slacks, stuffed with straw to resemble a real person. Whoever dressed the dummy topped it off with a long blonde wig. It looks very realistic, but why anyone would take potshots at a scarecrow is a mystery, so I thought I'd ask if you have any ideas.'

'I have lots of ideas, but none of them relevant to your problem.' There was silence for a moment as Nash thought over what Clara had told him, then suggested, 'Try to find out who owns the cottage. They might be able to shed some light on what happened up there.'

'That sounds sensible.'

'And before you go, tell me you didn't go alone to a potential murder scene.'

Clara looked embarrassed.

'Who did you call? Viv or Adil? You've already said everyone from uniform was tied up.' Nash was concerned — he couldn't believe Clara would be so foolish.

'Er . . . no . . . er, David was at a loose end, so I got him to drive me.' She bit her bottom lip. 'Look, I just wanted to check it out before I called out the troops. I wasn't in any danger.'

Nash shook his head, knowing full well that her husband, David Sutton, ex-SAS, wouldn't let anyone harm a hair on Clara's head. 'OK, you were safe — this time! Just don't do it again.'

'Yes, boss,' she said, as she headed for her desk to explain what she had seen to the waiting DCs.

Nash grabbed a folder and his car keys, and left.

CHAPTER NINE

'Have you any update on the mortuary corpses?'

Nash grimaced at Superintendent Fleming's question. 'None whatsoever, but it's early days yet. Mexican Pete has extracted samples and sent them for DNA testing, so with a bit of luck, if they're in the system, we might be able to get their ID. If not, we're back to square one.'

'Is there nothing you can do in the meantime?'

'Clara and the others are trying to track down the most recent occupants of that building. It's been a good many years since the old hospital closed, and all we know so far is that it was bought by a development company, who we believed leased it out in sections. Actually, even the development company is a bit of mystery.'

'Can't you send someone to their offices to get the information you need?'

'I could do, I suppose, and there'd be no shortage of volunteers. However, I doubt the chief would sanction the travel expenses.' Seeing Fleming's puzzled frown, he laughed. 'The only address we have for them is their registered office in the Cayman Islands.'

Jackie winced. 'Yes, I can imagine the chief constable's reaction to that request. It would probably blow our budget for the next five years. What about the directors of that development company? Have you tried to trace them?'

'We have, but with no positive result. The address registered at Companies House belongs to a firm of solicitors in London, who refused to divulge confidential information.' He paused before adding, 'Even the names of the directors are highly suspicious, to put it mildly.'

'What were they?'

Nash glanced down at the case notes he was carrying. 'Allegedly, they are listed as Lionel Blythe and William Pratt, and the company secretary as Betty Perske.'

'They sound fairly ordinary to me. Why do you believe they're dodgy?'

'Viv Pearce nearly wet himself laughing when he searched for them on the internet. Apparently, Lionel Blythe is the real name of the actor Lionel Barrymore, William Pratt was better known as Boris Karloff, and Betty Perske's stage name was Lauren Bacall. I don't think three dead Hollywood film stars would be running a development company with premises in Netherdale, do you?'

* * *

Nash was leaving the headquarters building, and wondered how he would pass the remaining hours of the working day. With progress on the mortuary corpses at a temporary standstill, the building scam solved, and no other serious crimes filling his in-tray, there was little to command his attention. Even as he unlocked his car door and fastened his seat belt, Nash was unaware that he had unwittingly invoked what he referred to as Sod's Law.

Moments after he returned to Helmsdale, Nash's office phone rang. He took the call, listening to the message, before thanking the informant. Having replaced the handset, he sat motionless, digesting the news he'd just received, which added an extra dimension to the most serious crime they were currently investigating.

Clara had gone to collect sandwiches, and when she returned Nash called for her to join him. 'Before you get tucked into your cheese and pickle, I've had some news. I got a call a few minutes ago from the ballistics expert who was testing the bullets removed from the bodies discovered at the cottage hospital. He's got a match — or should I say several matches. I suggest you sit down.'

Clara perched on the chair facing him. 'Go on then, tell me.'

'The gun that fired those bullets was also used in four gang-related murders, one in Manchester, another in Bristol, plus two in London.'

While Nash paused before delivering the even more startling revelation, Clara asked, 'And that helps us, how?'

'The bullets' striations also matched those removed from Gabriel Welham and Thelma Daley, shot at Kirk Bolton Lodge six months ago.'

'Really?' She sat forward, her eyes wide, as she remembered the unsolved murders they believed to be ordered by someone cleaning house.

Nash nodded. 'That suggests a direct link between the murder of Welham, who we know was involved in the killings of the ex-convicts, members of the Country House Bandits, and now the two killed in the old cottage hospital.'

Clara stared at Nash for several seconds as she absorbed this startling development. Eventually, something he'd said triggered a memory which she wasn't certain was accurate. 'I could be wrong, but when we were looking into Welham's murder and we checked his landline, we found one number that belonged to an investment company. I seem to remember the firm was called Dale Investments Ltd, but we dismissed it as irrelevant, because the company had gone into receivership.'

'I think you're right, but why bring it up now?'

'I need to check my facts, but I believe Dale Investments' trading address was the old cottage hospital, Netherdale.' Clara grinned cheekily, before adding, 'Of course, you could regard that as pure coincidence, but only if you believe that such things happen.'

'If you've got it right, and I don't for one minute doubt it, that means the mortuary victims could be tied into Welham, and therefore the Country House Bandits. I'm not sure if that helps us, or if the job's just got a whole lot more difficult.'

* * *

Later that afternoon, Clara reported the outcome of her enquiry into the holiday cottage incident. 'The owners are a local farming family and all they were able to tell me is they rented it out three weeks ago to a guy by the name of Graham Lawson. He paid cash to lease the property for three months, so there's no way of tracing him. I spoke to the farmer's wife, who handled the transaction, and all she could tell me was that Lawson was in his thirties, possibly a little more, and that he was really handsome.' Clara grinned. 'I think he made quite an impression, but that might have been down to what she referred to as, "the fancy BMW" he was driving. Because this was a trivial incident, with no crime being committed other than wasting my time, I don't think there's any mileage in trying to pursue it any further, do you?'

Nash agreed, and the detectives soon forgot about the strange event, concentrating on other, more urgent matters, until developments elsewhere brought the incident back into focus.

CHAPTER TEN

A couple of days passed on the canal before Jolene decided to broach the subject again, asking Graham Lawson when he was going to tell her what was behind his actions. 'You must admit the things you've been doing and the way you've been acting aren't exactly normal behaviour.'

He smiled, but without much humour. 'I'll explain after we've eaten. It's not a very nice tale.'

He served their meal, a pizza he split in two, and poured two glasses of red wine to accompany it. As they were dining, he began to tell her his story. 'I never knew who my birth parents were and, to be honest, I was abandoned as a baby so I didn't much care. My adoptive parents were all I needed, and they cared for me as if I was their own. Sadly, that wasn't for long. They contracted e-coli on a holiday they'd earmarked as their second honeymoon — as bad luck would have it, they chose Africa as a destination. This happened when I was only six years old. It looked as if I was going to be placed in an orphanage, but then my Aunt Agatha and Uncle Edward stepped in. When I say "aunt and uncle", I mean they were my adoptive mother's sister and brother-in-law. They weren't able to have children of their own, so they took me in, and lavished care, attention and love on me. They ensured

I got the best possible education, but when I was in my first year at university, Aunt Agatha passed away. That left Uncle Eddie alone, something he wasn't used to. He wasn't one for joining clubs or social groups, which might have helped, so he was totally isolated. It didn't help that he lived in a very remote location, and the nearest neighbour was over four miles away. Before long, I was travelling the world as a journalist, only touching base with Uncle Eddie each time I returned to England.'

He stared moodily into his empty wine glass. Jolene refilled it, and did the same with hers.

'A couple of years after I started out as a reporter I met a lovely girl, Angela, and we got married. We were very much in love. Soon after returning from honeymoon, I was sent to Asia to cover a big news story that was breaking. Angela got along very well with Eddie, so I suggested she should go and stay with him while I was away, and maybe accompany him to the Ebor meeting in York.' He paused. 'That has to be the worst suggestion of my life.'

Noticing Jolene's puzzled expression, he explained, 'Eddie loved horseracing, as did Angela, partly because her grandfather was a trainer. The Ebor Handicap meeting is one of the biggest events in the flat racing season. They went along, staying in York until the meeting ended, then drove back to Eddie's.'

There was a long pause.

'That was when everything went wrong. Eddie's house was a small mansion, with a long drive surrounded on both sides by an avenue of trees, what he jokingly referred to as his private arboretum.'

Graham took a hefty swig from his wine glass, before continuing, 'The crashed car was found on the drive by the postman, by which time Angela and Eddie were long dead. He called the police. From what they told me, they initially believed Eddie either suffered a stroke or a heart attack, causing the car to swerve off the drive and collide with a massive oak tree. It was when they went to the house they discovered it had been broken into, the burglars forcing entry via a smashed French window. Almost everything of value had been stolen, antique furniture, ornaments, jewellery, paintings, ceramics, the lot. That made the police rethink the cause of death.'

He took another large swig of his wine. 'I had to identify the bodies. Angela was a beautiful girl, but her face had sustained such injuries she was almost unrecognizable.'

He stared into space for a moment. Jolene could see unshed tears brimming in his eyes. Instinctively, she reached out and gently squeezed his arm.

'When the forensic blokes checked Eddie's car over, they believed they had been forced off the road. They found paint scrapings on the front wing and side panel. A week later, a Ford Transit with a dented wing and side panel was found burned out on the moors near the Lancashire border. The van had been reported stolen a couple of weeks before the robbery, and the paintwork matched the one that killed my wife and Uncle Eddie, the only two people I loved, and who cared for me.'

Graham took a deep breath, the emotion almost getting the better of him. 'I intended to tell you all this before now, but when you asked a couple of days ago, I couldn't bring myself to talk about it, because that would have been Angela's birthday.' He took another drink.

'This all happened eleven years ago. I was determined to identify the culprits. Even though I had a lot of contacts who might have been able to help, I was getting nowhere. But then I found out about a gang whose MO fitted this crime to a T. Despite four of the gang members being arrested and sentenced to ten years for a string of burglaries, others have never been identified. I've been investigating that gang and everyone remotely connected to it for years, but I'm no nearer finding out who is behind it than when I started. It was only when I discovered more recently that the convicted men and everyone around them had been murdered that I felt certain my theory was correct.'

He paused once more, and looked directly at Jolene. 'One of the other gang members was a skilled locksmith, who definitely wouldn't have needed to smash a window to gain entrance. He wasn't involved in the raid on Uncle Eddie's house, though. I tracked him down and met him, and from what I learned he wouldn't have countenanced violence of any description, certainly not murder. Known as Artful Artie, his real name was Arthur Fawcett. He was stabbed to death in Harrogate seven and a half years ago, but you already know that, don't you?'

Jolene looked shocked.

'Soon afterwards, his stepdaughter, Joanne Fawcett, disappeared. She knew she was in danger, and so she shed her former identity, changing her name. But I don't need to tell you that either.' He smiled. 'By the way, which do you prefer to be known as, Jo-Jo, Jolene Fraser, or Joanne Fawcett?'

Jolene stared at him, her expression one of complete astonishment mixed with a tinge of fear, until he reassured her.

'We have so much in common, because we have both suffered loss. And we have one overriding objective in life, to find the person responsible for the death of those loved ones. However, in order to do that, we need proof, something concrete, because all I have at present is a wild theory, which might or might not be relevant.'

When she eventually recovered the power of speech, she asked, 'How did you find out who I really am?'

'I watched Jo-Jo and the Tykes performing on television a few months before you were arrested, and I recognized you immediately.'

'How come?'

Graham smiled reminiscently. 'Although Uncle Eddie's house was over forty miles away, I went to boarding school in Harrogate. Even after I left, I naturally retained an interest in what happened in and around the town. The local papers were full of the story of Arthur Fawcett's murder, and one of the articles had a photo of you in it. Luckily, I have a photographic memory, which came in very handy as a reporter. In this instance, remembering your face wasn't difficult, as you were one of the most beautiful girls I'd ever seen. I have to admit I got a heck of a surprise when I saw the band performing. I'd wondered for ages what had happened to you, then I realized you'd simply changed your name, which I guessed was self-protection, after what had happened to Arthur. I also believe it was an extremely sensible decision. Now the murders of the other gang members and everyone close to them proves how wise you were to go into hiding.'

'If you've found out so much about the connection to your wife and your uncle's death, why not take it to the police?'

'Sadly, I have absolutely no evidence, merely a theory. Even though one of the senior detectives in this area is an old friend, the crime wasn't committed anywhere near here, so it was way out of his jurisdiction. There's no way he would be able to act without something more substantial than gossip and my wild ideas. I need far more, because I want justice for Angela and Eddie, just as you do for Arthur. And also, just like you, I believe the evil swine behind all this was the leading light in the burglary gang and so many more criminal activities. For long enough, like you, I thought Gabriel Welham was responsible, but when he was murdered, I realized he wasn't the head man.'

She blinked with surprise. 'How did you know I thought Welham was in charge?'

'I was keeping a discreet watch on Kirk Bolton Lodge when I saw you planting surveillance cameras pointing at the house. That's where I shot the video evidence that cleared you. I was about to come and talk to you about it a couple of weeks later, but then you went and got yourself arrested.'

'What put you onto Welham?'

'Your stepfather Artie told me a lot before he was killed. He revealed he'd parted company with the burglary gang once he learned they'd been involved in Angela and Eddie's murders. He told me as much as he knew, including the fact that the head honchos of the Country House Bandits always turned up in a top-of-the-range Mercedes, with a Netherdale dealer's name on the number plate. He also revealed he'd overheard one of them calling the other Gabe, which I assumed was short for Gabriel. Knowing that, I visited the dealer and told them I was interested in looking at a Mercedes similar to one my friend Gabriel had bought from them. The salesman asked if I meant Gabriel Welham. I looked him up, easy as that.' He refilled the glasses. 'Now tell me how you found Welham?'

'Very much the same way as you, but I used more devious tactics. I pretended I was more interested in the man rather than the car, but I wanted to get one to impress him.'

'Did Artie ever talk to you about the other man, the one who always accompanied Welham to the burglary sites?'

'He did, but in a roundabout way. All he said was the man always wore sunglasses, even at night, and he was referred to by the gang as the Keeper.'

CHAPTER ELEVEN

Jolene asked Graham, 'Weren't you afraid that pursuing whoever is behind the gang might put you in danger?'

'It did, because soon after I started asking questions about what happened to Angela and Eddie, there were a couple of attempts on my life. That was the reason I bought this boat, so I could be off the radar. I believe the people I was trying to find were determined to stop me asking questions. One of the incidents might have been put down as bad driving, when I was nearly run over by a speeding car. The other certainly couldn't have been written off as an accident. There cannot be an innocent explanation for someone firing a rifle bullet at you.'

Jolene stared at him in disbelief, until he pulled up his shirt and showed her the wound on the side of his waist. 'I suspect the gunman was Gabriel Welham. If he'd been a better shot, we wouldn't be having this conversation.'

'What makes you so certain the car was deliberately trying to run you over? It could have been bad driving, surely?'

'The car was a Toyota, and I managed to spot the number plate as it zoomed away. When police checked it out, they told me it must have been on cloned plates, because the actual car was on the forecourt of a motor dealership in

Birmingham at the time. The police thought it was nothing more sinister than some career criminals, such as drug dealers, trying to disguise their activities.'

'What led you to believe it was anything different?'

Graham grimaced as he replied, 'A week after I was released from hospital, as I was trying to deal with Uncle Eddie's paperwork and sort out the house, there was a knock at the door. Bear in mind, I hadn't bought this boat at that point in time. When I answered the door, there were two tough-looking characters standing there. They said they had a delivery. It was a cardboard box, around six feet in length and a couple of feet wide, which they deposited on the ground, then drove off in their van. I ripped the packaging open and stared at the contents. It was a coffin, complete with handles. There was a brass plaque screwed to the coffin lid, inscribed with my name. That was the moment I knew for certain I was being targeted.'

Jolene clasped her hands over her mouth. 'Oh my God, how awful. What did you do?'

'I got an axe from Eddie's workshop and hacked it to bits, then made a bonfire and lit it, ensuring I doused it with petrol first. I did all this in the large open area in front of the house, so anyone watching would get the message I was sending. Whatever they threatened me with, I wasn't going to stop.'

'How did you prevent them having another go at you?'

Graham smiled. 'I made it difficult for them. Realizing they weren't going to stop until they'd finished me off, I faked my own death. It isn't easy to kill a dead man.'

* * *

Seeing her bewildered expression Graham explained, 'Fifteen months after Angela and Eddie were murdered, I announced to the newspaper that I was quitting, then in my final article for them, I outlined my plans to take a solo hiking expedition through the Indian subcontinent, something Angela and I had always dreamed of. A load of baloney, of course, but I deliberately left ample evidence of my progress, even booking places to stay en route. When I didn't turn up at one of those venues, it got reported to the local police. Search parties were sent out, and eventually they discovered some of my belongings, including my passport, near the bank of a river that was in flood after the heavy monsoon rains. After a while, the search was called off and I was presumed to have drowned. As soon as possible, I headed back to the UK and went to ground here.' He smiled. '"Went to ground" isn't exactly the right expression, but you know what I mean.'

'If you no longer had your passport, how did you get back to Britain?'

'As a crime reporter, you get to meet a load of villains, and some of them have special talents. I used a master forger to manufacture a fake passport, which has never been challenged.' He paused. 'That's another thing we have in common. Like you, I changed my name for self-preservation.'

Seeing their glasses needed topping up, Jolene picked up the bottle and realized it was almost empty. Deciding a change of subject might help him, she asked a question regarding Graham's story of his upbringing that had puzzled her. 'If you were a foundling, how come you went to boarding school and from there to university? I thought those places were really expensive.'

If anything, Graham's reply heightened the sadness of his past life. 'That was down to my adoptive parents. Although I only learned about it when I was much older, they had set up a trust fund to cover such an eventuality. That, together with their life insurance policies, enabled Eddie and Agatha to pay for my education. Apart from that, Eddie was also a very wealthy man, having been a highly successful business tycoon.'

* * *

Two nights later, as she was getting ready for bed, Jolene pondered everything she'd been told. Graham was obviously still struggling to cope with the dreadful event that had caused the death of the only people close to him. It was easy to feel empathy, as she felt much the same about the murder of her stepfather. Artie had stepped up to the mark, caring for Joanne after her mother's death, even though they were unrelated by blood.

Jolene also acknowledged the debt she owed Graham. He had saved her from a long spell in prison, and more recently saved her life. She wanted to repay that debt, but it was a while before a possible solution came to her. She remembered his admiring glance as she'd been undressing at the cottage, and his remark about her good looks. He obviously found her attractive, and she realized the attraction was mutual.

Her plan might lessen his sadness, coupled with her own — feelings they had carried for too long. Even if it was only a distraction, a temporary abatement of their joint sorrow, that would be a bonus, and in the process, it would give them enjoyment too. She was still uncertain whether to act on her idea, when the decision was made for her. An enormous crack of thunder was followed almost immediately by a vivid flash of lightning which illuminated the cabin via the tiny windows. Although she wasn't easily scared, the one thing Jolene feared was a thunderstorm. She ran hurriedly across to his cabin, her bare feet making no sound on the carpeted floor. She turned the handle and dashed inside, where Graham had his back to her, preparing to climb into bed. Jolene's eyes were wide. 'I hate thunder. It terrifies me,' she stammered. 'Please, can I stay with you?' she pleaded.

He turned, surprise evident in his face. 'Oh, OK. In that case, you take the bed. I'll sleep on the floor.'

She began to undress, moving closer to him, until she was standing so near their bodies were almost touching. She put her hand on his shoulder. 'Forget the floor. I want us to go to bed and make love. That way we can forget all our sadness. If I'm in your arms I won't be frightened of the storm. We're both alone in this world, but there's no need for us to be lonely and sad when we can make each other happy, if only for a while. We should enjoy our time together, because it might be our only chance. It's not just what you told me about your past, it's about mine too. Believe me, I didn't decide to come in here on a whim. I'd already thought long and hard about it before the thunderstorm decided for me.'

At that moment, there was another loud crack of thunder. Jolene shrieked, and Graham slid his arms around her.

* * *

When Graham awoke next morning, Jolene was still close beside him, her arm across his chest. As he opened his eyes, she smiled at his question.

'Any regrets?'

'Certainly not. You?'

'No, I was too busy enjoying myself.'

'I'm glad about that, because I was too. You should know I don't go around forcing myself on men, but somehow I felt it was right for us to be together.' Her hand snaked down his body until she found her target, and as she began to caress him, she added, 'Making love with you was terrific, so now I want us to do it again.'

Later, as they were eating a belated breakfast, Jolene asked, 'What about my talent on the laptop? You said I might need it.'

'Not for the moment, but I'd like you to check the weather forecast. With a bit of luck, we might be in for another thunderstorm.'

CHAPTER TWELVE

It was two days before Vincent received the information he'd been waiting for. He stared at the details he'd scribbled down after his informant phoned them through. The man he'd been asked to dispose of was called Graham Lawson, and according to the registration details he'd acquired, he lived on a canal boat named *Angela*. The address was Mile Marina, Bishopton, North Yorkshire. Now he had the details, he'd be able to get the job tied down. Only then would he report back to his client and demand payment for his services.

Vincent began to plan his strategy. First item on the agenda was a vehicle. Given that the location was remote, with little traffic on the country lanes nearby, something as conspicuous as his Porsche would not be a sensible choice. Eventually, he decided the most nondescript option would be a small van of the type used by many delivery drivers. If he hired one for the day, he'd have it returned to the rental company before his victim's rigor mortis set in. It was a tactic he'd used before, more than once, and it had worked a treat.

Vincent followed the directions and left the van in a small parking area at the side of the canal. He reversed into a space, ensuring his route would be clear for a swift exit. Taking a fishing rod from the rear of the van, and a sack containing something heavy, he leaned casually on the gate and looked up and down the towpath, checking the area. It was deserted. He spotted the canal boat on his right and set off, aware of his surroundings. He didn't like fishing, had no intention of doing so, but if he was noticed, he had a valid reason for being there.

* * *

Graham told Jolene he needed to go shopping. 'We're all right for a lot of stuff, but we need milk, eggs and bread. I'm a bit out of practice at buying provisions for more than one person, and I didn't buy too much in because I wasn't sure how long we'd be staying. Added to which, you've a very healthy appetite. That might be down to all the exercise you're getting.'

Jolene blushed slightly at the insinuation, but told him, 'OK, but hold on a minute before you dash off. Did you check the toilet rolls?'

He shook his head.

'I'll go and look.' She headed for the toilet at the stern of the boat.

'OK, I'll wait. And make sure you lock the door behind me when I've gone,' he reminded her.

While he waited, Graham checked the door to the bow was secure, and walked across the cabin towards the door at the stern. He'd only got halfway when the door was kicked, bursting open. He was frozen into immobility by the gun pointing directly at him.

Vincent walked carefully down the steps, advancing as Graham backed away.

'Sit!'

Graham sank onto the banquette, watching in horror. The intruder smiled, lifted the gun, and pointed it directly at Graham's heart. Vincent removed a silencer from his pocket and was about to attach it to the pistol when he heard a noise behind him. He glanced back and stared in horror at the figure standing only two paces away. Days earlier, he'd put three bullets in her back from close range. Nobody could have survived that. Momentarily focused on the apparition, he failed to notice what she was holding. It was to be a fatal mistake.

Vincent felt a stunning blow, the impact causing him to discharge the pistol. The effect was not what he had planned. The bullet struck a copper frying pan hanging above the stove. The ricochet lodged it in the planking on the wall, doing nothing more harmful than glancing against the arm of his intended victim en route.

The would-be assassin slumped to the floor, blood pouring from a gaping wound in his neck, where the sharp end of the boathook had severed his carotid artery.

Jolene looked across at Graham, wide-eyed. 'Oh God, what have I done? I was aiming for his head. I didn't know the hook was so heavy.' Then she saw blood on Graham's shirt sleeve and ran to his side. 'Are you OK?'

'I am, thanks to you. This is only a flesh wound, but it was a damned close thing. I think we'd better scarper. They've obviously found out where we've been hiding.'

'Where can we go?'

'There's another place where they've no chance of finding us.' Graham glanced around. 'We should get away from here as soon as possible. I'll summon assistance. The people I'm going to call are totally trustworthy. They're the only ones who know I'm still alive.'

'Before we do anything, let me see to your arm.'

While Jolene applied a dressing, Graham made the phone call, saying, 'Yes, we'll be ready. Perhaps it would be wise not to come alone. If the assassin has an accomplice, he could be lurking nearby, so a lookout might be necessary. Send a text when it's safe for us to leave. We'll leave my car here — the number plate would be a dead giveaway. I think we need to use one of your chalets until the danger passes, if that's OK with you?'

He listened for a moment, then told his contact, 'No, I think we'll only need one bedroom.'

He glanced across at Jolene, who nodded agreement.

Ending the call, Graham told Jolene to grab what she could, explaining more about where they were heading. 'The guy is an old friend of mine, and he owes me a big favour. You'll like his wife. She's similar to you in some ways, being quite feisty and determined. We'll be absolutely safe there. Nobody would be able to guess where we are.'

As they were packing, neither of them was aware that a few hundred yards further along the canal, an angler had heard the gunshot that had pierced the silence. A former soldier, the fisherman knew instantly that this was not a car backfiring, nor the sound of a shotgun being discharged, as you might expect to hear in such a rural location. He recognized it as a handgun, and he was close enough to identify the location. As he headed away, running for safety, he pulled his mobile from his pocket and dialled 999.

* * *

Graham and Jolene waited until he received a brief text message before they left the safety of the cabin. Peering round anxiously, they moved to step ashore. It was only then Jolene noticed the petrol can on the deck. Alongside it was an empty sack and a fishing rod. She shuddered, clutched Graham's arm, and pointed. 'I think that petrol was meant for us.'

The discovery hastened their retreat, running towards the car park, where they saw a man by the gate. They hesitated, and saw him look around before he turned and waved to them. There, they scrambled into the back of the vehicle that would carry them to their new refuge. A small van has little in the way of comfort, even in the passenger section. In the rear, there is none whatsoever. Jolene and Graham were each laying on their side, their arms and legs interlinked to avoid them rolling from side to side during their journey along the narrow, winding country lanes. 'I never read about this position in the *Kama Sutra*, or *Fifty Shades of Grey*,' Graham muttered.

Jolene's reply made him chuckle. 'Really? Haven't you heard of "Cock au Van"?'

'Don't worry, we'll be there soon,' the driver reassured them. 'At least the back was empty when you called. Otherwise, you'd have been sharing the space with a load of fertilizer.'

CHAPTER THIRTEEN

Nash arrived at Helmsdale with the feeling he had forgotten to do something. The first thing he noticed on entering the CID suite was that both detective constables, Adil Hassan and Viv Pearce, were on the phone, pens poised as they made notes.

Clara followed Nash into his office. 'Good morning, Mike, how are you? And more important, how are Alondra and Lucy?'

He noticed she was clutching a sheet of paper. Eyeing this, he replied, 'We're all fine, but I've an idea you're about to change that, for me at least.'

'I'm not sure. This might be a crime. Alternatively, it could simply be the result of an elderly woman's absentmindedness.'

'I've already done this morning's cryptic crossword, so perhaps you could explain, preferably in English.'

Clara grinned. 'There's been a call from a Mrs Bagshaw, a widowed lady from Kirk Bolton who sounds to be getting on a bit. She said she took delivery of a tankful of domestic heating oil about four weeks ago, she's not sure exactly when. She's barely had to use any, but this morning, when she dipped the tank, it was almost empty.'

'If she only took delivery a few weeks ago, what prompted her to dip the tank?'

'She'd been away visiting her brother and sister-in-law, who live near Morecambe. She stayed with them for over a week, and when she returned, she noticed the filler cap from the oil tank was lying in the middle of the flower bed. At first, she thought it was down to the fuel company's delivery driver being careless, but now she's convinced someone has siphoned off somewhere in the region of two hundred litres of oil.'

'That's quite a haul, both in quantity and money, given the exorbitant cost of heating oil these days.'

'I agree, and I was about to send Viv or Adil to interview Mrs Bagshaw and obtain precise details of the delivery, and get them to dip the tank and take a photo of the level shown on the dipstick. However, by the sound of the calls they're taking at the moment, I think they'll have plenty on their plate today. So I was just waiting to brief you and then I'll set off.'

'Can't uniform deal with it?'

Clara laughed. 'Oh, they're all busy, and Steve's theory is it will get passed upstairs to us anyway, so we might as well take it now.'

Nash shook his head. 'Go on then.'

* * *

No sooner had Clara left his office when DC Hassan entered, and Nash noticed that he too was clutching a sheet of paper. 'I've just been talking to a man who works for a farmer near Drovers Halt. He told me his boss has been away for a few days — taken his family for a break to visit a couple of agricultural shows. They aren't due to return until the weekend. Anyway, the farmhand went to fill up one of the tractors, but the fuel tank was completely empty. He swears there was plenty of diesel in it, so he's certain somebody's nicked it, and he reckons he's got a bit of evidence. He spotted some tyre tracks in the soft ground alongside the tank, and they don't appear to match any of the farm vehicles.'

'He sounds as if he should be working for our CSI team.'

Adil smiled. 'The poor man is pretty unhappy about it. He told me his boss will be livid when he finds out. As he put it, "no doubt he'll blame me for it. If anything goes wrong round here, I'm always responsible".'

'Does our unhappy labourer live on site?'

'No, he has a cottage in Drover's Halt, a couple of miles from the farm.'

'In that case, you should tell him to point out to his boss that unless the farmer forks out for a huge telescope, there's no way the man can see what's going on at such a distance. I take it you're going to Drover's Halt now?'

'Yes. Is there anything special you want me to do?'

'Phone CSI and get them to send someone to take a cast of those tread marks, and also get the farmhand to dip the tank again, then take a photo of the dipstick for evidence.' Nash thought for a moment and then asked, 'I suppose we're talking about red diesel, aren't we?'

Adil looked shocked by the question. 'Of course, Mike! You don't think they'd pay full price when there's a cheaper option available. Not only is he a farmer, but he's also a Yorkshireman, and that's about as tight-fisted a combination as you can get.'

'I suppose if someone's going to nick a large quantity of diesel, they won't be too concerned what colour it is. OK, off you go, and liaise with Clara. She's checking out a possible domestic heating oil theft, and the two might just be connected.'

* * *

As Adil picked up his paperwork, Nash saw Viv Pearce hovering by the doorway. He signalled for the DC to enter and listened as Pearce told him about the call he'd received. During this, Nash was reminded of the expression 'it never rains but it pours', and this seemed highly appropriate.

'I've just taken a call from a guy called Andrew Ball. He lives in Bishop's Cross. He went to Harrogate theatre last night along with his girlfriend, who lives in Netherdale. After the show they went for dinner, then stayed at her place overnight. When he returned home this morning, he spotted the filler cap from his heating oil tank was missing. He found it tossed in his hedge. He'd dipped the tank only a couple of weeks back, so he dipped it again before he called us, and he reckons someone's had it away with over a hundred and fifty litres of oil.'

Nash thought this over for a while and then told Pearce, 'Here's what I want you to do. Give Mr Ball a call and let him know one of your colleagues will be round to see him later this morning. Then phone Adil and ask him to go to Bishop's Cross when he's finished at Drover's Halt. Once you've done that, hook up to any CCTV cameras operating near Bishop's Cross, Kirk Bolton or Drover's Halt. Give HQ a call and ask them to get someone on it as well. Adil can give you a hand when he returns.'

Having explained his reasoning, Nash continued, 'There might not be any cameras close to the crime scenes, but if this is all the work of one gang, they might have driven towards Bishopton, Helmsdale or Netherdale, and on any of those routes they would have to pass one or more camera. You'll be looking for activity late at night or in the early hours of the morning, when there's likely to be no one about.'

Nash added another thought. 'I think you should concentrate on a vehicle big enough to hold several containers with hundreds of litres of fuel inside, maybe even more. That way you can discount a Mini, a Fiat 500 or other small cars. In fact, I'd be tempted to cross cars off your list altogether, because the quantity, plus the different types of fuel reportedly stolen, would probably need a Transit van or bigger.'

Seeing Pearce's puzzled frown, Nash told him, 'Two of the thefts were of domestic heating oil, but the other was red diesel, and they would need to be kept separate. Given that it's extremely unlikely for two sets of fuel thieves working in such a small area, I think we're only after one crew of villains. Maybe even a lone operator.'

* * *

Three hours later, Nash was still trying to remember what had been bugging him all morning, but soon after Mironova and Hassan had both returned, his phone rang. He listened for a moment and then said, 'OK, Steve, we're on our way.'

He put the phone down and went into the general office. 'Clara, you're with me. An angler has just reported hearing a gunshot from inside a boat moored in a remote stretch of the canal at the far side of Bishopton. The fisherman's an ex-soldier and is convinced the discharged weapon was a handgun.'

Nash turned to DCs Pearce and Hassan. 'Viv, Adil, you'd better follow us as backup. Get your protective jackets on.'

Clara struggled into her Kevlar. 'Thank goodness we don't have to wear those helmets.'

'Worried about your hair, Clara?' Viv joked, then grinned at the scowl he received.

CHAPTER FOURTEEN

It was fifteen minutes before Nash and Mironova pulled to a halt in the designated assembly point, a lay-by on the main Bishopton Road some distance from the track leading to the canal. A marked police car was already there. The officer jumped out and reported to Nash. 'Sir, I was the nearest when the shout went out. There's another of our cars on the way. The lane that leads to the canal car park is just round that bend. I wish we could see the junction and spot any cars leaving. Do you want me to block it?'

'No, wait for the ARU team. We have to follow protocol.'

The two DCs parked behind Nash's Range Rover and Clara went to speak to them, leaning on the bonnet and complaining about the wait. Viv, however, was complaining that they should have brought one of the drones, with Adil in agreement.

Thankfully traffic was light, and Clara watched the vehicles manoeuvring to pass what was becoming a car park on the wrong side of the road. None of the detectives paid much attention to the nondescript-looking van that passed them, although Clara spotted a man in the passenger seat, who turned his head away and spoke to the driver. He seemed vaguely familiar, but she couldn't think how.

Moments later, two cars pulled to a halt ahead of the lay-by. The ARU team had arrived.

'Right, who's in charge here? What have we got?' the leader demanded.

Nash explained.

'So, we only have the word of an ex-soldier that he heard what he thought was a gunshot.' The ARU officer looked very sceptical. 'I hope this isn't a waste of time. If it was a gunshot, they're probably long gone by now.' He issued instructions to follow, and the convoy drove down the narrow track to the car park near the canal. There were three vehicles already occupying the site, leaving room for only three more. Nash told Pearce, Hassan and the patrol officers to remain behind and keep their eyes open for anyone acting suspiciously.

He and Mironova followed the ARU team along the towpath. To ease the tension, Clara told Nash about the van passenger she had seen, remembering who it had reminded her of. Had she not been distracted by their colleague's signal to wait, she might have noticed the change in Nash's expression when she mentioned the name.

While they watched and waited, Nash signalled to a man standing further along the canal, whom he assumed to be the angler by his mode of dress, to remain where he was and wait.

Clara read the sign painted on the bow of the vessel and wondered if the owner had bestowed the name *Angela* on his boat as a tribute to his wife, girlfriend or mistress. With little else to do, she glanced round, her training in examining potential crime scenes coming to the fore.

* * *

With an ARU officer on the bank stationed at the prow, and a second at the stern, their Glock machine pistols poised, the leader shouted, 'Armed police! Come out with your hands where I can see them!' He waited, then repeated the call. 'Armed police! Come out now!'

With no response, a third armed officer holding a riot shield climbed aboard and cautiously approached the broken cabin door, the senior officer close behind.

The leader of the ARU team emerged onto the deck. 'There's a dead man in the main cabin. We've checked the boat over and he's the only occupant. There's also an automatic pistol and silencer alongside the body.' He looked round at the location. 'There doesn't look to be anyone around. Probably got away in the time it took us to attend. You don't need us anymore, but I'll leave one of my men. You'll need him to remove the pistol when the photographer's finished. I'll report in and ask for the usual circus to turn out for you.' He spoke to his team and left.

Clara grinned. 'I dread to think what Mexican Pete would say if he knew he and his team are referred to as the "circus". He has enough to cope with when he sees you.'

* * *

Nash walked along and spoke to the fisherman, who seemed aggrieved at having his fishing interrupted. 'Did you see anyone enter or leave the boat?'

'No, because I was further along the canal, at the point where it bends.' The man pointed with his right hand. 'My vision was obscured by those weeping willows. But I know what I heard,' he added defiantly. 'I didn't rush to get here. In fact, I ran the other way. Self-preservation — I've been shot at enough times in my life, and I didn't want to risk another one.'

'It's quite remote here, so I assume you drove. Is your car in the car park?'

'Yes, mine's the old banger, ideal for ferrying fish around. If I ever get chance to catch some, that is.' He looked dejected at the loss of his day's leisure.

Nash indicated the boat. 'If you head back to the car park, give your details to one of the officers and you can leave. We can arrange to take an official statement from you later.'

Nash took his mobile and updated Viv. 'The angler is heading for you. Take his details and let him go. You can both remove your Kevlar, and then bring two sets of incident suits to us, please. There's some in the boot of the Rover in the plastic crate.'

'Mike, is that really necessary? I've got some gloves and overshoes in my pocket we can use,' Clara told him.

'It's too confined a space, too risky. We need to preserve the scene.'

Viv and Adil arrived carrying the plastic bags. 'Er, Mike,' Viv said, 'is Alondra doing anything today?'

'I think she's going to visit Lisa, see how she and the baby are doing.' The fifth member of the team, DC Lisa Andrews, was currently on maternity leave, caring for her baby son, born on Christmas Day. 'Why do you ask?'

'Do you like humble pie?' Both Viv and Adil were struggling not to laugh.

'Viv, explain.'

'We were just wondering why you've got Lucy's pram in your boot.'

'Bugger!' Nash's face was a picture as he grabbed his mobile and stepped away. Now he remembered what had been bugging him all day, what he should have done before leaving home. Would he be in trouble!

* * *

Suitably clad, they entered the cabin. The dead man was laid face down, a pool of blood surrounding his head. On the floor behind the body was a long piece of timber with a brass hook attached. The pistol mentioned by the ARU leader was under the corpse's right hand.

Nash bent down and sniffed. 'This is the gun our angler friend heard being fired. So where's his victim? It would take a spectacularly bad shot to miss at such close range — unless, of course . . .' His sentence tailed off as he surveyed the scene a second time.

'Unless what, Mike?'

'Unless someone clobbered him with that boathook just as he was in the act of discharging his weapon. A clout on the head is likely to affect anyone's aim.'

Moments later, Clara recognized the accuracy of Nash's guesswork. As they continued their visual search, she noticed small spots on the cabin floor. 'Those look like bloodstains, but they're a few feet away from where the dead man's lying,' she told Nash.

He turned to the waste bin alongside him, flipped the lid with his gloved hand, and peered inside. 'Maybe that guy isn't the only one who got wounded. Look here.'

Clara saw a number of bloodstained tissues, cotton wool and the wrapper from a bandage. 'We might need to search the canal bank and surrounding area,' Nash told her. 'There might be another body nearby. Before that, once Mexican Pete and CSI get here, we need to find out who this guy is, and equally important, if he owns this boat. If not, our priority has to be finding the owner and checking for other potential victims.'

Nash paused, and after inspecting the corpse again climbed back up onto the deck. 'Viv, I want you to check the vehicles in the car park — do a DVLA search. If this guy isn't the boat owner, that could be the quickest way to identify him. Before that, however, I want you to get onto the relevant waterways authority and find out who owns this vessel. Adil, will you run the log and send those two officers to walk along the canal beyond the barge, just in case there's another victim? Keep your eyes open, all of you.'

Clara pointed to the fuel can on the deck. 'Do you think that's significant?' she asked.

'It could be.' Nash unscrewed the top and sniffed. 'Well spotted, Clara. I think this is definitely relevant.'

'How do you know for certain?'

'This can has petrol in it. As far as I know, all canal boats use either diesel or electric engines.'

* * *

81

Nash was about to call Detective Superintendent Fleming to inform her of the development, when his phone rang. 'Yes, Viv,' he answered.

As he listened to DC Pearce, Clara saw his expression change to a puzzled frown. What, she wondered, could Viv have told him that he found so baffling?

'Do you know anything else? The name sounds familiar, but for the life of me, I can't think where I've heard or seen it,' Nash commented. 'I'll have to get my thinking cap on, and hopefully I'll remember before long. And no comments about my memory, thank you.'

He ended the call and stared at Clara, but she guessed his thoughts were elsewhere. After a prolonged silence, she asked, a trifle hesitantly, 'What did Viv tell you?'

Nash's response surprised her. 'The dead man might, or might not, be the owner. Viv checked out the boat and gave me the details. I'm sure I should know the name, but I can't think from where. Viv said the vessel is registered to someone by the name of Graham Lawson.'

Clara was immediately able to provide the answer to his conundrum. 'Graham Lawson. That's the name of the man who rented the holiday cottage where the fake shooting incident took place.'

'I knew it sounded familiar. The two events are obviously linked, but I can't for the life of me think how.'

CHAPTER FIFTEEN

In the track leading to the car park, a convoy of vehicles arrived. Heading the procession was the pathologist, followed by a coroner's van driven by one of his mortuary assistants. In sharp contrast to this drab vehicle, the last to arrive was a gaudily painted CSI van.

When he reached the boat, Ramirez was predictably sarcastic. 'Have your superiors offered you a productivity bonus, Nash, or are you taking backhanders from the local Undertakers' Guild?'

Nash smiled sweetly at him. 'Neither of those, Professor. I just couldn't bear the thought of you sitting in your office, bored and lonely, with nothing else to occupy your time and nobody to make jokes about.'

Ramirez snorted. 'There is no chance of getting bored the way you keep producing corpses. What's the tally now, ten bodies or more within the past six months? Eleven, with this one? There have been so many, I've almost lost count, but it must be close to a record, even for you.' He paused. 'Please don't regard that as a challenge, though.'

Nash and Mironova waited on the towpath for the pathologist's initial findings.

When he emerged, only a few minutes later, his first few sentences confirmed at least part of Nash's guess. 'The man was killed by a single blow to the head. There is a large open wound to the neck which appears to have pierced the carotid artery, which would have proved fatal. I have little doubt the weapon used was the boathook found alongside the body. His pockets contained a car key.' He handed this to Nash. 'You may need it.'

'Thank you, Professor,' Nash said.

'And the post-mortem will have to wait a couple of days, as I will be away. I will expect you at nine o'clock on my return. I doubt whether the findings will provide any great surprises.' Ramirez returned to sarcastic mode as he added, 'I trust you'll be able to find your way to the mortuary without needing directions.'

With little reason to remain, Nash spoke briefly to the CSI team leader before he and Mironova returned to the car park, where Viv and Adil were waiting. 'Any luck with the vehicle check?' Nash asked.

Viv winked at Clara before replying, 'We have found a car belonging to an extremely dodgy character.' He pointed to where Nash's Range Rover was parked.

'Oh, very funny.' He scowled.

'Have you finished checking them over?' Clara intervened hastily.

'Yes, the Ford Transit Connect van belongs to a vehicle rental company, Carline, based in Netherdale.' He pointed to a BMW. 'That belongs to the boat owner, Graham Lawson.'

'We'll have a look at the van.' Nash took the key and opened the driver's door for Viv to check inside.

In the glove box, Viv found a mobile phone along with the hire agreement, and a set of house keys attached to a car key for a Porsche. He whistled. 'Look what I've found.' He dangled the car key in the air.

Nash went round to the back. Inside was a holdall containing a fresh set of clothing. 'Bag it all,' Nash said. 'We have to assume this van belonged to the dead man on the boat — otherwise, how did he get here? It's a long walk, even along the towpath.'

As they were doing so, Viv said, 'We allowed Mr Fisher to take his car away, once we'd checked it over.'

'Fisher? Who's Mr Fisher?' Clara asked.

Viv grinned. 'Mr Fisher, the angler.'

'You're having us on.'

'Afraid not.'

* * *

It was late afternoon when the detectives arrived back in Helmsdale, to be greeted by Sergeant Meadows on the desk. He handed Nash a Post-it note with a phone number scrawled on it. 'I took a phone call a while back from the head of Forensics. I explained that you were at a crime scene, and she asked me to ensure you call her back as soon as you can.'

Nash was puzzled. 'The head of our Forensic team is a man. You said "she".'

'Sorry, the call was from West Yorkshire Forensics. The woman said she had an important update for you regarding the corpses from the old cottage hospital.'

That comment, Nash thought later, had to be one of the biggest understatements of the year.

He made the call, and enquired as to the reason West Yorkshire had become involved in one of their investigations. He listened for a long while, and Clara, who was watching from the general office, saw his expression change from surprise to disbelief, and finally acceptance. She also saw he wasn't making any notes about the topic they were discussing, which puzzled her.

Having asked the officer to send him an email containing the information, he assured the woman of their cooperation, promising to keep her up to date with developments, and ended the call. Despite his colleagues pressing him for information, Nash refused, saying only that he preferred to wait until he could deliver them the full story. Before the email arrived, Nash re-examined the file on the cottage hospital incident, and in particular, the details of the previous occupants of the building.

Half an hour later, Nash printed the email off and assembled the team. 'Because of the fire damage at the cottage hospital, our forensic guys felt they had to get a second opinion on the DNA results.' He smiled wryly. 'In fact, I think they were so shocked they hardly believed the evidence their tests threw up. With that in mind, they sent the samples to West Yorkshire, because the original information stemmed from DNA logged on the PNC database by them.

'Their names are Byron Harvey Morris and his wife Audrey, but given their history, it's more than possible that these might be aliases. Several years ago, they were arrested and charged in connection with an alleged major fraud, amounting to somewhere in the region of twenty-seven million pounds. They were released on bail. The case never came to court because they were dead.'

'We already know that, Mike. We found the bodies, remember?' Clara commented a trifle sarcastically.

'Clara, I'm talking about the *previous* time they died.'

CHAPTER SIXTEEN

Nash grinned at his colleagues' bemused expressions. 'Years ago, Byron Morris and his wife ran a company which sold life insurance and, supposedly, massive investment opportunities, targeting people over the age of fifty. They also traded in cryptocurrency, marketing it as a safe investment option. With the unstable economy, the firm went into receivership, and investigators acting on behalf of a group of investors discovered there had been fraud and embezzlement on a massive scale.

'Both directors were due in court for the initial hearing, but failed to turn up. As a result, warrants were issued, but when police went to execute those warrants, the couple had disappeared. There was no further development until a month after that scheduled court appearance, when Morris's BMW, covered in parking tickets, was discovered in a car park in Whitby close to the harbour where his yacht had been moored. But this boat, like its owner, had vanished.

'When police followed up on this, a local fisherman claimed to have seen the vessel set sail over three weeks earlier. The eyewitness was absolutely certain there were two people on board, a man and a woman. Initially, it was believed the fugitives had made a successful escape and were living it up in some tropical paradise on the proceeds of their crimes, but two further developments caused a complete reversal of that theory.

'The first was the discovery of the yacht, adrift in the middle of the North Sea, its sails torn to shreds, steering gear unworkable, and the engine malfunctioning. According to the eyewitness, there was one inflatable attached to the back when the yacht left Whitby harbour. This was missing when the yacht was recovered. The second discovery came several days later, when an inflatable was found on the shore near to Flamborough Head. Examination revealed there were multiple large, jagged holes below the water line, consistent with the fragile craft hitting rocks with considerable force. Given that there had been several near-gale-force winds over the previous weeks, it was assumed the fugitives had abandoned ship, taken to the dingy, been hurled onto the rocks and drowned.'

'If the boat engine failed, why didn't they call out a Mayday?' Adil asked.

'Think about it. Would you call out the RNLI to be rescued if you were on the run? And who says the boat actually broke down?'

Nash turned to Clara, smiled sweetly and told her, 'That means they've actually died twice. They survived drowning, but were unable to dodge the bullets that put them in the mortuary.'

* * *

There was a long, stunned silence as the detectives tried to grapple with this startling information. Eventually, Clara asked a two-part question that scarcely seemed relevant at the time. 'What was this company they ran called, and where was it based?'

Nash glanced at the file notes from West Yorkshire. 'The company was named Janus Investments, and according to their letterhead they had offices in Leeds and Manchester. Their registered office was care of a firm of accountants in Rochdale.

Although they claimed to trade from the premises shown on the letterhead, these were only used for postal deliveries, and in fact, almost all their activity took place via the internet. That tallies with their dabbling in cryptocurrency, I guess.'

'Staging the scene so that everyone believed they were dead must have taken some arranging,' DC Hassan observed.

'That's a very good point, Adil, and it leads onto another very interesting question. Who helped them stage it?'

'You think someone else was involved?' Pearce asked.

'There must have been. If, as we now believe, they sabotaged the yacht and the inflatable, they would have needed help to get ashore, unless they were cross-Channel swimmers. Even when they were back on dry land, they'd require transport, accommodation, new passports and driving licences, plus assistance in setting up their new enterprise. While I was waiting for the information from West Yorkshire, I re-examined the file on Dale Investments, a previous occupier of the old cottage hospital building. This had also gone into receivership. The directors are listed as Maurice and Anita Harvey.'

'What?' Viv laughed. 'Maurice Harvey — Byron Harvey Morris. Well, that really took some ingenuity to think up a name like that.'

'I think you're right, Viv. Given all the evidence, I think it's safe to assume these two are the same people as the directors of Janus Investments.'

* * *

Something Nash had said caused Mironova to puzzle, but it was a few minutes before she realized the significance of the trigger word 'accommodation'.

'We ought to concentrate on finding out where they lived,' she suggested, 'because there might be some useful evidence in their home.'

'Excellent idea,' Nash agreed.

'How will we be able to find out their home address?' Pearce asked.

'That's going to be tricky,' Nash replied. He thought for a moment and then suggested, 'I don't believe they will have bought a property, because that would involve too much paperwork, and if they applied for a mortgage, they would need to provide proof of identity.'

'What if they'd bought one for cash?' Hassan queried.

'I don't think they'd do that. There would still be too much paperwork, and given their propensity for acquiring money, particularly other people's, I doubt they'd be prepared to shell out a six-figure sum if they could avoid it. So all in all, that virtually rules out a purchase.'

'We need a plan of action,' Clara said.

Nash nodded. 'We need to identify the property they rented and do so without delay, because if we don't examine the place as soon as possible, we could miss out on vital evidence, should it be cleared by the owner. We might already be too late, but we can't afford to take that chance. So, tomorrow morning, let's start by contacting all the local estate agents, plus the national ones with branches in our area, concentrating primarily on those who act as letting agents. Run the names of the deceased past them, and see if they come up with any matches. Can one of you also contact the local council, water services, et cetera? See if they have any means of finding them by name with no address.'

'What happens if we find the place they've been living?' Hassan wanted to know.

'I want a CSI team to enter the property and conduct a microscopic forensic sweep of the interior and check every item of the contents inside, plus any outbuildings.'

He saw Pearce and Hassan's puzzled frowns and explained, 'Given that we believe our two fraudsters had at least one accomplice, if not more, this could be our only opportunity to identify him — or her, or them. Their fingerprints or DNA would be ideal, and if they happen to be on the PNC, that would be even better. That's jumping the gun, though. Before we start planning our strategy, we have to find the property.'

'What if they rented from a private landlord, not through an agency?' Pearce asked.

'That's what I like about you, Viv, your undying optimism. We'll cross that bridge when we come to it. Try the professionals first, and if we draw a blank, we'll have to think up a way to tackle the others. Now, get off home. It's getting late and we'll be busy tomorrow.'

* * *

Before he left, Viv Pearce told Nash, 'I phoned the rental company in Netherdale about the Ford van parked at the marina. They told me the vehicle was hired yesterday and is due to be returned tomorrow. The man who rented had to produce his photo driving licence, which they photocopy as part of their routine. They've just emailed me it, and the guy's name is Vincent Brown, with an address in Shadwell, just outside Leeds.'

He passed a printout of the licence to Nash, who took one glance before handing it to Clara. 'That's the man we found dead in the canal boat.'

Clara nodded agreement, and then commented, 'What we need to find out is why he'd come all the way from Leeds to such a remote location, carrying a gun. And what he did to get himself killed.'

'We also need to find this Graham Lawson, the boat owner. He might be the one who was wounded, but could also be our prime suspect,' Nash added.

* * *

Later the following day, the detectives reported to Nash. They had been unable to locate the residence used by the directors of Dale Investments. 'We've checked, but drawn a complete blank,' Viv told him. 'There is one possibility I didn't think of until I was trying the third or fourth agent, and that is they might have taken the tenancy out in a totally different name.'

'I think that's unlikely,' Nash pointed out. 'That would involve arranging yet another set of ID paperwork.'

Although it looked to be a complete dead end, Clara still had one contact outstanding. 'All the others on my list can be discounted, but when I phoned Tophams, their partner was unavailable. All I could glean from their receptionist was that he'd gone to view one of their rental properties, and from there, he was heading straight home. I thought that was a bit odd, as it was only early afternoon, but the girl in the office said he had to pick up his child from school. The receptionist promised to get him to call me first thing in the morning.'

Next day, Clara had only been in the CID suite a few minutes when her phone rang. Five minutes later, she was able to report to Nash that she'd struck gold.

'Simon Finlay from Tophams Estate agents has just phoned me. Yesterday afternoon he went to a property on High Grove Crescent in Netherdale. The tenants had defaulted on their rent and are now several months in arrears, despite several reminders being sent. The house was locked up, and it looked as if it had been that way for quite a while. At first, he thought the tenants had simply done a moonlight flit, but when he went inside, he found lots of their possessions and personal effects, including clothing, in situ. There was also some extremely mouldy and very smelly food in the fridge. He was intending to call a firm of cleaners this morning and instruct them to clear and sanitize the house throughout, ready for re-letting.' Clara smiled. 'However, I asked him not to do anything, because we need to access the property first, and would be treating it as a potential crime scene.'

Clara paused before delivering the punch line to her story. 'The client who signed the lease was Maurice Harvey. Occupation — company director for Dale Investments Ltd. I've asked Mr Finlay to provide us with a photocopy of the lease agreement. We can collect that along with the house keys later this morning.'

CHAPTER SEVENTEEN

When the detectives arrived outside the semi-detached house on High Grove Crescent, the CSI van was already there. Nash issued specific instructions to their team leader, which provoked a mild protest.

'Unless the house has been stripped bare, what you're asking for is going to involve a mountain of work. We're already snowed under with one of our team on leave, and we're still handling that canal boat crime scene plus several other jobs. Is all that effort absolutely necessary?'

'It most certainly is. This is the home of the two people whose bodies we recovered from the old cottage hospital, and could represent our only chance of identifying their partners in crime, and from there, tracking down their killer. As things stand, we're almost bereft of factual information, and what little we do have is purely theoretical. We need every microscopic piece of concrete evidence we can get, no matter how insignificant or irrelevant it might appear to be. This house could be our only opportunity to obtain something useful. Before you go in, DS Mironova and I will give the place the once-over.'

Nash gave it some more thought as he was putting on his protective suit and turned back to the officer. 'OK, I take your point. I'm trying to look at it from your perspective. As this search relates to murders that took place several months before we uncovered the bodies, I suppose it's not fair of me to ask you to prioritize it. Maybe you can put it on the back burner until other pressures ease, and then conduct the microscopic examination of any contents you are able to remove from the property. That leaves only the immovable objects to deal with now.'

The look of relief on the CSI team leader's face told Nash the man hadn't exaggerated the pressure they were under.

'One thing's for certain,' Clara commented, after they'd been inside the house for a while, 'this place hasn't been stripped bare like the boffin hoped.'

They were standing in one of the bedrooms, where the open wardrobe door revealed a rich variety of men's quality clothing on hangers and shelves. 'That's true enough, but whether it's good news or bad, only time will tell.'

Nash's remark puzzled Clara, causing her to ask, 'Why might it be bad news?'

'It could imply the killer, or the victims' accomplice, is confident there will be nothing inside this house worthy of our attention.'

'A couple of days ago you accused Viv Pearce of being pessimistic, but that sounds as if you've been taking lessons from him.'

Half an hour later, Nash handed over the house keys to the CSI team leader. As he accepted these, he asked Nash if they had noticed anything of potential significance inside the property.

'Apart from the trio of corpses inside the chest freezer, the fifty-kilo bag of what looks like cocaine, and a couple of stolen Lowry paintings, very little of interest,' Nash replied, and turned to leave.

'I don't think our friend believed you,' Clara said as they walked across to Nash's car.

'OK, so I exaggerated. Maybe there were only two corpses and one painting.'

* * *

Without forensic results from either the property rented by the cottage hospital murder victims or the canal boat crime scene, the detectives were at an impasse. Seeking a positive slant on their steadily increasing workload, Nash asked for an update on the fuel and heating oil thefts.

Unfortunately, as Pearce and Hassan reported, there was a lack of progress in that investigation too. 'We've checked what sparse CCTV footage is available,' Pearce reported, 'but we've been unable to find a vehicle which appears on all the cameras.'

'Actually, what Viv said isn't strictly accurate,' Hassan chipped in. 'There was one van which appeared in all the footage, and what's more, it was the right size to carry stolen fuel. It had been registered in Kingston-Upon-Hull, and for a while we got excited, believing we were onto the villains. However, when I checked it out, I discovered the vehicle was one used by an Amazon delivery driver, and their schedule is far too tight to allow time for nefarious activities such as fuel thefts.'

'In other words, we're back to square one,' Clara responded.

'Pretty much so, and to be fair, we've run out of ideas,' Pearce told them.

'Have you checked other similar vehicles, to see if there's a common denominator, such as the ownership, or if they belong to a hire fleet?' Nash asked.

'No, to be honest, we hadn't thought of that,' Pearce admitted. 'We'll get on with it immediately.'

'While you've got the registration numbers on screen, it might also be worth checking them against the vehicle type. One of the simplest ways of avoiding detection is by switching registration numbers, as we know. If that's been going on, the van used by the thieves could well be on cloned plates, possibly more than once.'

Nash watched as they left his office, wondering whether it was time for a coffee. Before he could act on the idea, his phone rang. The ensuing call postponed any thought of refreshment for several hours.

'OK, Steve, Clara and I will attend. We'll need a CSI team there. Would you ring them please, Steve, and if they start whining about their workload, remind them that's what we pay them for.'

* * *

Nash put the phone down and signalled Clara to join him, telling Pearce and Hassan, 'Clara and I are going slumming. Steve's had a report from Traffic Division of a Hanoi burglary at some shack this side of Bishopton. The hovel goes by the name of Fellside Manor.'

Pearce whistled with surprise. 'I know that house. It's an absolutely magnificent property. Lianne and I go walking around there with little Brian. The woodland and scenery is beautiful, and makes a stunning setting for such an impressive building.'

As they were driving to the crime scene, Clara asked more about the incident they'd been called to. 'As you referred to it as a Hanoi burglary, I take it the thieves broke into the house, stole some belongings and then made off in the owner's car.'

'That's correct, but it gets a bit confusing, because Hanoi burglaries have different names in various parts of the country. In some places they're called Millennium burglaries, whereas in others they're known as two-in-ones.'

'I think I'll stick with Hanoi burglaries, rather than increase the confusion.'

'Anyway, in this instance, going from what Steve Meadows told me, the victims had been away on holiday and returned to find the house had been burgled. They rang Netherdale control room and reported that all three of the family's cars had also been taken. That's one Mercedes, one Audi and one Mini Cooper. Apparently, there are three family members resident at the manor, Mr and Mrs Payne plus their daughter. There is also a son, but he lives and works in London.'

'If the house is as grand as Viv Pearce suggested, I'm surprised they don't have a sophisticated burglar alarm fitted.'

'Apparently they do, together with CCTV. It will be interesting to see what the camera footage reveals.'

* * *

After passing through the village of Bishop's Cross, Nash drove north for three miles, before turning off the country lane, where a couple of large, wrought-iron gates were suspended from imposing stone pillars, these surmounted by griffins.

The long drive leading to the manor house was flanked on either side by huge rhododendron bushes, which Clara estimated were somewhere in the region of six feet tall, possibly even more. 'I bet those are a magnificent sight when they're in full bloom,' she commented.

'Yes, it's a pity the burglary took place too early. Perhaps you should ask the house owners to arrange another robbery in April or May.'

The tarmac driveway yielded to a wide sweep covering the area directly facing the imposing facade of the building. Nash pulled to a halt behind a patrol car, the only other vehicle there. Indicating this, he told Clara, 'Steve mentioned Starsky and Hutch were at the crime scene.'

Two of their recent additions to the uniform branch were Traffic Officers Peter Starkey and David Hutchinson, who, from the moment they were paired together, had gained the nickname Starsky and Hutch, after the popular 1970s US crime-fighting duo.

As Nash and Mironova approached the sturdy oak front door, it swung open, with one of their uniform colleagues having adopted the guise of butler. Nash responded to the officer's greeting, noting with approval he was wearing protective gloves as he welcomed them to the property.

'It's like a scene from *Downton Abbey*,' Clara muttered, referring to the popular TV drama.

Nash smiled. 'If Jim Carter, who plays the butler in *Downton*, had opened the door to greet us, you'd know we're on the film set.'

'I didn't realize you were such a fan!'

CHAPTER EIGHTEEN

The detectives were ushered into a large sitting room, where the other officer was standing along with the householders. The man stepped forward and made the introductions. 'I'm Thomas Payne, and this is my wife, Jennifer, and our daughter, Georgina.'

Nash reciprocated, showing his warrant card, as Clara did likewise.

'I assume you won't have had chance to identify what's been stolen — apart from the cars, of course.'

'Not as yet. Your control room advised us to touch as little as possible for fear of possibly contaminating evidence. Which means,' Payne added with a grimace, 'that we haven't even been able to make a cup of coffee.'

'Have you found out how they got into the house? I'm assuming the car keys were kept inside, not in your garage.'

'That's correct, and we knew the entry point from the moment we arrived home. The taxi dropped us and our luggage by the back door — that way Jenny could drop the used clothing into the washing machine. One glance at the back door was enough. It looks as if they took a sledgehammer to it.'

'I was told you have a good burglar alarm. Why didn't the break-in trigger it?'

'I can answer that, Inspector Nash,' one of the traffic officers told him. 'We had the same thought. We checked, and the burglars simply cut through the cable, severing the power supply to the alarm system.'

'What about the CCTV?'

Thomas Payne's expression became even more sombre, if that was possible. 'The CCTV is on a separate cable, and the footage shows a man in the act of cutting the alarm cable. He even had the nerve to wave at the camera. Unfortunately, he was wearing a mask, unless of course Mickey Mouse has taken up a new career as a burglar.'

'Was he the only person the camera picked up?'

'No,' Payne sighed sadly. 'There was one other. He was disguised as Donald Duck.'

Nash turned to the traffic officers, thanked them, and said, 'We'll handle it now, until Forensics get here.'

After they left, he told the householders, 'I don't think we need to wait for our CSI team. I'd like you to accompany DS Mironova and myself as we do a tour of the house, identifying any obvious missing items. Before we start, it would be helpful if everyone puts on protective gloves and overshoes.'

When the search of the large house was over, the detectives and the victims compared notes. Jennifer Payne was the first to report. 'My jewellery box has gone, but there was little of value inside it, merely costume jewellery. Oh, and there was my old watch, but that will be of little use to them as it stopped working years ago. I'd been meaning to throw it away, but never got round to it.'

Her daughter's account was along similar lines. 'I only left a pair of earrings and a pendant in my room, and they weren't worth much. Anything of value, Mum and I give to Dad, and he puts it in the safe.'

Seeing Nash's puzzled expression, Thomas Payne explained, 'I had a combination safe installed in the bedroom, secreted behind a wall mirror. Once I realized we'd been burgled, it was the first place I checked. It's completely intact, and so are the contents.'

* * *

After handing the crime scene over to Forensics, Nash and Mironova headed back to Helmsdale. 'What do you make of that?' Clara asked once they were en route. 'It seems like a lot of effort for very little reward.'

'There are two possibilities that spring to mind. Either the thieves underestimated the Payne family's caution and were deeply disappointed by what little they could steal, or the house contents weren't the prime objective. I tend towards the latter line of thinking.'

'In other words, you believe they were simply after the cars, and burglary was committed to hide their true objective, yes?'

'That would be my guess, and it leads to another possibility.'

'What might that be?'

'If you check out the retail value of the three stolen vehicles — a Mercedes S Class, an Audi A8 and a Mini Cooper — they would probably set you back in excess of two hundred thousand pounds new. Even second-hand, they're going to be worth well into six figures. Given that all three cars are relatively uncommon and highly distinctive, I reckon the burglars must have a source for disposal of the booty.'

'What source are you thinking of?'

'Again, this is pure speculation, but the best way of earning substantial sums of money from those vehicles, and doing so in relative safety, would be by taking them to a friendly breaker's yard and getting them stripped down for spare parts. Once they've been taken to bits, the components would be completely untraceable.'

Nash paused and thought for a moment. 'My other guess is that Forensics won't pick up anything useful from their sweep of the house. That would mark the thieves down as highly professional. Also, if they had been after some of the house contents and were thwarted, amateurs would have been likely to commit one or two acts of vandalism, purely out of spite.'

'All of which is going to make catching them doubly difficult.'

'True. But I've a couple of ideas that might be of some use. First of all, we ought to get our tech wizards to suspend operations on the fuel thefts and check CCTV footage from all roads leading to the nearby towns, to see if they can spot which direction the stolen cars were taken. We should also check with other forces in nearby areas, to see if they've had a spike in high-end vehicle thefts.'

* * *

The more he thought about the outbreak of comparatively minor crimes, the more irritated Nash was that they were being distracted from what he saw as their main goal — to identify and apprehend the driving force behind the cottage hospital and canal boat murders. It was a long time before he realized how erroneous that line of thought was.

It was only when they pulled into the car park outside Helmsdale station that Nash remembered he'd failed to switch his mobile back on after leaving Fellside Manor. He confessed the omission, adding, 'I must be getting old.'

'You're not the only one,' Clara told him. 'I forgot as well.'

As they entered reception, Nash said, 'Daniel's on half-term break. I've a missed call from him. I wonder what that's about?'

Clara stopped in mid-stride. 'Daniel tried me too — perhaps we should ring him back.'

Before they had chance to do so, Steve Meadows hailed them. 'You've missed all the excitement. We've just appre-hended the fuel thief, thanks to a vigilant member of the public. He's in the CID suite at the moment, giving his statement to Viv and Adil.' Meadows grinned at the detectives. 'I'm sure you'll both want to see him. As for the suspect, he's in the cells awaiting a solicitor prior to interview, but you can't be present during that, Mike. I'm sure you'll understand why when you go upstairs.'

If this statement was designed to intrigue Nash and Mironova, it succeeded, and they both hurried up to the first floor.

CHAPTER NINETEEN

Daniel Nash was home alone. Normally, his father would have taken leave so they could spend time together. However, with the recent increase in workload the detectives were struggling to cope with, that was not possible.

Daniel had quite understood, and was comforted by the fact that he would have the company of his stepmother, Alondra, who he loved deeply, and his tiny half-sister, Lucy, who he also adored — except when she cried in the middle of the night and woke him up.

On this day, however, Alondra had to take Lucy for the baby's development review, conducted by the health visitor at the surgery in Helmsdale. Alondra had offered to take Daniel along, but he had refused point blank, the reason for which amused her.

'If you think I'm going to sit for an hour or longer in a room full of screaming, wailing infants, you can think again.' Gesturing towards his sibling, Daniel added, 'This one makes more than enough racket, without the encouragement of a full choir to back her up.'

That conversation had taken place the previous evening, and later, when they were alone, Nash had wondered how

Daniel would pass the day, with little to amuse him, and only their Labrador, Teal, for company.

'I hope he won't be glued to his laptop all day,' he told Alondra.

'I doubt it,' she replied. 'I'd be willing to bet he'll be occupied writing a love letter to his girlfriend.'

Nash had looked at Alondra in astonishment. 'I wasn't aware he had a girlfriend. Who is she? Someone from his school, or a lass who lives round here? How long has this being going on, and why didn't you tell me?'

'I've only found out recently, and you were too preoccupied with all the problems at work, so I didn't want to burden you with it.'

'Hang on, Daniel's not sixteen yet. How serious is it? I hope he hasn't been taking things too far, because he's still under the age of consent — and the girl might be too.'

Alondra shook her head and laughed. 'Stop panicking. It's serious, alright, but there's no chance of him "taking things too far", as you politely put it, not for the foreseeable future, anyway.'

'How can you be certain?'

'Because unless things change in the near future, the girl is well out of Daniel's reach — she's over a thousand miles away.'

'You obviously know a lot about it. Did Daniel confide in you?'

'No, he was pretty taken aback when he realized I'd discovered his secret. It was the sub-postmaster in Wintersett who let the cat out of the bag.'

'You're going to have to explain that.'

'A couple of weeks ago, I was in the shop for stamps, and the postmaster asked me if Daniel's special Christmas card had reached Romania in time. When he saw I was baffled by his question, he explained that back in December, Daniel had insisted the card went first class. He was concerned he'd missed last posting date for Romania and he got the card posted on the final day.'

'Romania, does that mean . . . ?'

Alondra gave her husband a cheeky grin and told him, 'I interviewed the suspect and obtained a full confession. He admitted that he and Nicola Sinclair have been writing to each other since she left England eighteen months ago. The Sinclair family wanted to be out of the glare of publicity after everything they'd been through, but whether they'll remain overseas or return to the UK is still uncertain. Daniel hopes they're going to come back once the media circus stops following them everywhere.'

Nash remembered the case vividly, having been instrumental in overturning a massive miscarriage of justice, which led to Nicholas Sinclair being released from prison after many years. He was reunited with his wife, Demetra, and met his daughter, Nicoleta, known as Nicola, for the first time.

'Hang on. If this all started after the Sinclair family left England, how did it happen?'

'If you remember, I told you I'd noticed Daniel was attracted to Nicola when they first met, and warned him to behave himself. What I didn't know was that Nicola was equally attracted to him. You recall the family came here to thank you before they left? That was when Nicola gave Daniel her email address. They've been corresponding online whenever possible, but apparently the internet in the town where Nicola and her parents are staying is virtually non-existent, so they've been using the old-fashioned method.'

'How come we've never seen letters to Daniel with a Romanian stamp?'

'He's been really crafty. He gave Nicola his address at school, plus the dates of each term. She sends her letters there. If they want to correspond when he's at home, she writes to him via Jonas Turner, who has been sworn to secrecy. I reckon Daniel's about as devious as you, Mike.'

Alondra paused. 'Was I right, allowing them to continue the relationship, or do you disapprove?'

Nash considered the question for a few seconds. 'I think it was the best way to handle it. If teenagers are banned from doing something, it seems to make them more determined to carry on. Apart from that, as I recall, Nicola is not only a very good-looking young lady, she's also a really nice person, which shows what excellent taste he's got. If it's meant to be, that's all well and good, if not, it'll probably fizzle out given time. Besides which, for me to object with my history would be extremely hypocritical.'

* * *

If Daniel had been aware of that conversation, he would have been impressed by the accuracy of Alondra's guess as to how he intended to spend the time alone. He took Teal for her morning walk, but the fresh air and exercise was curtailed by a sudden squally shower. They returned to the house, where his first task was to spend time drying the Labrador's coat, a process Teal enjoyed immensely.

Daniel then returned to his bedroom, and, seated at his desk, he slid the photo of Nicola from the drawer where he'd secreted it. Having placed it against the desk lamp, he stared at her image, drinking in her striking features, the dark eyes and splendid figure. He had asked Nicola's permission to take the photo, saying it would give him something to remember her by. She had agreed, but only on condition that she could take one of him using Daniel's mobile, as she didn't possess one.

'How will I get it to you?' Daniel had asked.

'You could post it to me, but maybe it would be better if I give you my email address to send it, and then I can download and print it. That way we could also remain in touch, which would be nice. I'm not sure if we'll stay in Romania permanently or not, and email would ensure we remain in contact, wherever we are, if you'd like that.'

Daniel's enthusiastic agreement to the plan had caused Nicola to blush slightly, which he thought made her look even prettier. After spending several minutes daydreaming of her, he took out a sheet of paper and began to compose what he privately acknowledged was a love letter.

* * *

The sole occupant of the van glanced sideways as he drove past the isolated house. No vehicles were parked in front of the building, which to him meant the occupants were out. When he'd reconnoitred the property ten days earlier, he'd identified the residents as a man, a woman, and a baby. He'd reckoned without the twin factors of a boarding school and the half-term break.

He reached the end of the lane and turned his vehicle round, which would make for an easier getaway should he be disturbed, then pulled to a halt alongside the front entrance to the target house.

There was a momentary panic as he heard a dog barking. It sounded to be a large animal. He didn't like dogs. Dogs presented a bigger threat than humans. Then he relaxed, identifying the location of the sound. The dog was inside the house, and therefore posed no danger.

After opening the van's rear doors, he removed a long pipe from within and commenced operations by unravelling it, heading towards the large fuel tank alongside the building. He eyed the tank approvingly, hoping it was full, or close to it. If it was near to capacity, this would be a highly profitable morning's work. Having removed the cap from the tank, he lowered the pipe inside and began to siphon off the contents.

* * *

Daniel heard Teal barking, but initially this didn't concern him. When the sound continued, he glanced at his watch. It was far too early for the postman, so what had disturbed the dog? She was normally placid, not given to displays of unrest. When the noise didn't abate, Daniel put his biro down and left his room, determined to discover what had agitated the Labrador. On reaching the half-landing, he glanced out of the window, which faced the front of the house.

It was then he saw the van — and the equipment alongside it. Daniel stopped in his tracks, staring in disbelief for several seconds, before returning to his bedroom. Picking up his mobile, he rang his father. The call went straight to voicemail, so he tried again, this time using the number for DS Mironova — his unofficial Aunt Clara — but got the same outcome.

'Third time lucky,' he muttered, using the number of Helmsdale Police Station from his contacts list. He got through immediately, and cut into Sergeant Meadows' standard greeting. 'It's Daniel Nash, Mike's son. I'm at home, on my own, and there's a van pulled up outside the house. Someone's siphoning fuel from our central heating oil tank.'

'OK, Daniel, stay on the line and I'll get someone there ASAP.' Seconds later, Meadows updated him, 'There's a patrol car heading to you. They'll be with you in less than ten minutes.'

'Right. In the meantime, I'm going to video the van and activity using my mobile.'

'Just be careful you're not seen, Daniel. Whatever you do, stay inside the house without being spotted — and check to ensure all the doors are locked. I've just had an update from the guys who are en route. They're currently passing through Wintersett village, so with a bit of luck, we should have your fuel thief in handcuffs in a few minutes.'

CHAPTER TWENTY

As soon as Nash crossed the threshold into the CID suite, he stopped dead. He remained motionless, staring in disbelief at the person sitting on the corner of Viv Pearce's desk.

'Daniel, what are you doing here? Has something gone wrong at home?'

'No, Pa, everything's fine. I'm here to give my statement. The traffic officer gave me a lift.' He grinned as he added, 'Seeing who I was, Starsky, he said his name was, let me sit in the front!'

Seeing his father's baffled expression, he continued, 'I'd taken Teal for her walk and when I got back home I was in my bedroom . . . er . . . messing about, when she started barking and wouldn't stop. I went to find out what was wrong and that's when I noticed a van outside with a guy helping himself to our heating oil. I tried your phone, and Aunt Clara's, but they both went to voicemail, so I rang here and reported what was happening to Sergeant Meadows. Luckily, there was a patrol car nearby, and ten minutes later, they'd arrested the bloke. Sergeant Meadows sent a van to collect him and the other officer drove his vehicle back here.'

'Bravo, Daniel, that was really quick thinking,' Clara told him.

Once Nash had recovered from the shock, he was immensely proud of his son. But as he told him so, Nash couldn't resist the chance to tease him. 'When you said you were messing about, I don't suppose that means you were writing love letters, does it?' Seeing Daniel's embarrassed and anxious expression, he relented, telling him, 'It's OK, Mum told me all about it, and I certainly don't disapprove, so there's no need for you to keep it secret any longer. I might even raise your pocket money to cover the cost of postage. Above all, I agree with Clara. What you did this morning was extremely intelligent and should result in a serial thief being put behind bars.'

'It's a good job it happened this week,' Daniel told him. 'Next week I'd be back at school and would have missed all the excitement.'

'And we'd be short of heating oil,' his father said.

'Oh, I didn't think of that. But I did think to send Mum a text to explain why I'm not at home.'

'That was very thoughtful.' Turning to Pearce, Nash asked, 'Now, what about the petrol pincher?'

'We checked his van. The rear compartment was packed with large tanks marked up as "red", "heating oil", "diesel", and "petrol". There were also eight sets of number plates, some of which correspond with those picked up by the CCTV cameras.'

'That sounds like game, set, and match to me. Thanks to Daniel's quick thinking, we should be able to draw a line under a series of crimes that have occupied too much of our time.'

'He must get those talents from his mother,' Clara suggested, winking at Daniel.

Nash glared at his deputy, but his expression changed to a warm smile as the door behind her opened. The others followed his gaze and saw Alondra standing on the threshold, with baby Lucy in her arms.

'We've come to collect the hero of the hour and take him home,' she announced. 'Sergeant Meadows told me what happened.'

After a few minutes, during which Clara and Viv took it in turns to bounce Lucy on their laps and play with her, Nash escorted his family downstairs. On his return, he told the team, 'We should concentrate on getting the case notes for the fuel thefts ready, including a recording of an interview with the suspect. Then we can forward it all to Tom Pratt to prepare a file for submission to CPS. Once we've got that out of the way, we can perhaps focus on trying to make headway in our other investigations.' He paused before adding, 'That reminds me, I'll be absent tomorrow morning. Mexican Pete scheduled the post-mortem for the canal boat victim and I'll be the attending officer.'

He was about to return to his office when Clara asked, 'What was that about love letters? I could tell Daniel was embarrassed when you mentioned it.'

Nash explained, causing Clara to remark, 'Like father, like son, I guess.'

* * *

One of the more popular winter pastimes of those frequenting hostelries within the dale was the game of dominoes. There was even a league, founded many years earlier to meet the needs of those players and landlords with a competitive nature.

For the previous three years, one public house had dominated the competition, winning the trophy each season. The Bull Inn at Gorton had seemed unassailable, but now their supremacy was being challenged. The Miners Arms in Wintersett village was an unlikely candidate for a strong contender, but in recent times they had recruited several talented new players.

One of the newcomers, Tony Jackson, had joined the team at the suggestion of a friend. He wasn't overly competitive, but saw the outings as a way to ease the discomfort of his solitary existence. He had, he admitted to his close circle of friends, been lonely since his wife had walked out deciding she preferred the warmth of a Spanish winter, and the additional warmth of a Spanish lover.

Tony lived some distance from the Miners Arms, but a scheme was devised to share the driving to and from matches on a rota basis. This meant that all the players with one exception could indulge in copious amounts of alcohol to celebrate their success, or to drown their sorrows in the event of failure. This could be done in perfect safety, without attracting the attention of the police with their breathalyser kits.

As Tony awaited the arrival of his chauffeur for the evening, he suddenly remembered he had left his mobile in the car. He hurried outside, retrieved the phone, placed it in his pocket, and returned indoors. He had barely time to place the Range Rover keys on the hall table when the sound of a car horn signalled the arrival of his free taxi ride.

The evening was a resounding success, and the celebrations had continued until well after midnight. The solitary lemonade drinker had borne the carousal with fortitude, knowing it would be someone else's turn to miss out the following week.

He commenced the shuttle service, returning his teammates to their homes. Last to be delivered was Tony Jackson. As he pulled up at the end of the drive leading to Tony's house, the driver noticed something amiss. 'Ayup, Tony, where's thy motor?'

Jackson peered a trifle myopically out of the passenger window. Sobriety returned instantaneously. 'Oh, bloody hell, some bastard's nicked my car.'

Several miles away, the driver of a Range Rover began to sing. The rendition was a corruption of a popular television advertisement, 'Just stole your car, 'cos we nick any car. Just stole your car, 'cos we nick any car.'

* * *

As Ramirez had predicted, the post-mortem on the corpse from the canal boat was fairly routine, merely confirming his assumptions made at the time, backed up by gunshot residue tests from his hands and clothing proving the dead man had fired the pistol found alongside his body.

As usual, Nash had turned his mobile off whilst inside the mortuary, and when he left, his first task was to check for messages. There was only one, from DS Mironova. It read, *Call me when you get this. There was another Hanoi last night.*

Minutes later, Nash learned of the theft, and the minimal amount of valuables taken from inside Tony Jackson's house. 'This looks like the same gang who stole the Payne family's cars,' Clara suggested. 'But what interests me is how the thieves knew Mr Jackson would be out playing dominoes yesterday evening.'

'That would tend to suggest they're on the lookout for particular vehicles, and once they've identified a potential target, they conduct surveillance until they can establish a weak point in their routine.'

'That seems logical,' Clara agreed.

'The other thing it suggests is that they aren't picking cars at random. It's beginning to look as if they've a shopping list. That's bad news for the victims, because it's logical to assume they also have a place to take the stolen goods, where they will soon become unrecoverable. While I'm in Netherdale, I'm going to have a word with Paul Grant. I appreciate this is a CID matter, but it's all about cars, so I think Traffic Division's input could prove useful.'

Inspector Grant had been transferred to their region only three or four years earlier, but had already proved his worth in many ways as he headed up their Traffic division. For the meantime, however, neither branch of the force had sufficient evidence to do more than theorise about the car thefts.

Other reports continued to come in. A top-of-the-range BMW was now missing, while the couple's other vehicle, a Renault Clio, had been ignored by the thieves — giving credence to Nash's theory about the burglars' working from a shopping list. Having taken three vehicles on a previous incursion, this seemed the only logical solution.

* * *

Nash took a couple of days' leave, designed to spend time with his son prior to Daniel's return to boarding school. When he returned to work, Clara reported yet another Hanoi burglary. 'Again, there was little of value taken from the property.'

'But we've still no idea where they're taking the stolen cars. Has anyone looked at CCTV images, so we can at least get some clue as to which direction they take after they've nicked the vehicles?'

'Yes, but all that's done is provide us with another puzzle. Viv and Adil, along with officers at HQ, spent hours looking at footage from the few cameras in those remote areas, but apart from a brief glimpse of Mr Payne's Mercedes in Bishopton town centre, there's absolutely no sign of the other stolen cars.'

'That's really odd.' Nash thought it over for a few moments. 'In that case, they have to be using the back roads, which implies they know the area or have their route planned in advance.'

Up to that point, although the car thefts were categorized as serious crimes, the detectives nevertheless viewed them as an unwelcome distraction from the far more violent crimes they were investigating. That would all change later, when news of yet another incident began to emerge.

CHAPTER TWENTY-ONE

At long last, Nash received the report from the CSI team charged with examining the canal boat. He'd been immensely relieved there were no other victims in the vicinity, but remained puzzled by what exactly had taken place aboard the *Angela*. Viv had only been able to establish one fact — the ownership details for the barge in the name of Graham Lawson. He had confirmed this with the registration details of the BMW, plus the photograph on the driving licence provided by the DVLA. However, Graham Lawson remained as mysterious a figure as ever.

Nash called Mironova into his office. 'The superintendent's on her way. She wants an update before she briefs the media. Let's see what we can tell her from this report.'

The file contained a few surprises, and when Jackie Fleming arrived, Nash suggested they sit in the general office so the others could hear the discussion.

'I think you'll find what CSI discovered quite interesting. Let's start with the man who was clobbered to death at the marina. We found a driving licence, fake. The home address in Shadwell, Leeds, is bogus — no such place. The keys found on the body did match the rental van found in the nearby parking area. The mobile phone found in a holdall in the back appears to be a burner and is with the Forensic team. We also have a set of keys.'

There was a shaking of heads as the team looked at one another, realizing it was yet another dead end.

'However,' — Nash smiled — 'luckily for us, his fingerprints were on the PNC. Real name Richard Petersen, of Dutch parents, not Vincent Brown, the name shown on the driving licence he produced when he hired the van. Several years ago, Petersen, a former soldier, had several convictions for burglary and later assault.

'Our CSI man was sufficiently curious to enquire about Petersen with West Yorkshire CID. They thought it unlikely he was going straight. I think they were correct with that assumption. We should ask West Yorkshire Police to see if there are any other properties linked to him.'

Jackie agreed. 'I'll sort that.'

'CSI's next task is to run ballistics tests on the gun and the bullet they dug out of the cabin floor. They'll run the results through the PNC and hope they get matches to any previous crimes, which will tidy them up.'

'Is that everything from the report?'

'Far from it. The rest makes even more interesting reading. CSI found fingerprints and DNA from two people within the sleeping accommodation and elsewhere on the barge. Richard Petersen's DNA and prints weren't found anywhere, but the boffins did obtain samples of semen and vaginal fluid on the bedding in one of the cabins. The semen is from the male whose blood was on the tissues found in the waste bin. They are in the process of analysing the samples and will let us know within the next twenty-four hours if either the man or the woman is on the PNC.'

* * *

The timescale was shortened considerably, because the meeting was still in process when the head of Forensics rang back. Nash listened to the first part, scribbling notes as he did so, but after a couple of minutes, Clara saw his expression change to one of disbelief. He asked the caller to repeat the information, before he reacted. 'That's impossible,' he said, which clearly provoked an angry reaction from the scientific officer.

'Sorry, I didn't mean to doubt your word, but it came as a terrible shock. No, you don't have to email the file to me. We already have it. Now we know the full facts, we might be able to make some progress.'

Clara could tell Nash was struggling to come to terms with what he'd just been told. It was a long while before he gathered his thoughts sufficiently to tell them what he'd learned. Before that, he asked Viv Pearce to get him the driving licence photo ID from DVLA of the man who owned the BMW parked near the marina. Having examined this, he began to explain what had shocked him so much.

'Two people have been staying on the canal boat and both are in the PNC system. The woman's name is Jolene Fraser, and she has very recently been released from Blackwell Prison, following a successful appeal against a conviction for attempted murder. She was declared totally innocent.'

'Jolene Fraser . . . that name sounds familiar, but I can't think where from,' Clara said.

Nash continued, 'Before her conviction, Jolene was lead singer of a highly successful pop group called Jo-Jo and the Tykes. What makes me curious is why she was on the canal boat — apart from having sex, that is. Her fingerprints are in the cabin and inside the sleeping quarters along with her DNA. Crucially, Jolene's fingerprints were also on the boat-hook that was used to clobber Richard Petersen.'

'I think "interesting" is a massive understatement,' Jackie commented. 'What about the DNA from the blood and semen?'

'That person is also in the PNC,' Nash told them, and paused. 'I'm absolutely baffled as to why his name has cropped up after such a long time — unless, like Clara, you believe in ghosts.'

'Why are you so puzzled?' Clara asked.

'Forensics identified the DNA as belonging to Geoffrey Lister, a former foreign correspondent. Although he's a few years younger than me, we went to the same school, and later, when I was working in the Met, he covered several cases I was involved in. That was when he was a mere crime reporter. However, the reason I'm so shocked is that around ten years ago, Geoff Lister was presumed dead.'

He saw the confusion on his colleagues' faces. 'I attended his memorial service.'

'I think you'd better tell us more,' Jackie told him.

'Geoff had gone missing during a hiking expedition in India. Despite extensive searches, he was never found.' Nash pointed to the image he held. 'However, if you exclude the designer stubble, the photo of Graham Lawson on this driving licence is pretty much how I imagine Geoff Lister would look after the passage of ten years. I think it's safe to conclude they're one and the same person.'

'Not another puzzle to solve.' Clara shook her head in disbelief.

* * *

The meeting had been scheduled to end, but Nash's explanation extended it considerably as the team expounded theories as to the reason Lister would wish to hide. Jackie went in search of coffee, but Clara remained at Nash's side, aware that the shock revelation had upset him deeply.

'It seems to me,' she began rather tentatively, 'your friend Geoff Lister was sleeping with Jolene Fraser. And their idyll got rudely interrupted.'

'I'm not sure sleep had much to do with what was going on in that cabin. When he was young, Geoff had quite a reputation where girls were concerned. That all changed though, when life went sour on him.'

Clara seized the opportunity to tease Nash, which she hoped might cheer him up. 'Didn't you say that Lister went to the same school as you? Tell me, was seduction part of the curriculum, or did they add Viagra to the drinking water? They certainly didn't put bromide in it. Come to think of it, your Daniel also goes to that school, and we've just discovered he's a budding Casanova.'

'I'll have you know I'm a respectable married man,' Nash stated with mock umbrage.

'I'll agree with two-thirds of that remark,' Clara retorted. 'Man, yes. Married, yes. But respectable — that's going too far.'

She smiled at Nash's vulgar two-fingered gesture, but then said, 'I wonder what caused Lister to disappear. And what made him take up with someone like Jolene Fraser? They seem to have little in common.'

Jackie Fleming returned, accompanied by Viv Pearce acting as barista. She watched Nash, who was studying the photo of Jolene that accompanied the report. It had been taken shortly after her arrest.

'I think that's easy to answer. She's an extremely attractive young woman, just the sort who would appeal to Geoff.' He flipped the photo across the desk as he spoke. They stared at it for several seconds, before Clara gasped aloud.

'What is it? Do you recognize her?'

'No . . . or rather, I do and I don't.'

'What does that mean?'

'I don't recognize Jolene Fraser as such, but I've certainly seen that highly distinctive blouse before. It was on the dummy at the holiday cottage, with three bullet holes through the back. And Jolene has long, blonde hair, which looks pretty similar to the wig on the dummy someone used for target practice.'

'That puts a totally different slant on what we think happened in the canal boat. Maybe it was Jolene, not Geoff, who was being targeted. I think we should examine Jolene Fraser's file. Something in her past might give us a clue as to why somebody might want to shoot her.'

He thought for a moment. 'Clara, what did you do with the scarecrow at the cottage?'

'I left it where it was. Why?'

'When we've finished here, take Adil and go and get the bullets out of it. Take them to Forensics and let's see if they match, and Jolene is actually the target.'

'I think that confirms our theory as to Richard Petersen's new occupation — hitman!' Jackie said, as she sipped her coffee. Then she brought up the principal reason for her visit. 'OK, so, in the light of all this confusion, what do you suggest I tell the media?'

Nash was still pondering this when Clara came up with a possible solution. 'Why not release the dead man's name, say we're treating the death as suspicious, and that we're anxious to trace the owner of the boat, plus one other person we believe was on board. We could do so without mentioning Lister's name, or his alias, and certainly make no mention whatsoever of Jolene Fraser.'

'What would that achieve?'

'It would tell whoever hired the assassin their man is dead and that Lister is still at large. If he was the target, they'll know their attempt to silence him has failed. They'll also wonder who the other person mentioned in the press as being aboard the canal boat might be. However, if Jolene Fraser was their target, by excluding any mention of her at the canal boat, they might still believe they disposed of her during the pantomime at the holiday cottage.'

Nash smiled at Mironova's description of the staged crime scene, but applauded her reasoning, with one notable exception. 'I think Clara's got it pretty much right, but I'd prefer to put in a couple of amendments. If we add "as a matter of urgency" to our statement about tracing the boat owner and the mystery person, it might send a message to Geoff Lister and Jolene Fraser that we need to speak to them. However, I believe we should withhold identification of the dead man, and merely tell the press that a body has been found in a canal boat at Mile Marina, and that we are treating the death as suspicious.'

'What would withholding the dead man's identity achieve?'

'It would leave whoever hired Petersen in a state of uncertainty as to who got killed and who survived. That could provoke a reaction, which might help us identify who employed him.'

CHAPTER TWENTY-TWO

When Jackie Fleming had left, Clara asked the question she'd been puzzling over since Nash mentioned it, 'What did you mean about Lister's life turning sour? And why is his DNA on file?'

'Geoff was a very successful journalist, and had just got married. Shortly after his return from honeymoon he was sent abroad. I can't remember the exact details because I wasn't involved, and as I recall, Geoff's uncle lived somewhere over the other side of the county. But while he was away Geoff's wife and his uncle were killed in what at first seemed to be a tragic accident, however, it then became a murder enquiry. Apparently, their car was in collision with a van being driven by thieves who had burgled the uncle's house. His DNA would have been taken at the time for elimination.'

'Surely it would have been destroyed if he was innocent.'

'I believe the case was never solved. It would have been retained.'

'That's all very sad, but it sounds as if Jolene's now consoling him.'

Nash grinned. '"Consoling", that's a new word for it.'

Clara's mention of Jolene's name provoked a reaction from Nash, one which, together with further information, would provide much food for thought.

'Pass me that woman's file,' he asked.

Nash stared at the image of Jolene Fraser for several seconds before calling DC Hassan into his office. He instructed Adil as to what he required, which puzzled Clara.

'Why do you want those files in particular?'

'Because if I'm right, I think I could have just solved something that's been baffling me for months, and it might tie everything we've just learned together.'

When he took delivery of the first file, Nash flipped it open and withdrew a photograph. He slid this alongside the image of Jolene Fraser and stared at them for a few seconds. 'I knew it,' he muttered. 'That's got to be the answer.'

'What has?' Clara was becoming impatient.

'This is a photo of Joanne Fawcett, stepdaughter of Arthur Fawcett, aka Artful Artie, who was one of the Country House Bandits burglary team. Joanne was twenty when Arthur was murdered, and she disappeared shortly afterwards. I've wondered for ages what happened to her, but now I know. She simply changed her name to Jolene Fraser.' Nash pointed to the second image. 'That's the same young woman.'

Clara picked up the photos and compared them. 'I think you're right, Mike, and trust you to remember such a strikingly attractive female. Hang on, though, why wasn't she identified as Joanne after her attempted-murder conviction, via her DNA? Oh, of course, she was Arthur Fawcett's stepdaughter, wasn't she? She wouldn't have any of his genetic makeup.'

'Well done, Clara, I can see the makings of a good detective in you.' He ignored the face she pulled. 'I think I've an idea as to why Jolene/Joanne and Geoff are together. It also explains why someone tried to kill her at the holiday cottage. Remember, Geoff is an investigative reporter. What if he was on to something? He could have needed to disappear for his own safety.'

Nash paced about, thinking. Moments later he said, 'I reckon Geoff believes his wife and uncle were killed during a robbery committed by the Country House Bandits who were active at that time — and we know Joanne's stepfather was one of the gang. Everyone connected to the burglaries has been murdered, both the members who were convicted and those close to them, with the exception of Terry Palmer and Joanne Fawcett. That suggests Geoff is protecting Joanne.'

'The other thing I find odd is, why did Geoff Lister fake his own death and change his name?'

'That's something we'll hopefully be able to ask him.'

DC Hassan entered Nash's office, bearing the second folder. 'I think this is the one you asked about, Mike. It's to do with an unsolved cold case involving the murders of a Mrs Angela Lister and Mr Edward Lawson, somewhere near Skipton over ten years ago.'

As Nash took hold of the file, Clara said, 'That'll be why he named the boat *Angela* — in memory of his late wife.'

* * *

They spent the next quarter of an hour studying the details of the cold case, and eventually Nash passed a sheet of paper to Clara. 'This makes very interesting reading, when you couple it with what we believe went on at the canal boat.'

Clara perused the document, which comprised a report from the SIO investigating the Angela Lister and Eddie Lawson murders. In the memo, written almost six months after the fatalities, the officer gave a significant update.

'*Geoffrey Lister, the husband of Angela Lister, was admitted to Leeds General Infirmary yesterday, and is currently in ICU, recovering after surgeons removed a bullet from his abdomen. Early analysis of the ammunition round reveals it was fired from a high-powered weapon, most probably a sporting rifle.*'

Clara looked across at Nash, before tapping the document with her finger. 'Have you reached the same conclusion as me? That this could be another example of the burglary gang leaders eliminating anyone they perceive might be a threat?'

'Absolutely, Clara, because I don't think for one minute Geoff would simply mourn his dead wife and uncle. He would want their murderers brought to justice. And in the process, he probably started asking some extremely awkward questions. However, I think he must have hit a brick wall and decided he was in too much danger, which is probably the reason he took such an extreme measure as faking his own death, so he could continue the search without as much risk.'

Later, as she was about to leave with Adil to collect the bullets from the scarecrow, Clara asked Nash, 'When you spoke to Forensics, did the guy give you any news about the house and contents used by the cottage hospital victims?'

'He did, in part, but it was all negative. He told me they'd gone through the house and outbuildings, testing every surface, but came up with nothing other than prints and DNA from the victims. They haven't started work on the contents yet, because they've been a bit busy with all the other work we've sent their way. He said he hopes they'll be able to get round to it over the next few days, providing there are no further interruptions. Which, I suppose, is the best we can expect. I did tell him it wasn't a priority, and it's a bit of a long shot there will be anything useful among the paperwork and personal possessions anyway.'

Nash reflected on that remark later, and ruefully admitted how wrong that surmise was.

The *Netherdale Gazette* headline was suitably dramatic, the article that followed barely less so.

DEATH ON THE MILE

Yesterday, police revealed that a body had been found in a canal boat moored at Mile Marina, Bishopton, under what they described as suspicious circumstances. They are currently trying to identify the deceased and a police spokesperson said they are anxious to trace the owner of the vessel, plus anyone else who might have been aboard, as a matter of urgency.

* * *

Nash had only been in the CID suite a few moments the following morning when his phone rang. Abandoning his task of filling the coffee machine, he answered the call from the ballistics expert, who had a report which confirmed his suspicions. He was thanking the man for the update when Clara walked in.

Nash signalled her to join him and told her what he'd just learned. 'The gun and bullet recovered from the canal boat are a match to the ones used to kill Gabriel Welham and his mistress, Thelma Daley, at Kirk Bolton Lodge six months ago. Add to those the gangland murders, the killing of the victims at the old cottage hospital and one dead scarecrow.' Nash smiled. 'I think Richard Petersen has been a very busy fellow, and whoever put paid to him deserves a medal, don't you?'

It took Clara a few minutes before the full impact of what Nash had said struck home. 'That proves our theory was correct, doesn't it? If Petersen murdered Gabriel Welham and his mistress, and he also shot the old hospital victims before having a go at Geoff Lister or Joanne Fawcett, everything that's happened must be connected to the Country House Bandits.'

'I agree, and our next problem is going to be trying to work out what that connection is. I think we ought to pass this new information to our colleagues in Leeds, and that will emphasize the importance of finding Petersen's home for a thorough search.'

CHAPTER TWENTY-THREE

Nash arrived at Helmsdale early the following morning. He walked into the reception area to be greeted by Steve Meadows, who told him, 'There was a phone call for you a few minutes ago. The lady didn't give her name. All she said was she would ring back in half an hour, and it was a personal matter.'

Once he'd spoken to the caller, Nash was completely baffled. Again, she didn't reveal her name, at least not directly. Having confirmed that she was speaking to DI Mike Nash, she told him she wished to protect her privacy, and explained they had met many years earlier when he'd been working for the Met. She asked him not to mention her name aloud. Even then, it took a moment before he realized who he was speaking to.

'I'm calling because I want to ask you about the canal boat death reported in the *Netherdale Gazette*. I'd prefer not to go into detail over the phone. Neither would I want to come into the police station, for obvious reasons. Would it be possible to visit you at home — say, this evening?'

'Looking for a story, are you?' Nash asked.

'Certainly not! I'm retired now. I'm looking for information, that's all. You may remember I always did,' she said pointedly. 'I told you, it's personal.'

'OK. I understand why you don't want to be seen. So I'll see you this evening, as long as you can put up with my daughter's teething screams.'

'That's OK. I doubt whether she can match the racket made in a TV studio when the technicians are preparing for a show to go on air.'

Having elicited Nash's address and his promise not to discuss the call, or reveal her name in the interim, she told him she would visit him at teatime.

'If I'm not home, my wife will entertain you until I arrive,' he responded.

'I thought she'd have enough to cope with, keeping house for you and your son, plus caring for an infant and creating artistic masterpieces.'

'I see you're still well informed about current affairs, even after so long away.'

'Very witty, Inspector Nash.' Her laughter was followed by the dialling tone.

* * *

When DS Mironova arrived, she had clearly heard about the mystery caller, but was unable to get Nash to discuss the subject. Having been told by Meadows that the topic was personal, she wondered if this might be one of Nash's old flames, possibly keen to rekindle the fire.

He assured her this was not the case. 'The caller is coming to our house tonight. If I can, I'll explain everything tomorrow.'

With little occurring to delay him, Nash was able to leave early. Having called first to forewarn Alondra of their visitor, he arrived at Smelt Mill Cottage in time to update her. 'The lady who is coming to see me is very famous, or rather, she was until several years ago. She was a TV news-caster and presenter for one of the major channels. But she suddenly quit her job and retired, having suffered what her agent referred to as a "cataclysmic nervous breakdown". Since then, nothing's been seen or heard of her. Then she rang me first thing this morning, completely out of the blue, and told me she needs to speak to me. That's all I know.'

'Does this celebrity have a name?'

'Yes. Sylvia Cross.'

Alondra's eyes widened with surprise. 'I don't know much about British TV back then, but even so, I have heard of her.'

'She hosted a highly successful programme called *Current Affairs*, which principally involved in-depth investigations into organized crime, plus other scandals such as misdemeanours in public office. I met her once when I worked in London. She interviewed me after I'd been involved in trying to bring a notorious serial killer to justice. He killed one of my colleagues and committed suicide before we could detain him. That event was pivotal in my decision to leave the Met and return to Yorkshire.'

* * *

Just as Nash had finished telling Alondra this, the doorbell rang. 'This will be Sylvia,' he said, hurrying to answer before Lucy woke up. Having performed the introductions, he invited their guest to have a coffee, and wandered through to the kitchen, leaving Alondra to entertain her.

Having delivered the drinks, Nash listened for a while to the ongoing discussion, which ranged from Alondra's success and reputation in the art world, to the difference in lifestyle between Spain and North Yorkshire, plus the new challenges the vastly different scenery and climate posed for a landscape painter.

Eventually, sensing a degree of reluctance in their visitor to turn to the reason for her call, he forced the issue by asking, 'OK, Sylvia, you mentioned the incident on the canal boat, so what do you want to talk about? Would you prefer if Alondra wasn't here?'

'I'd rather she stayed, if that's OK?'

'It is for me, but I might have to leave if Lucy wakes up,' Alondra warned.

Sylvia took a deep breath, which Nash guessed was only partly physical, more a mental preparation. 'I want to ask you about the canal boat. Was it named *Angela*?'

'Why do you ask?'

'If that's the case, I have what I suppose you could call a personal connection.'

'Before I reveal anything confidential, you're going to have to explain what your interest in all this is.'

Alondra was watching their guest, and noticed Sylvia's expression change to one she later described as the most haunted, saddened look she'd ever seen. Sylvia began her tale, a story that harked back over thirty years, and one, moreover, that was filled with grief.

* * *

'Long before I was on TV, I was a junior reporter for a local radio station in Leeds, and during that time I fell in love with a colleague. Colin was a couple of years older than me, and everyone said he was destined to go far. In fact, it was the pursuit of stardom that resulted in his death. He'd been selected to audition for a new TV show and went to London for the interview. I saw him off at Leeds City station and wished him luck with the job. I was on the point of telling him my news, but thought it better to wait, rather than distract him. I wish now I'd revealed it, but hindsight isn't always the best. That was the last time I saw Colin. He attended the audition and they offered him the job there and then. As he was walking back to his hotel, Colin was hit and killed by a drunk driver. He never knew he was the father of the child I was carrying.'

There was a long pause before Sylvia was able to continue.

'Then I had to face the future without him, with no means of support apart from my meagre salary. Naturally, I wanted to keep the baby — any mother worth her salt would — but in my situation, that was impossible. My job was all I had, and being an only child, with both my parents dead, I had no family members to call on. I couldn't stop working, because I had to fend for myself. That wouldn't have been possible with a child to care for. That was where I got lucky. I'd met most of Colin's family and they were all really nice people — with one terrible exception.' She shuddered.

'When the family realized my predicament, Colin's cousin stepped in. He and his wife offered to adopt the baby, that way I'd be able to remain in touch with them and hear about my child. Everything went well at first, but when my son was only six years old, they both died, and I believed I was back to square one, until the wife's sister and her husband took over.'

Sylvia took a sip of her coffee, before continuing. 'By then I was becoming successful, which meant moving — first to Manchester, then to London, so I only got to hear about my son via letters updating me on his progress. This continued even when he became an adult, and eventually I heard he'd got married. There were many occasions when I wanted to reach out to him, and the news of his forthcoming wedding was probably the biggest of these. But I was scared — scared he would reject me for having abandoned him. He'd been told early on he was adopted, but from what I gathered, he'd expressed no interest in finding out who his birth parents were, which I found rather sad. Then, tragically, it all went wrong for him. His wife and the man who'd brought him up were murdered, and then my son also died in a tragic accident.'

Seeing the torment in Sylvia's expression, Alondra realized that, behind the facade and trappings of a successful career, the fame and fortune that accompanied it, all that remained was a grieving woman who had lost everything precious to her, and whose future must seem to be little more than a progressively steep downhill path.

Nash had been listening with increased perplexity until the final part of Sylvia's history. He knew she was talking about Geoff Lister, and knew he had to be very careful what he said. Maintaining a level voice and demeanour he asked, 'So what's your interest in the canal boat?'

'My son, Geoffrey, bought a canal boat and moored it at Mile Marina soon after his wife and adoptive uncle were murdered. He promptly renamed it *Angela*. I thought this was such a touching gesture, and it demonstrated again that everything I'd been told about him was true, and that he was a good, kind and caring person.'

Sylvia began to weep, and instantly Alondra was alongside her, a comforting arm around her shoulder.

* * *

'My poor boy, everything went wrong for him, almost from the day he was born, and to have so much tragedy in his young life was so unfair, before it ended so horribly. When he died, I knew I couldn't continue my career. Everything I'd worked so hard to achieve, the sacrifices I'd made, instantly became meaningless. I decided to quit, and I've spent the last few years grieving, and regretting almost all the choices I've made, because every one of them seemed to make things worse. The loss of someone you have given life to is an indescribable torment.'

'How did you know your son had bought the canal boat, if you were no longer able to get reports about him?'

'I hired a private investigator to keep me up to date on how Geoffrey was coping after his wife's death, and he told me about the boat. I think the fact it was well away from the area he associated with such unhappiness might be why he used it as a base. That was much the same reason as I chose this part of Yorkshire to return to when I left London. Further west there were too many painful reminders of the past. I just want to know if this incident, as the press are calling it, was on a canal boat called *Angela*.'

Nash looked directly at Sylvia. 'I suppose you still have old contacts who might be interested in the facts about this "incident", as you refer to it?'

Sylvia was indignant. 'I told you this was purely personal.' She dabbed her eyes with her handkerchief, then sighed. 'I'm not even sure why I want to know. I don't even know why I'm here. I just feel that if it is Geoffrey's boat, I'd be happy to know it still has the same name.'

'So why come to me?'

'You're in charge of the case, and I believe you knew Geoffrey because I saw you at the memorial service.' Seeing Nash's surprised expression, Sylvia explained, 'I was there, but I kept out of sight at the back of the church and left before the service ended. I assumed you knew Geoffrey from his reporting career.'

'Yes, we met up a few times. Geoffrey and I also went to the same school.' Nash paused and thought for a moment before saying, 'OK, Sylvia, strictly between you and me, the boat still has the same name. And *Angela* would seem to have been well cared for under the current ownership.'

That, Nash thought, was the best way of saying nothing.

CHAPTER TWENTY-FOUR

Sylvia Cross stood up to leave. She thanked them both and hugged Alondra, before saying, 'I'll leave you in peace now.'

As she went into the hallway, upstairs, Lucy began to cry, causing Alondra to bid Sylvia a hasty farewell.

Nash smiled. 'I doubt there'll be much peace and quiet until Lucy's settled. One thing you mentioned earlier had me puzzled. You said Colin's family were all nice people, but with one exception. What did you mean by that?'

'I got to know almost all of Colin's family, and I liked them, apart from a cousin of Colin's I met a couple of times. He and his closest relatives lived near here. Right from the beginning I knew I couldn't trust him as far as I could throw him. That might sound like a snap judgment, but it's part of a reporter's job to form an opinion of people based on first impressions. To me, he came across as shifty. He only seemed interested in money, and probably wasn't too scrupulous as to how he got it. He had an affluent lifestyle, which made me wonder how he funded it. It certainly wasn't from his so-called career. In the end, it was all immaterial, because he no longer posed a threat to anyone. Having said I disliked him so much, I wouldn't have wished him to die in such horrific circumstances.'

Seeing Nash's puzzled expression, Sylvia explained, mentioning the man's name in the process. It rang vague bells with him, but as it referred to something he had little interest in, he soon forgot what she'd told him.

She had opened her car door and was about to step inside, when he called her back. 'As you're aware, the death of the man on Geoff's boat is now a police investigation. That being so, I am bound by regulations to share the information you've given me about previous ownership. However, I believe it's only necessary at this stage for my deputy, Detective Sergeant Mironova, to learn the facts. Clara is totally trustworthy, and you can rely on her discretion completely. I hope you're OK with that?'

* * *

Next morning, as soon as Clara entered the CID suite she was summoned into Nash's office and told to close the door. She wondered what this was about, because it was obvious Nash had something to share, and equally clear that it wasn't bad news.

'Before I say anything, what I am about to reveal must go no further. I promised not to tell anyone, but you already know the facts.'

Clara nodded, so Nash continued, 'You recall the mystery woman who phoned me yesterday?'

'Yes, didn't she say it was something personal?'

'That's right, and it was only as she was telling me the reason behind her need for discretion that she revealed her history. That, coupled with what we knew about the canal boat incident, enabled me to confirm that she is actually Geoff Lister's mother.'

Clara was puzzled. 'I thought you said you knew this woman?'

'I do, because we met once, a long time ago. I think you'll also remember her, unless you don't own a TV set. Her name is Sylvia Cross.'

Clara stared at him, her eyes wide with surprise. Eventually, she managed to say, 'How did you find out the TV star Sylvia Cross is Geoff Lister's mother? Did she tell you?'

'Yes, but by then I'd already worked it out from her question about the canal boat. Let's grab a coffee — the filter machine should be ready by now — and then I can explain.'

As their colleagues arrived, they noticed that Nash's door remained closed, and there was much speculation as to what was being discussed. Despite their detective talents, neither of them could have come close to guessing what Nash and Mironova were talking about.

When she'd heard the full story, Clara reacted much as Nash expected. 'That poor woman! What she must have gone through all these years, believing her son was dead, and after suffering so much tragedy. It's no wonder she quit her TV job and retired. She must have felt there was no point in carrying on.'

'That was more or less word for word what she told us. Alondra was a great help, comforting her and supporting her, until Sylvia told me enough for me to work out the connection.'

'Did you tell her Lister is alive?'

'No. And I don't plan to. Until we know what's going on, I'm not prepared to take any risks. If the news got out, there's more than his life at risk. And we've got to find him first.'

'One thing that intrigues me,' Clara told him, 'is that although Geoff Lister was unaware of his mother and father's careers, he too became a reporter. That's mildly spooky, like a subconscious genetic inheritance.'

It was only much later, after further information came to light, that the need to locate Geoff Lister became more urgent.

* * *

'I'm getting worried.'

'What about? I thought everything had been sorted.'

'Not everything. Now Vincent hasn't been in contact, which is most unlike him. It's been over three weeks since I gave him instructions to waste the bloke who was with the Fawcett bitch. Vincent told me he'd dealt with the cow, put three bullets in her, but there was a man with her in some place back of beyond. Vincent told me this character picked Fawcett up from outside Blackwell Prison and drove her to the cottage.'

'Yes, I remember you telling me all that. So what's the problem?'

'Vincent always reports back when he's finished a job, like he did after he sorted Wellie out, or when he did for those two in the mortuary, plus the hit-and-run and the others I paid him for. This time — nothing. He hasn't even asked for the money owing to him.'

'What do you plan to do?'

'Not sure. I tried phoning him, but it went straight to voicemail. I daren't leave a message, and I can't risk phoning him again or sending him a text.'

'Why not?'

'I'm worried the phone might have ended up in the wrong hands. If something has gone badly wrong — say, if Vincent got arrested — I don't want some nosey copper reading the message or trying to track the number.'

'Oh, I get your point, but you're using a burner, aren't you? I don't think they can track that.'

'Who knows? But I'm not taking any chances.'

There was a long silence as they mulled over the dilemma, but eventually a suggestion was made, 'Why not ask Mr Nobody to help? He could go to Vincent's address and look around. Maybe ask the neighbours if they've seen him, or know what's happened to him. That way, there's no risk of it being traced back to you.'

'There's one minor drawback to that.'

'What?'

'I have absolutely no idea where Vincent lives. All our transactions have been done over the phone or digitally.'

That was another unforeseen problem, but again, a solution soon came to mind. 'What about the bloke who put you in touch with Vincent in the first place? He might know where he lives.'

'That's another good idea. You're really on form. I'll ask Mr Nobody to start with him.' He smiled as he uttered the name "Nobody".

His smile caused his companion to look away hastily. The image of his features, disfigured as they were, could not be disguised. The movement of his facial muscles was still enough to turn one's stomach. Despite the passage of time, which should have lessened the impact on someone who was almost constantly alongside him, was deeply distressing.

A change of topic was definitely called for.

'One thing that puzzles me is why you trust Mr Nobody so implicitly. And why this man is so loyal to you. He seems prepared to do anything you ask of him.'

'That's because he owes me — big time. If I hadn't intervened, he would have been dead years ago. I thought we could trust Welham — he was supposed to be my right-hand man — but he let us down badly. That won't happen again, and certainly not with Mr Nobody.'

'I don't remember you saving his life.'

'That's because you weren't in the country at the time. It was during the early days of the trouble we had with the Albanians. I'd sent you away for your own safety. Then I got a call from one of my dealers. He and a couple of his heavies had rescued someone from a grow house that had been crashed by the opposition. They escaped just in time. He was so grateful he came on board and has proved his worth time and again. After that snitch Corey Davies blew our operation to bits, Mr Nobody was the only one left I could trust.'

'So why did you employ this Vincent character to do the cleaning-up when you already had Mr Nobody available?'

'Because Vincent was highly recommended and has no connection to us.'

Twenty-four hours later, that trust had to be raised to another level. As he listened to what Mr Nobody told him about another matter, the Keeper's reaction was immediate — and angry in the extreme. 'I want you to clean up. Do it, and dump the rubbish somewhere remote. You'll need help with transport, but that's easily organized. Once that's complete, we'll have to rethink the whole operation.'

CHAPTER TWENTY-FIVE

Penny Watkins was looking forward to the weekend. It would provide the first opportunity for years to spend some quality time with her father. After her mother died when Penny was eight years old, Raymond Watkins had stepped up to the mark, raising the child on his own. With no siblings, Penny had received all his attention. He had helped and encouraged her through her education and to fulfil her ambition in life.

His reward was bittersweet. Delighted and proud though he was by her achievement, her success within the banking sector meant that Penny, now a senior executive working for one of the Big Four British banks, was based full-time in London.

Although they spoke regularly on the phone, they hadn't met up in over two years. He would have gladly travelled to the capital to see her, but the demands of her job were such that a visit would have meant nothing more than swapping being alone in one location for another.

As the weekend approached, Penny decided to phone her father and make him aware of her proposed itinerary and ETA. Her first attempt on Wednesday evening met with no success, the call going straight to voicemail. Following a hectic day in the office on Thursday, it was only after she returned to her apartment that she realized her father hadn't called her back. This was most unlike him, but even then, she wasn't unduly worried. She tried again, not once but three times over the course of the evening. When she got no reply, only then did she become concerned.

After some consideration, Penny resorted to the only option she could think of to resolve the issue, a course of action she never believed she would have to take. With no immediate neighbours, close friends or family, her father was as remote as if he was stranded on a desert island.

After some research, she rang the number she had found. Her call was answered immediately. 'North Yorkshire Police, how can I help?'

'My name is Penny Watkins. I live in London, but I'm scheduled to visit my father this weekend. However, I've been trying repeatedly to contact him for over twenty-four hours, but I can't get any reply, only a voicemail message, and now I'm really worried, because this is so unlike him. He lives alone, and I wondered if your officers could carry out one of those, er, welfare checks, I believe they're called?'

'Could I have your father's details, please?'

'His name is Raymond Watkins, and he lives at the Old Mill, at Gorton village. I've tried his landline repeatedly. He doesn't own a mobile, so I'm a bit stuck.'

'What age is your father?'

'He's sixty-one.'

'Very well, we'll get officers to call at his house as soon as possible. Can we contact you at any time on this number?'

Having agreed to that, Penny waited — and waited.

* * *

It was a relatively quiet evening in the Netherdale control room, the operator thought. Apart from the welfare check request, there hadn't been a single call. It would be different the following night, when England's next soccer match would be shown in every pub in the area. What was it about football that caused spectators to drink so heavily and provoked so much aggression, even among the most mild-mannered spectators? That wouldn't concern her, because she wouldn't be on duty. As soon as this quiet shift was over, she'd be on leave all weekend. Later, as things changed rapidly and dramatically, she recalled her father's saying, 'Don't tempt Providence'.

With no other priorities, she had been able to assign a two-man uniform unit to carry out the welfare check. It was a little after nine thirty when their squad car reached the village of Gorton, in the upper reaches of the dale.

They soon located the property, a fine, stone-built Victorian house standing in its own grounds on the edge of Gorton, directly opposite the village green. As they were about to announce their arrival, they received an update from the control room. Obviously, with nothing else to command her attention, she had been able to carry out research which would produce useful backup information.

'I've done a DVLA check, plus a voters' roll scan, and Raymond Watkins is the only person listed at the property. He is also the registered keeper of a 2022 Lexus ES.' She recited the vehicle registration number before ending the call.

* * *

The house was in total darkness, and with no other form of illumination, not even a street light, the officers switched their torches on before passing through the open five-bar gate leading to the gravel driveway.

Alongside the imposing main building was a smaller structure, which was obviously the source of the property name. Long since disused as a flour production site, the windmill had at some point been converted, the ground floor now serving as a double garage. Roller shutter doors had been fitted, but their torchlight revealed that one of these was open, and there was no vehicle visible inside.

'Looks as if Mr Watkins has gone away,' one of the officers remarked.

'That doesn't make sense. His daughter's supposed to be visiting him this weekend. Besides, nobody in their right mind would go off on a jaunt leaving their garage open to the elements and any light-fingered locals. Let's try the house.'

They had been fairly relaxed so far, but as they approached the front of the building, they were alarmed by a sudden burst of illumination from a PIR light above the front door. With the aid of this, they were able to switch their torches off and concentrate on attracting the occupant's attention. One of the men reached forward, pressed the bell attached to the frame, and they heard the mellow sound of the ringtone echoing from within the building.

Getting no response, they waited a couple of minutes, which seemed to them longer, before trying once again. This met with an equal lack of success, so one of them reached forward and tried the door handle. It opened easily to his touch, which caused the officers to look at one another in surprise. 'This isn't right,' the senior of them muttered. 'We'd better update Control before we go any further.'

Having reported to Netherdale and received the go-ahead, the officers entered the building, calling Mr Watkins' name repeatedly as they moved slowly and cautiously down the large hallway. Again, no reaction. 'I don't like the feel of this one iota,' the senior officer muttered.

As he was speaking, his colleague located the hall light switch and turned it on. Once their eyes had become accustomed to the brightness, he gestured to his left. 'I'll have a look in there,' he said.

'OK, I'll go for the other one.' He gestured to his right.

He was reaching for the door handle when his colleague came hurtling past him, going like an express train as he headed for the open front door. Halfway through their shift, they had stopped for a takeaway during their break. The officer managed to reach the garden in front of the house before depositing most of his Chicken Tikka Masala onto a flower bed.

Inside, the second officer checked the room to his left, and immediately spotted the cause of his colleague's distress. 'Oh my God.'

He reached for his radio, still staring at the obscene sight as he called the control room once more.

'We need CID, a CSI team and a pathologist here ASAP. We've found Mr Watkins, or at least I assume it's him, because he's wearing pyjamas and a dressing gown. He's lying on the hearth rug in the lounge, and his head's been beaten in. There's blood all over the place. I'd check for a pulse, but I reckon it would be a waste of time. Nobody could have withstood such a violent attack.'

* * *

Nash was on call and his mobile rang. His grimace made Alondra smile, but as she watched his facial expression change, she knew there was nothing amusing in the message he was receiving.

'OK, I'm on my way. Please alert Professor Ramirez, plus CSI. DC Hassan is second on the duty roster. I'll summon him.' He ended the call and turned to Alondra. 'Sorry, darling, I've got to go.'

He kissed Alondra, headed for the door, and patted Teal on the head. He told the dog to take care of her mistress and the baby, then set off for Gorton village.

Nash was first to arrive. The uniform officers had already strung incident tape across the front of the building, supporting it with some purloined garden canes. Nash donned protective clothing and joined them outside the front door.

'We'll have to go as soon as the others arrive,' the senior officer said. 'Apparently there's a fight outside a nightclub in Netherdale needs sorting out. Apart from that, Sonny Jim here' — he gestured to the pale-looking constable — 'will probably want another supper. He chucked the previous one among the gladioli.'

Nash looked at the junior officer, noting his distress. 'That bad, is it?'

'I've seen some bad stuff, RTAs and such, but nothing to compare with this. I thought it best to warn you.'

'OK, I'll go take a look and see if I can keep hold of my dinner. Have you checked the rest of the house?'

'Er . . . no, sir, we thought we should preserve the scene first.'

Nash nodded and headed for the door. He gave the room a cursory glance, before concentrating his attention on the victim. From what he could see, it appeared the householder had put up quite a fight, before being overpowered and clubbed to death. There were bruises around the knuckles of both hands, and at least three of the visible fingernails were broken. Assuming that to have happened during the struggle, Nash thought they might yield valuable DNA, which in turn might help identify the assailant — or assailants.

His thought process was interrupted at that point by the arrival of the pathologist and his retinue. 'Why couldn't you settle for a nice romantic, peaceful evening at home with your beautiful wife?' Ramirez asked by way of greeting.

'Romantic and peaceful with a trainee banshee in the next room? You must be joking,' Nash retorted.

Having glanced at the victim, Ramirez shook his head. 'Very unpleasant. Am I to assume this is the only victim? If that's the case, you must be slipping. I suppose old age catches up with all of us — even you, Mike.'

Ramirez smiled at Nash's response. 'I love a challenge. I'll take a look round and see if I can find some more.'

CHAPTER TWENTY-SIX

While the scene at Gorton was being dealt with, an employee of Good Buys supermarket was driving home from the late shift. Trevor Jenkins had taken the job as a security guard following his discharge from the army on medical grounds. It wasn't the best paid work around, but, along with his military pension, it was sufficient to provide for his wife and their two children.

Jenny had taken the kids to visit her parents on the island of Anglesey, a trip that was scheduled to last all week. To save cooking when he got home, he stopped for a meal at a local hostelry, and was much later than usual on his drive home. Halfway along his journey to the village of Rowandale, at the far side of Black Fell, his headlights picked up something in his peripheral vision. He slowed the car to little more than walking pace, which was hardly a risky undertaking on such a deserted country lane. As he edged closer, he got a better view of the object that had caught his attention. He frowned. 'What on earth?'

His question was greeted with silence, hardly surprising as he was alone. He pulled to a halt, put the handbrake and hazard warning lights on, and continued to stare at the scene for several seconds. Try as he might, Trevor couldn't think

146

of a logical explanation for a Transit van being ditched in the entrance to Lady Luck Quarry. Having passed that way en route for work, he knew the vehicle hadn't been there that morning, so it must have been abandoned more recently.

Curiosity got the better of him. He reached into the glove compartment of his car and took out his torch. The van had been parked facing the quarry, its rear end towards the road. He squeezed through the narrow gap between the side panels and the fencing to reach the front. He tried the driver's door. The handle turned easily, so he swung the door open, simultaneously shining his torch inside. Empty.

There was a distinctive smell.

He moved to the rear and cautiously opened a door. During his active service in Iraq and Afghanistan, Trevor had witnessed the effects of extreme violence many times. But here, in the dead of night, along a sleepy country lane in a remote part of his home county, he was totally unprepared for such a horrible sight. He took an involuntary pace backwards, muttering, 'Oh dear Lord,' as he slammed the door shut to blot out the atrocity from his vision. Seconds later, securely locked inside his vehicle, with the engine already running, he dialled triple nine, his fingers trembling.

* * *

Mike Nash returned to the interior of the Old Mill and sought out Ramirez. 'Have you any idea how long the victim's been dead?' he asked.

'Judging by the condition of the body and the congealed blood, I'd say somewhere around forty-eight hours, but I'll be able to give a more accurate time once I've conducted the post-mortem.'

They were interrupted at that point when Nash's mobile rang. He moved away from the CSI team and listened to the message imparted by the caller. A few minutes later he rejoined Ramirez, who was supervising his assistants as they checked over the body for any forensic evidence. He looked up as Nash spoke to him.

'You should be careful what you wish for, Professor.'

The pathologist frowned, clearly puzzled.

Nash continued, 'I've just had a call from Control. A van has been found, parked in the entrance to Lady Luck Quarry. There are two occupants, both of whom are dead. The man who found them is a former soldier, so he was easily able to establish the cause of death. They had both been shot in the head. DC Hassan is here, so he can take over this crime scene and liaise with CSI. I'll ring Viv and get him to meet me at the quarry. I'm off, so if you wouldn't mind following me there when you can, I'd be obliged.'

Nash rang Viv Pearce, asking him to attend, before he phoned home and updated Alondra, adding, 'At this rate, I'll be lucky if I'm home in time for breakfast.'

* * *

The following morning when DS Mironova arrived at Helmsdale, she was surprised to find the reception area unmanned, despite Steve Meadows', Mike Nash's, and DC Hassan's cars being in the car park. On entering CID, she was further confused, as that too was unoccupied. After a few seconds, she heard the faint sound of conversation, and tracked down her colleagues to the kitchen, where they were gathered round the coffee machine, waiting for it to deliver.

'Ah, I might have known I'd find you here,' she said, with a cheeky grin.

Her smile faded as she noted their sombre expressions, plus the fact that Nash appeared unshaven and without a tie, something he would never allow under normal circumstances. 'Has something happened?' she asked.

'See, Adil, I told you Clara was a good detective, didn't I?'

Without awaiting a response, Nash began to explain the events of the previous hours. 'We've what looks like a Hanoi burglary gone wrong, with the homeowner bludgeoned to death. We're awaiting a positive identification, but there's little doubt the victim is Raymond Watkins, and he lives — lived — at the Old Mill in Gorton village. I now have the unenviable task of breaking the news to his daughter, who lives and works in London. What will make it even harder is that she was apparently scheduled to visit him this weekend.

'That was merely the start of things. Whilst we were at the Gorton crime scene, a man driving home from work spotted a van parked across the entrance to Lady Luck Quarry. He was intrigued enough to look inside and found two occupants in the back who had been shot in the head, from extremely close range. Whoever killed them was either a sadistic psychopath, or wasn't prepared to take any chances, because they were both shot twice. One of them had bruising about the face, which implied he had been in a recent fight.'

Nash waited as Clara absorbed this shocking development.

'I called Viv to that one. He'll be in later. The CSI team leader had one of those fingerprint-reading gizmos, but neither of the victims is on the PNC database. We're waiting on a DNA test, but I doubt whether it will lead anywhere.'

He ended by telling Clara, 'I'm leaving you in charge. I'm off to Netherdale to update Jackie Fleming, then I'm going home for a spot of shut-eye. Do me a favour,' he said, as he paused by the door. 'I'd be grateful if you can manage to keep the body count down to single figures while I'm absent. Oh, and by the way, Forensics are arranging for recovery of the van to Netherdale for a closer inspection. Who knows, the killer might have left his calling card.'

* * *

It was the beginning of the following week when there was an unexpected development in what the team referred to as the 'quarry murders'. The CSI team leader conveyed the news in two parts.

'When we examined the van, we noticed something puzzling, so I checked with Professor Ramirez and he confirmed our suspicions. Whether resolving the anomaly will be helpful is another matter. We can now confirm that neither of the occupants of the van drove it on its final journey.'

'How can you be sure?' Nash asked.

'Judging by the position of the driver's seat, and the distance from it to the accelerator, clutch and brake pedals, we ascertained that the person who did drive the vehicle was at least six inches taller than either of the victims, possibly even more.'

'That's useful to know, but like you said, I'm not certain it gets us any further with the investigation,' Nash pointed out.

'Possibly not on its own, but the other information might prove more useful.'

Nash listened with growing interest as the scientific officer continued.

'As you're aware, we checked the victims' fingerprints and found there was no match on the database. However, as per your request, we also did a DNA test, and from this we were able to identify one of the dead men, albeit via the back door, so to speak.'

'What do you mean by "via the back door"?'

'Although one of the men has never been convicted of a criminal offence, when we ran his DNA we established a familial link, and were thereby able to identify him. His sibling, a full brother by the name of Roy Proctor, is twenty-six years old and is currently serving a three-year stretch as a resident of Felling Prison for burglary and car theft. Proctor has only one sibling, a younger brother by the name of Joshua. I'm about to email the dead man's details, including his full name and last known address, to you.' With a touch of what Nash identified as gallows humour, the officer added, 'By "last known address", I'm not referring to Lady Luck Quarry.'

Five minutes later, Nash walked into the CID general office asking for everyone's attention. The trio of detectives listened as he outlined what he had just been told. 'Thanks to some good work by our CSI colleagues, we now have the identity of one of the occupants of the van. And we now know neither of the men drove the van to the quarry. They were murdered elsewhere.'

He explained about the disparity in height of the victims, leading Clara to ask, 'Where do we take it from here? This might prove useful as background information, but we can hardly interview the dead men.'

Nash smiled. 'I agree, but once he knew the name of the deceased's brother, our CSI man was able to run a search of his home area. The dead man's family comes from the Pontefract and Castleford area, and a search of the voter's roll revealed a name and address. According to this, our victim, whose name is Joshua Proctor, was twenty-three years old and lived in Castleford, along with a young woman of the same age, who we assume to have been his girlfriend. I suggest we contact our colleagues in West Yorkshire, and ask them to interview the girlfriend, Tamsin Charlton. They can pass on the bad news. And at the same time, try and elicit some information about Joshua's activities from her.'

CHAPTER TWENTY-SEVEN

Twenty-four hours later, Nash addressed his colleagues once more, and this time imparted some shocking news. 'I've just heard back from West Yorkshire Police.' He looked across the room to where DCs Pearce and Hassan were seated. 'Viv, you and Adil are going to be in charge today, because Clara and I are going to Castleford. As a result of what I've just been told, we're going to visit a patient in their District Hospital. The patient's name is Tamsin Charlton — Joshua Proctor's girlfriend.

'From what they told me, Tamsin works behind a bar at a pub in Castleford. She was on her way home from work two nights ago when she was the victim of a hit-and-run incident, having been struck by a van. This was no accident. It was a deliberate attempt to kill her, and it nearly succeeded. Fortunately, someone passing by intervened, throwing a brick at the van's windscreen as the driver was about to reverse over Tamsin. The van drove away, and the Good Samaritan called the emergency services. The hospital told our colleagues Tamsin would most certainly have died from her injuries had the van driver succeeded. According to the medics, she was lucky she didn't bulls-eye the windscreen and suffer severe head injuries. However, she has a broken femur, which punctured an artery, causing internal bleeding. Had it not been stopped in time this could have proved fatal. She also has a broken arm and a dislocated shoulder. Despite the damage she has suffered, the specialists treating her are confident she will make a good recovery.'

Nash paused to allow the team to absorb this information, before adding, 'Our trip might be in vain on two counts. It could be that Tamsin has no knowledge of what Joshua was involved in, and even if she does know something, she might not be willing to disclose it.'

Half an hour later, having brought Superintendent Fleming up to date with this development, Nash and Clara set off. One statement Clara overheard him make during the phone call had puzzled her. During the early part of their journey, she quizzed him about this. 'What did you mean when you told Jackie Fleming this has an all-too-familiar ring about it?'

'What we believe to be a criminal and his partner-in-crime are shot to death, and shortly afterwards there's a near-fatal "accident".' Nash took one hand off the wheel to make the apostrophe air sign. 'An alleged accident, involving someone who just happens to be the girlfriend of one of those victims. Doesn't that bear a remarkable similarity to something we've investigated previously? Something where we believe the head honcho is still at large? Something we've discussed recently.'

'You're thinking about what happened to people who were connected to the Country House Bandits burglary gang, aren't you? They were all got rid of.'

'I am indeed, and I believe we should also include the cottage hospital victims in the mix. If I'm right, I believe the same person is behind all the different crimes committed by those people, who, when they were of no further use to the mastermind, were simply disposed of.'

'If you are right,' she told him, 'this so-called mastermind has to be a contender for the most ruthless, evil and cold-blooded criminal we've ever had to deal with.' She paused before adding, 'And that's saying a heck of a lot, given some of the villains we've encountered over the years.'

* * *

Tamsin Charlton might have been a pretty girl prior to the attack, Clara thought, but there was little evidence of this in the bruised, battered, and bandaged woman lying on the hospital bed. Her leg was encased in plaster. One of her arms had also clearly been broken and was similarly covered.

It was clear she had already been informed of her partner's fate, for when Nash introduced himself and Mironova, Tamsin spoke, her voice little more than a husky croak. 'This is about Joshua, isn't it? How did he die? Was it a car accident, or was he murdered?'

'Why do you think he might have been murdered?' Nash asked.

Tamsin bit her lip and remained silent.

Nash told her, as gently as possible, that Joshua's death was being treated as suspicious, which Clara thought had to be the biggest euphemism of all time. He went on to attempt to reassure her, saying Joshua hadn't suffered prolonged agony. Whether this was of any comfort or not was highly doubtful.

It was towards the end of their visit, which was curtailed by the demands of the ward sister, that Tamsin revealed something. In itself, it was little more than supportive evidence for what Nash had theorized, but which, in time, might prove useful to their investigation.

During the drive back to Helmsdale, Clara broached the subject raised by Tamsin, albeit via a circuitous route. 'I think Joshua and his partner-in-crime might have been far more active than we believed. When Tamsin told us Joshua had phoned her on several occasions, from different locations across the north of England, it tends to suggest they didn't restrict their activities to the Yorkshire area.'

'I agree, and although that was useful background, I have a feeling the other thing she revealed could prove far more useful. I was rather surprised by it, and I reckon it adds a different dimension to the term "a family business".'

'You mean the bit about Josh starting his travels after a discussion with his brother, Roy? The conversation she overheard that took place shortly before Roy Proctor was sent to prison?'

'That's it. And her other comment, that "Josh's death is probably Roy's fault" was equally illuminating. She heard Roy tell Joshua "this job is far too lucrative to give up on, a bloody sight better paid than nicking stuff from supermarkets, so I want you to handle it while I'm out of action". I feel sure he was asking Joshua to take over the burglaries while he was inside. West Yorkshire Police didn't make the connection, but supposing there's a link to the Hanoi burglaries? One way we might find out is by visiting Roy and asking him point blank.'

'Do you think he'll tell us anything, or will he keep silent out of fear, knowing what happened to Joshua?'

'We'll only know for certain when we ask him. I'm hoping Tamsin's other comment might be the persuading factor. She said Josh and his brother Roy were really close. If he feels angry and guilty because he involved Josh in something that led to him being murdered, Roy might be willing to spill the beans and tell us what he knows. I think my first task when we return is to get Jackie Fleming to obtain an interview at Felling with Roy Proctor ASAP.'

* * *

When they reached Helmsdale, there was an update regarding Joshua Proctor, relayed by Steve Meadows. 'West Yorkshire have had no luck tracing Proctor's parents. In the case of his father, that's hardly surprising, because according to a neighbour, he left the family home to set up with his mistress over twenty years ago. The neighbour also revealed that Mrs Proctor was believed to be, and I quote, "somewhere in France, having it off with her fancy man". They also want to know if they should visit Proctor's brother, or if you want that pleasure.'

'Do me a favour, Steve, call them back and tell them we'll handle it all. They'll probably be delighted to have the job taken off their hands.'

Having updated Jackie Fleming, Nash asked her to organize a visit for himself and DS Mironova. 'The reason I want us to handle it is threefold,' he explained. 'First off, we have to inform the family of the death, and as the dead man's parents are not contactable, Roy Proctor is the closest family member. Second, with a bit of luck, if Proctor is forthcoming, he might give us a clue as to the identity of the other man shot dead alongside Joshua, because at present we've no idea who he is . . . or was.

'Those are both reasons enough for the visit, but I think the third part is equally, if not more, important. I'm hoping the news of his brother's murder might persuade Proctor to tell us what he knows about the people we believe organized the car thefts. Even if he's only willing to reveal where the vehicles were taken after they were stolen, that would be a big step forward. We're planning to approach Proctor by piling guilt on him for causing his younger brother to become involved in a scheme that led to him being murdered. Joshua's girlfriend told us Roy persuaded Joshua to take over during the time he was in prison. That might induce Roy to reveal everything.'

CHAPTER TWENTY-EIGHT

Two days later, Nash and Mironova travelled to Felling Prison to conduct what promised to be a difficult interview. 'If we only get him to tell us who the other victim is, it'll be worth the drive,' Clara commented as they were en route.

'That's true, although the downside to learning the second man's identity is we'll have to face the unpleasant task of informing another set of relatives that a family member has been killed. My hope is we'll be able to persuade Proctor to tell us far more than that, though.'

When Proctor had been placed opposite them in the interview room, Nash performed the introductions, watched by the prison officer as he and Clara displayed their warrant cards.

'This conversation is not being recorded, and we're here to talk about your brother Josh.'

'If this is summat to do wi' Josh, we're both from Castleford. So why are North Yorkshire police involved?' Proctor asked. 'Has he been arrested for summat he's supposed to have done on your patch?' He laughed.

'No, I'm sorry to have to inform you that it's far worse than that, Roy. There's no easy way to break this to you. The reason we're here is because Joshua is dead.'

The horrified expression on Proctor's face was clear indication of how deeply the news was affecting him.

'Dead?' he stammered after a long silence. 'Josh is dead? How did it happen? Accident?'

'No, Roy, what happened to Joshua certainly wasn't accidental. His body, along with that of another young man, was found in the back of a van abandoned in our area.' Nash paused, and as Proctor was still assimilating this information, added, 'Both of them had been shot at point-blank range. We know from the crime scene they weren't killed inside that van. The murderer loaded them into the vehicle, drove to an isolated spot and left them there.'

The interview had to be suspended at this point, owing to Proctor's extreme distress on learning of the cold-blooded way Joshua had been gunned down. When he had recovered sufficiently, they resumed.

'I'm sorry we had to come here and bring you such awful news,' Nash began, 'but it's our duty to inform the deceased's next of kin. As we were unable to contact your parents, we had no alternative.'

Proctor nodded his understanding, enabling Nash to continue.

'We spoke to Josh's girlfriend, Tamsin, and she told us that several months ago she overheard a conversation which seemed to suggest you were persuading Josh to take over some job you'd been doing. She said it involved travelling. We'd like to know more about what that entailed, and ask if you could help us by identifying the other person found with your brother. Neither of them had any ID on them, so we have no idea who he might be, which in turn means we're unable to inform his next of kin that he is dead.'

Nash waited, and there was a long silence, during which Clara thought Proctor was unlikely to cooperate.

Eventually, however, Nash prompted him with a suggestion that was to prove pivotal. 'If it's any help, I do have a photograph of the other man. If he's known to you, I think you might be able to recognize him, although I should warn you it isn't a pretty sight. All the bullets were fired at extremely close range.'

Proctor looked up, clearly startled by Nash's statement. 'All the bullets?'

'Yes, both Josh and his companion were shot twice, and the range was so close we found gunshot residue on their skin and clothing.'

Proctor was again distressed.

* * *

It was some while before Proctor agreed to examine the photo of the second victim. As he stared at the image, Clara saw Proctor's face whiten and his fingers tremble to the extent he almost dropped the paper. Had Nash gone a step too far?

'Del Boy,' Proctor muttered. He turned the paper over, so the image was out of sight, before looking at Nash. 'His name's Derek Bates, but all his mates call him Del Boy after that TV bloke. Josh an' 'im have bin mates since they were at school.'

Having made a note of Bates' address, Nash returned to the prime reason for their visit. 'I told you earlier that we spoke with Josh's girlfriend, Tamsin. We had to visit Castleford Hospital to talk with her. She's lucky not to need the services of their Intensive Care Unit. She's recovering from injuries caused by a hit-and-run incident. She very nearly died.'

Proctor looked shocked.

'From what she said about your conversation with Josh and the outcome, I now believe I know what the job you asked him to take on was. I reckon Josh and Bates were committing Hanoi burglaries.'

The look on Proctor's face implied Nash was right.

'They had been remarkably successful, but the latest escapade went badly wrong. A house was broken into, and the owner was found bludgeoned to death. As a result of that, I also believe whoever is behind those car thefts was afraid the investigation might lead back to them.' Nash paused. 'Therefore, Josh and Bates had to be eliminated.'

Proctor was clearly appalled by the accuracy of Nash's guesswork, but there was no indication he would cooperate until Nash pushed him further.

'Tamsin told us how close you and Josh were, and how your mother raised you both single-handed after your father walked out when you were toddlers. How do you think your mother will react when she learns you persuaded Josh to take on a job that ended with him being murdered in cold blood? For that matter, how will you ever be able to look your mother in the face, knowing you had a hand in killing her younger child?'

* * *

During the earlier part of the interview, Nash had done most of the talking, trying to encourage Roy Proctor to cooperate. But once he responded to Nash's questions, it was as if a flood gate had opened, and he revealed everything he knew in a gushing tide of information.

'You can begin by telling us how the operation works,' Nash asked.

'I've no idea who's behind it,' Proctor replied. 'I got into it the same way as Josh. Last time I was inside, I got a new cellmate. I could tell he was worried about something. A couple of days before I was released, he told me he'd taken on a job to support his partner, who'd just given birth to twins. He needed someone to take his place while he was inside.' Proctor shook his head. 'He never got chance to return to the job. He was killed a couple of days after he got out, hit by a speeding car in a lane near Ilkley. They never got whoever hit him. No one even knew what he was doing on that road, miles away from where he lived.'

Nash and Mironova exchanged glances, which Proctor failed to pick up on. He continued his story, which Clara thought was more like a confession, or a way of expiating the guilt he must feel over what had happened to his brother.

'The bloke told me he'd done a lot of work for a guy, work that paid really well. Then he asked him to do something different, something that would pay even better. But he couldn't do it, 'cos he'd never learned to drive.'

Proctor paused and took several sips of water.

'When I said I was interested, he gave me the contact's mobile phone number, and explained this was a one-chance number.'

'What does that mean?'

Proctor smiled slightly. 'You can only call that number once. After that, if you got the job, you get instructions on a text and each time the sender's number is different. I rang the bloke and told him how I'd got the number. He took my details and promised to call me back. Said he'd have to carry out some checks. I didn't hear anything for more than six weeks. I'd almost forgotten about it when he called and set the thing up.'

'How exactly did it work?'

'Like I said, I'd get a text. The only way I knew it was kosher was his name at the end. The text had the location, description of the house and the car. I could nick things if I wanted, but I never did — just in, keys, and out.'

'How were you paid?'

'A week after delivering the motor, I'd get another text with instructions on where to pick up the cash from him. Each time it was a different place. All I had to do was get there and have some ID.'

'Did you have any other contact with him?'

'Yes, there was a rush job, and he met me near the site of the burglary beforehand. Said this one was special, and I was told that under no circumstances was I to steal anything from inside, just get the car keys and drive the motor away. He threatened me too, telling me if I disobeyed and anything went missing, they'd find out and punish me.'

'Can you describe him?'

Proctor shrugged. 'Average sort of bloke, taller than me, fair hair, mid-thirties, I guess. The only thing out of the ordinary about him was his name. A weird one I'd never heard before.'

'What was so unusual about it?'

'He signed all the texts "Mr Ningun".'

'You told us that when he threatened you before that burglary, he said "they" would find out. That implies there was someone else involved. Can you explain that?'

'I'm only guessing, but in the texts he'd put, "Next job. We want you to go to . . ." and give the details. After I delivered the vehicle, I'd get another text, saying. "We will deliver your payment to . . ." and give the place. It was always Ningun who arrived, but soon after I delivered one of the motors, I saw Ningun talking to another guy close to the drop-off. It was early evening and there were few people about, so I guessed this might be the other driver, or one of them.'

'Can you describe the man he was talking to?'

'He was sitting behind the steering wheel of a fancy Merc, all muffled up. Dark-haired, but that's about it. Oh, and it was quite gloomy, but he was wearing sunglasses.'

There was a long pause as Nash digested this seemingly irrelevant piece of information, and Clara saw the faraway expression on his face. Something had obviously crossed his mind, but what was it? There seemed to be little or nothing significant in Proctor's story about this chance encounter. Later, when Nash told her the thought he'd had, she was shocked beyond measure at the implication.

* * *

Eventually Nash resumed his questioning, switching to a completely different aspect of their investigation. 'One thing you haven't mentioned. Where did you deliver the stolen cars?'

'It was always a unit on an industrial estate in Netherdale. When I arrived, the door would be open. My job was to drive the motor inside, ensure the door was closed, and then make my way home with my mate.'

'Your mate?' Nash was puzzled.

'How do you think I got to the houses to nick the bloody cars? They were all out in the sticks. I didn't walk. I got dropped off and then picked up at the unit after I'd delivered.'

'I don't suppose you want to tell us the name of your chauffeur, do you?'

'I'm no nark.' Proctor sneered.

'OK then, just one more question and then we're through. What was the name of the cellmate who introduced you to the car theft outfit?'

'Balderstone, Nick Balderstone.'

CHAPTER TWENTY-NINE

On the return journey, Clara contacted their office to pass on the instructions she and Nash had agreed. Viv Pearce answered the call and immediately put her on speakerphone, so that Adil Hassan could also hear what was being said.

'We need you to contact West Yorkshire Police and request a file regarding a hit-and-run fatality twelve months or so ago near Ilkley.' She recited the name Proctor gave them and added, 'You'll also find the dead man had been in prison, probably more than once, so we would like his records as well. That's the first job. The next is to contact the company who operate an industrial unit in Netherdale. You need to find out if anyone rented a unit long-term, covering the dates that coincide from when the Hanoi burglaries began. The person or persons concerned will have returned to the unit on several occasions. The other job we have for you is to do a person search. The man we're anxious to trace has a most unusual surname, so it should be quite easy. His name is Ningun.' Clara spelled out the surname to ensure there was no chance of error.

'Hopefully, by the time we get back to Helmsdale, they'll have some results,' she told Nash, unaware she had just invoked Sod's Law.

She saw that he seemed preoccupied and asked what he was thinking about.

'I was pondering the description of the man Proctor saw, the one Mr Ningun was talking to. Didn't it remind you of anyone? Concentrate on what Proctor said. As I recall, it was "a man muffled up, wearing sunglasses, and driving a fancy Merc", yes?'

'OK, what about it?'

'Think back to the Country House Bandits, and the description Corey Davies and Terry Palmer gave of the man they referred to as "the Keeper". That sounds identical to the guy Proctor's just told us about, even down to the car.'

'We thought the Merc belonged to Gabriel Welham.'

'Welham certainly owned a Mercedes, but that's not to say there's only one criminal driving around in them. They're quite popular.'

Clara thought this over for a while. 'I think you might be onto something. The way people who have become an encumbrance finish up dead seems to tally with what happened to the Country House Bandits, under the direction of the Keeper. You think he's responsible.'

'We'll keep this theory to ourselves for now — otherwise it might distract the others.'

'One thing puzzles me, though,' Clara told him. 'I accept most of your theory as being feasible, but there's one aspect that doesn't seem right.'

'And what is that?'

'Thinking back to the Keeper's various operations, this seems completely different. The Country House Bandits were involved in stealing treasures worth six or seven figures. From there, he switched to drugs and people trafficking, which was also highly lucrative. Finally, we believe he was behind the internet scams that yielded millions and millions. All those were big-ticket operations, but these Hanoi burglaries seem like chicken feed in comparison.'

Nash thought for a moment. 'You could be right, but look at it another way. If those other routes were closed off to him, that's three sources of income no longer available. Given his immense capacity for greed, he'd want something to maintain the cash flow. Maybe we're looking at the car thefts from too narrow an angle. I'd hazard a guess that if the Keeper is behind it, he'll also be involved in the sale and distribution of the end product, via breaker's yards or parts supply chains. That would make it far more lucrative. He could even be shipping them abroad.'

* * *

When they entered the CID suite, one glance at their colleagues told Nash the news they had to impart was probably going to be of the negative kind. DC Pearce began to tell them of their all-but-fruitless search for the requested information. 'I checked the industrial estate, and there is a unit rented by one particular outfit from the dates we know Hanoi burglaries took place. The unit is leased to a company by the name of N.A.D.A. Trading Ltd, so I checked them out, but with very little success. Their registered office is care of a firm of solicitors in Manchester, but they were no help.'

'Manchester?' Nash asked as he glanced sideways as Clara.

'Yes, they refused point blank to reveal anything about N.A.D.A. Trading, citing client confidentiality. I also did a Companies House search, and there have been no accounting records filed for that firm. Neither is there any recorded trading address.'

'That tends to suggest it's a shell company,' Nash suggested. 'Did you ask how they paid the rent?'

'Yes, apparently it was paid for up front via a banker's draft.'

'That's another anonymity cloak. Anything else to report? What about the man we asked you to research?'

'We had even less luck there,' Hassan told them. 'We couldn't find anyone with the surname Ningun in the UK, and even the Births, Marriages and Deaths records yielded no result.'

'Whoever is running this operation seems to be going to extreme lengths to cover their tracks,' Clara suggested. 'We know little more about them than we did when we started, apart from a vague description supplied by Roy Proctor, and even that could fit millions of men.' She glanced sideways at Nash and saw him shake his head fractionally, and left it to him to continue.

'Maybe we'll have more luck when West Yorkshire has contacted Derek Bates' next of kin. Speaking of them, did you get the files on the Ilkley hit-and-run victim?'

'Their computer is down for routine maintenance,' Pearce told them. 'But we should be able to download the information tomorrow. His criminal record is on your desk. It contains three convictions for burglary, nothing else.'

'If that's everything, I'm going to leave you to set the ball rolling with West Yorkshire about Derek Bates, Clara. I'm leaving early, as I've some important shopping to do.'

'How important is it?'

Nash laughed. 'Nappies and dog food. I don't think it gets much more important than that for family harmony.'

* * *

Nash reached Smelt Mill Cottage, and Alondra could tell immediately that his day hadn't been a successful one. He'd told her of his visit to Felling Prison with Clara, even outlining part of the reason for their journey, so she wondered what had gone wrong.

Later, after their evening meal, once they had put Lucy to bed, she returned to the subject.

'It was extremely frustrating,' Nash told her. 'And the worst part of it is that when we left the prison, we were quite upbeat, because what the prisoner told us suggested we were about to make real progress. He was most forthcoming, and from him we learned the name of one of the men behind all these car thefts. We also discovered the name of the company that rented the place where the stolen cars were taken, but in both cases, it appeared to be a dead end. The company is only a shell, and there is no record of anyone living in the UK with such a surname, even though it's a highly distinctive one.'

'What are these strange names?'

'The guy is called Mr Ningun and the company goes by the name N.A.D.A. Trading Ltd. That's about all we know about them.'

Alondra started laughing, and seeing Nash's puzzled expression, explained, 'One thing I can tell you, to add to your scant knowledge, is that whoever invented the name of the man and the company can speak fluent Spanish.'

Nash blinked with surprise. 'How on earth do you work that out?'

'*Ningun* is a variant of *ninguno* which is Spanish for "nobody", so your mystery man is actually calling himself Mr Nobody. And the company, *Nada*, is Spanish for "nothing", hence Nothing Trading. That's very clever — nobody's doing anything.' She grinned at her joke.

* * *

When Nash revealed these facts to his colleagues, Clara's response was immediate. 'I think we owe Alondra a huge vote of thanks. She's saved us countless hours of wasted effort attempting to trace a man and a company who simply don't exist.'

'What we do have is the knowledge that the person behind the car thefts is a fluent Spanish speaker,' Pearce pointed out. 'Whether that will be of any help is anybody's guess.'

'OK,' Nash told them, 'let's examine what we learned from Roy Proctor and see whether it provides us anything useful.'

'There is one thing,' Hassan volunteered, 'but it might be a long shot.'

'Let's hear it, Adil. Even long shots sometimes hit the target.'

'I was thinking about the industrial estate where the stolen cars were taken. If the estate has operational CCTV cameras, we might get lucky and pick up images of what happened to the vehicles after Proctor or his brother left them inside the specified unit.'

'Some of those offences took place a while back,' Pearce pointed out, 'so the CCTV footage relevant to those dates will probably have been wiped long since.'

'That's what I like about you too, Viv,' Clara told him. 'As Mike said before, your unflagging optimism.'

'I agree,' Nash said. 'But he does have a point. I still think it's an excellent idea, though. Maybe we'll get lucky with some of the most recent incidents. Will you follow up on it, Adil?'

'There is another titbit Proctor gave us that might lead somewhere,' Pearce said, 'regarding that trading company with the spurious name. I know we hit a dead end with the company title, but we didn't check out the directors. As far as I'm aware, whenever a company is registered, they have to supply details of the appointed executives, giving their full names and addresses.'

'Good point, Viv, although if the company name is fictitious, those of the directors might also be imaginary.'

'Now who's being negative?'

Nash smiled at Clara's comment, but told Pearce, 'Go ahead and check them out, Viv. Even if it's another dead end, at least we'll have eliminated it from our workload.'

Pearce was the first to report, and the result of his research proved as disappointing as Nash had predicted. 'The directors of N.A.D.A. Trading are listed as George Butterworth and John Dryden, and the company secretary as Elizabeth Barrett. Unlike Mr Ningun, I was able to trace all three of them, even though they are all dead.'

He glanced at his colleagues, noticing Clara and Adil's puzzled frowns, and Nash's look of recognition. 'Shall I tell them or will you, Mike?'

'Go ahead, Viv.'

'George Butterworth was a composer, John Dryden was England's first ever Poet Laureate, and Elizabeth Barrett was also a poet, better known by her married name, Elizabeth Barrett Browning. I'm afraid that means we've hit yet another brick wall.'

Later, when they were alone, Nash told Clara, 'I'm now becoming more confident that the crimes being connected isn't as wild an idea as I first thought. Corey Davies came here from Manchester where a lot of the drug element of the Country House Bandits started.'

'Of course! That's why you weren't surprised at Viv's information about Manchester,' Clara said.

'Now we have another connection. And remember the spurious development company involved in the old cottage hospital? Unless I'm mistaken, that firm also had directors with fictitious names.'

'You're right, Mike, and they were also those of dead celebrities.'

CHAPTER THIRTY

A couple of days passed before their other research project yielded results, and these were more promising. DC Hassan presented his findings, which began with some negative news, much as Viv Pearce had predicted. 'I had no luck with the older dates the vehicle thefts occurred, because they were too long ago for the footage from their CCTV cameras still to be stored.'

Adil paused before switching to the positive news. 'I got lucky with the more recent ones. If I'd waited a week longer, their CCTV would also have been updated and we'd have lost some of the images. They sent them to me, and as I watched it, I struck gold. On the night we believe Mr Watkins' Lexus was stolen, a similar-looking car was driven into the unit. Another car was already parked outside and the driver got out, wandered inside and looked round the car with the delivery driver. It all looked quite casual. Then a Transit arrived, reversed inside and blocked my view. A man got out, but I was unable to see what he was doing.'

Hassan paused, before delivering his bombshell. 'A few minutes later, someone lowered the roller shutter door, almost closed. Despite that, I was able to make out four bright flashes in quick succession from inside. Ten minutes later, someone re-opened the shutter and drove the van away. The registration number of the Transit matches the one found at Lady Luck Quarry. That's not everything. Shortly before the van left, a car pulled into a remote corner of the industrial estate, where it was barely visible on the CCTV footage. It looked like a Mercedes. It remained there until the van drove away, and then followed it. Unfortunately, the car's number plate was obscured, but it was definitely a Merc.

'Several hours later, a pedestrian walked up to the unit and opened the door. Minutes later, a low loader turned up and reversed inside. It was empty when it arrived, but when it drove away, there was what looked like a vehicle on the back, although it was covered with a tarpaulin. I managed to make out the low loader registration — it was cloned from a Ford Fiesta belonging to someone in Cheltenham. My next task was to find out where the low loader went after it left the industrial estate, but so far, I haven't had any success.'

'That's both promising and frustrating,' Nash said. 'But it was good work, Adil. Stick with it and your efforts might be rewarded. Ask for some help from HQ. Get someone looking at the ANPR with you.'

* * *

As Nash and Mironova discussed Hassan's update, Clara mentioned their theory again. 'The Mercedes at the industrial estate adds more weight to the idea that the same person is behind all these crimes.'

'True, but we're no nearer identifying him than we were when we started. Putting a name to the Mercedes driver who always wears sunglasses and appears to hide his face would be a giant leap forward.'

'Even if and when we learn the man's name, that might not be the end of our problems,' Clara pointed out. 'We still have to pin all those crimes on him.'

What neither of them knew was that learning the mystery man's identity would present a bigger problem than any they could have envisaged.

Another twenty-four hours brought a further update from Hassan, with even more promising results. 'The low loader pinged an ANPR camera on the outskirts of Middlesbrough later on the night in question, and alerted the local police to the false registration number. However, when officers went to intercept it, the vehicle had vanished.' He paused. 'I spoke to the local CID, and they confirmed there's a scrapyard nearby. Moreover, the yard has a website offering a range of spare parts for luxury cars.'

'I think we need to check with Cleveland Police again and find out if they know or suspect anything dodgy about that scrap dealer,' Nash suggested. 'Follow up on it, will you, Adil?'

* * *

With the West Yorkshire computer maintenance now complete, the results confirmed Nash and Mironova's worst suspicions regarding the fate of Roy Proctor's cellmate. The file on ex-prisoner Nick Balderstone contained the post-mortem results, plus the findings from the coroner's inquest. Balderstone had lived in Kirkstall, close to the centre of Leeds.

'Where was his body found?' Nash asked, as the team examined the paperwork they had downloaded. The first document was the attending officers' report from the place where Balderstone's corpse had been spotted by a local farmer. 'It was somewhere between Timble village and Fewston reservoir,' Clara told him.

'That is a very isolated rural area, and it must be nearly twenty miles away from his home address,' Nash responded. 'I know that neck of the woods reasonably well from when I was growing up, because my parents lived near there. So

173

how did Balderstone get from Kirkstall to the place where he died?'

'Good question, Mike, because we've already been told he couldn't drive. There's no record of him owning a car or a motorbike, and there was no vehicle found near the crime scene. There doesn't appear to be any explanation on the file, either. Incidentally, you were right about the mileage too, because according to Google the distance is just over sixteen miles. That's a long walk.'

They turned next to the post-mortem results, and any remaining doubt they might have entertained vanished abruptly as they read the pathologist's report. Tests revealed that there was a significant amount of alcohol and GHB in Balderstone's bloodstream. From the force of impact, plus the tread marks across the dead man's torso, the pathologist deduced that the vehicle which had caused Balderstone's death was heavier than a saloon car, most probably a light commercial vehicle. He was also able to determine that the driver, having struck the victim once, had then reversed over the body, in the process crushing every bone in his ribcage and rupturing several organs, causing severe internal bleeding. The pathologist ended his summary on a grim note, adding that the offender had repeated this process several times, although his victim must already have been dead.

Faced with such incontestable evidence, the coroner's inquest verdict had been a foregone conclusion. When delivering this, the coroner had added that this was one of the cruellest, most cold-blooded and calculating murders he had ever encountered.

'It looks as though he was drugged and taken to the kill site,' Clara said. 'Probably in the van.' She shuddered at the thought.

These findings left Nash and Mironova with little doubt that the deaths related to the Country House Bandits. The scam investment company and the vehicle thefts were connected, and the person behind those offences was still in the process of cleaning house, eliminating anyone who might pose a threat, or could provide something that would incriminate him. This master criminal, known only as the Keeper, had evaded capture for nearly two decades — his range of activities covering almost every profitable criminal activity. His sphere of operation had stretched across the north of England, from coast to coast. There was nothing he would not touch in order to satisfy his insatiable greed for money — and yet, apart from a vague description, they knew little or nothing more about him than when he had begun.

Nash called DC Pearce into his office and instructed him, 'Contact that van rental company in Netherdale, Viv. I want them to look through their records and check if Vincent Brown, AKA Richard Petersen, rented a van around the date Nick Balderstone was murdered. If I'm right, and he did so, that's yet another homicide to add to his tally.'

The answer came back almost immediately. 'Vincent Brown hired a Transit a couple of days before Balderstone was killed. Not only that, but there is a note on the file saying that when he returned it, he mentioned there might be blood on the underside of the van, because he'd run over a badger.'

'That sounds fairly conclusive to me,' Nash commented. 'Thanks, Viv.'

Having discussed the situation at great length, Nash and Mironova decided it was time to share their line of thinking with their colleagues, and from there, to take it to a higher level by bringing it to the attention of the chief and Superintendent Fleming.

CHAPTER THIRTY-ONE

The immediate reaction from both senior officers reflected a similar level of incredulity to that shown earlier by Pearce and Hassan. However, as Nash and Mironova continued to outline the facts to support their theory, both Chief Constable Ruth Edwards and Superintendent Jackie Fleming began to see logic in their reasoning. Once they had been made aware of each and every event that led the detectives to form this line of reasoning, they accepted the premise as being sound, and Ruth Edwards signalled this by asking the all-important question.

She prefaced it by remarking, 'This man has to be the most ruthless and cold-blooded criminal any of us has had to deal with, and that's saying a lot. What we need to know is how to smoke him out, and once we've identified this monster, how can we ensure he pays the penalty for the countless inhumane crimes he's committed?'

'I was going to say we need a miracle,' Nash responded, 'but I realize they're in short supply, especially as it's nowhere near Christmas. What I'd like to do is speak to someone who I believe has been hunting the Keeper for much longer than us, because I believe they might have some ideas or information that could point us in the right direction. It might even be something they don't regard as significant, but if we tie it to what we know, it could prove useful.'

'Have you anybody specific in mind?' Jackie Fleming asked. 'I'd have thought officers from other forces might have faced similar difficulties to us, otherwise they would surely have made arrests by now.'

'I actually have two people in mind, and neither of them are police officers. I was thinking of Geoff Lister and Joanne Fawcett. I'm fairly certain they went off the radar for self-preservation while they tried to discover who was responsible for the deaths of their loved ones. I believe they're seeking revenge, be it via the legal process or more direct action. I can't think of any other reason for one of them to fake his own death and the other one to disappear and assume a new identity within weeks of her stepfather's murder. The problem is, now we know they're both still alive, we've no idea where they are, or how to contact them.'

The meeting broke up with no firm resolution as to how to tackle their problems. The only crumb of comfort Nash and Mironova took from it was the knowledge that both their senior officers were now onside with their idea. Although they felt deflated by the seemingly impossible task of identifying the Keeper, information would soon surface that would give them the first piece of solid evidence they needed. Before then, however, they had other problems to deal with.

Although the detectives were unaware of it, as they were driving back to Helmsdale, another meeting covering the same topic was underway only a few miles distant from them.

* * *

In the chalet they had been sharing since they had been forced to abandon the canal boat, Geoff Lister and Joanne Fawcett were also discussing ways to expose the man who had caused them so much heartbreak and suffering, and who had attempted to have both of them murdered.

'I've come up with an idea that might work, and prompt this vile creature to show his hand,' Geoff said.

'What's that?'

'I could give a newspaper interview, declaring myself alive and well, and explaining the reason I've spent years undercover. If he knows I'm still hunting him and won't give up, that might just provoke him enough to tip his hand and thereby bring him out into the open.'

Joanne's reaction was diametrically opposite to the one he'd expected. She thought about the short time they had spent together, and how Geoff had saved her life, plus the dangers they had shared, and — even more important to her — how close they had become. Joanne realized, with something of a shock, that although their intimacy might not mean as much to him as it did to her, she was now in love with Geoff.

'You can't do that. You mustn't do that. Please, I beg of you, forget such a wild idea. I've had so much taken from my life already. I know you've also lost the people who were so dear to you, but I couldn't bear the thought of anything bad happening to you. I've been alone for such a long time. Now I've found someone I care about. I don't want to lose you.'

Joanne stopped abruptly, aware that her emotions had given her away, and that she had unwittingly admitted the strength of her feelings for him. She tried to change the emphasis, hoping Geoff hadn't noticed her confession. 'Think of it this way, Geoff, if your attempt fails to draw him out, all he has to do is sit back and wait, then he can strike at any time. It could be six months or six years later, and you'd be unaware of what was about to happen. Do you really want to spend the rest of your life looking over your shoulder, or wondering if the man standing alongside you is carrying a gun, a knife, or even a hypodermic needle?'

Her diatribe confused him, and to cover up his jumble of thoughts, he protested. 'I wasn't thinking of going ahead with the idea without taking some safety precautions. There's our host and hostess here, for example; they're both used to battling the forces of evil. And Inspector Mike Nash, the lead detective in this area, is an old friend who would put all his resources at our disposal. But I take your point,' he conceded, 'because if my idea didn't work out, it could leave me exposed to danger. I wouldn't want that especially if you were alongside me.'

'This Mike Nash, is he intelligent?'

'He is, and a brilliant detective into the bargain.'

'In that case, he'd probably tell you not to go ahead with something so idiotic.'

Geoff resigned himself to defeat. 'OK, I'll forget the idea, if it makes you happy. Accepting that a big announcement of my rebirth is out of the question, have you any alternative ideas?'

'I was thinking we should talk to our host and hostess. When I spoke to her yesterday, she confirmed much of what you said about your policeman friend.'

'I don't recall you talking to her yesterday.'

'You wouldn't, because you were taking a shower at the time. Anyway, if they're OK with it, perhaps they would be prepared to talk to Inspector Nash on our behalf, and maybe even set up a meeting, if it's safe to do so.'

'That sounds like a better plan than my public exposure. Let's see if we can get them on board with it.'

As it transpired, the decision as to whether they should contact Mike Nash became irrelevant, but on seeing the look of relief on Joanne's face, Geoff smiled, saying, 'One really good thing has come out of this conversation.'

'What might that be?'

'It stemmed from what you said, when I realized you cared for me in the same way as I've come to care about you.' He looked at Joanne and smiled. 'So, before we do anything else, I'm going to check the weather forecast and see if there's going to be another thunderstorm.'

Joanne grinned.

Although he was completely unaware of it, something in Geoff Lister's past held the key that would unlock the mystery to the Keeper's identity. However, even when that secret was revealed, it would be by no means the end of their troubles.

* * *

'With any luck, unless we get sidetracked again, we might be able to concentrate on trying to solve the five-plus unsolved murders on our books.'

Hassan frowned, clearly puzzled by something Nash had said. 'Why did you say five-plus murders, Mike?'

'I'm including the murder of Roy Proctor's former cell-mate, Nick Balderstone, in the equation. I know his death occurred out of our area, but I'm convinced it's linked to the killings which took place within our patch. Added to that, there might be others we don't know of as yet. There's also the attempted murder of Josh Proctor's girlfriend, Tamsin Charlton. We have all that on our hands, but we haven't the slightest idea who is behind it, and even the connection is currently little more than theoretical.'

Nash's office phone was ringing. He went to answer it, and was soon back with more information. 'That call was from West Yorkshire CID. Having spent ages trying to track down Richard Petersen, somebody decided to try Google.' Nash laughed. 'Why we didn't think of that surprises me. Viv, get it up on screen.'

Moments later, they had everything they needed.

'He's so blatant about it,' Clara said. 'A businessman! Living in one of the best parts of Leeds. I don't believe it.'

Adil was working on his computer. 'Don't get too excited, Clara, it's a shell company. But it is registered with Companies House, and we have an address.'

'Quite correct,' Nash told him. 'And West Yorkshire will be putting together a search of that address in the next couple of days. There's no rush. According to the local council he lived alone.'

CHAPTER THIRTY-TWO

On Friday, it was Clara's turn to cover the late shift, which she later described as 'the night that turned into nightmare'. She had barely reached home and greeted her husband, David Sutton, when she received her first call-out.

She apologized, but David just shrugged. 'It's all part of the job. Don't worry, I'll keep your dinner warm. I won't give it to the dog.'

'We don't have a dog.' Clara was still smiling as she left to attend to the call-out. As a former soldier, David was far more understanding than many husbands would have been in similar circumstances.

She headed towards Netherdale railway station, the site of the incident. The report relayed to her from the force control room referred to a triple-nine call from an angry commuter. He had returned from a long and tiring working day in Leeds, and having disembarked from the early evening train, he'd headed to the car park, only to find his car was missing.

The Range Rover was his pride and joy, a top-of-the-range model that was only seven months old. As Clara was questioning him, in between trying to calm his outrage, she wondered if this was a variant to the recent spate of Hanoi burglaries they had been investigating. The car was certainly one the thieves could have chosen as a prime target.

After informing her that the only spare keys to the vehicle were secure at his house, as his wife had just confirmed, Clara asked him a question that clearly baffled him. 'Can I assume this is a contactless key?'

'Yes, it is. But I keep it on a ring along with my house and office keys.'

Clara explained, 'Contactless keys emit a constant signal, which can be intercepted by thieves to enter a vehicle and drive it away. They clone that signal to a device they use. That's how your car got stolen, of that I'm fairly certain.' Having taken note of his and the car details, she allowed him to leave, assuring him that every effort would be made to apprehend the thieves and return his beloved Range Rover as soon as possible. Whether this was of any comfort was extremely doubtful.

Once the aggrieved victim was on his way, Clara updated Control with the information and asked that all duty officers were made aware of the stolen vehicle, and that the ANPR camera system be uploaded with the car details. Before leaving the site, Clara looked round in vain for a CCTV camera which could have identified the miscreants, or given a clue as to which direction they had taken the purloined Range Rover. Meeting with no success, she returned to her apartment and the delayed dinner.

* * *

She and David had barely put their knives and forks down after completing the meal when her mobile buzzed again. This call was to a totally different incident, one that normally would not have involved CID, but for one important aspect. 'There's been a fight outside the Ram's Head pub,' the operator told her. 'It involved more than half a dozen men by all accounts, and one of them has been stabbed. We're awaiting CCTV images to see if we can identify the assailant. Paramedics are on site, but there's been no update as to the victim's condition. Starsky and Hutch, plus four other uniforms, have detained the other men involved in the brawl. With all our uniforms tied up, I hoped you'd give us a hand with another call we've just received, and if possible, help settle the outcome of the brawl. The other incident is close to where you live.'

'What's the problem?'

'Someone has just rung in because they're concerned about one of their neighbours. The woman lives alone, and the neighbour looked out of her window and noticed the back door was open. When she looked out again an hour later, the door was still open, but there's no sign of anyone moving about, either inside the house or in the garden. When I checked the name on our system, I saw the woman has some mental health issues. They're not severe, so it might be something or nothing. Alternatively, it could be serious.'

'OK, give me the name and address, plus the neighbour's details, and I'll go straight there.'

* * *

Less than half an hour later, Clara reported back to Control. 'Everything's OK, it was a false alarm. The occupant of the house accidentally dropped a bottle of bleach on the kitchen floor. As soon as it hit the tiles, the top came off and the bleach went everywhere. She's had a go at mopping it up, but even now the smell was so strong it made my eyes water, and I was only inside the property for a few minutes. I was able to reassure the concerned neighbour, so at least we can put that one to bed.'

'That's good news,' the operator responded, then paused so Clara knew there was more to come. 'Now that's been dealt with, would you come to HQ? Uniform have brought in six men from the Ram's Head brawl, and we now have footage of the incident, which might enable you to identify the person who carried out the stabbing.'

'OK, I'll be along straightaway. Any news on the victim?'

'He's been taken to hospital. The paramedics reckon his injuries aren't life-threatening.'

Identification of the perpetrator proved to be a simple task. The CCTV image showed him clearly, his brightly coloured floral shirt unmistakable, as was the small lock knife he used to carry out the assault. A second image, via an officer's bodycam, showed him still holding the knife as he was detained. Finally, his admission of guilt when interviewed ensured his detention. The others involved in the brawl were also held in custody, charged with affray. Now, all Clara had to deal with was the paperwork, and that promised to be fun. No sooner had she relayed the outcome to Control than she was handed another assignment.

* * *

Clara was heading for Helmsdale, wondering what she would find next. All Control had been able to tell her was that a vehicle had crashed through the window of a shop in the market square. Several reports had come in, one from the shop owner. This might be nothing more serious than the driver's overindulgence in alcohol or narcotics, because Friday nights were prone to such happenings. Only when she arrived and was able to liaise with the officers there would she know for certain.

In the event, one glance at the rear end of the vehicle buried in the shop window of the local jeweller's was sufficient for Clara to suspect the worst. The colour of the Range Rover, together with the personalized number plate, identified it as the car stolen earlier that evening from Netherdale railway station car park. She approached the officers, one of whom was roping off the area with the statutory blue-and-white tape.

'We're waiting for the keyholder,' the officer told her. 'Not that we need a key,' he said, indicating the mess in front of them. 'We haven't entered the premises. The fact this is a stolen car suggests it was a ram raid. Added to that, my mate shone his torch inside the store, and it looks as if several glass-fronted wall cabinets and counters have been smashed. And they're well away from where the car ended up.' His information was delivered in a virtual shout, as he competed with the strident protest of the shop's alarm system.

It was only after the shopkeeper arrived and disabled the device that peace was restored. Before then, Clara examined the scene with the use of her powerful torch and confirmed the accuracy of the uniform officer's statement. She decided it was time to call in reinforcements. Having instructed Control to send a CSI team to the site, she reluctantly pressed the short code for Mike Nash's mobile.

Clara smiled ironically at his sleepy tone as he greeted her. 'I hope this is business,' he muttered. 'Or has David left you and you've locked yourself out of your flat?'

'It's business right enough. Some villains stole a Range Rover from Netherdale railway station earlier this evening and they've just used it as a battering ram to force their way into Bell's, the jewellers in Helmsdale marketplace.'

'OK, I'm on my way. Meantime, you'd better raise the rest of the troops.'

While she waited, Clara spoke to the shop owner, Mr Bell. He was anxious to get inside and see what damage had been done, not just to his store, but more importantly, to his stock.

CHAPTER THIRTY-THREE

After what seemed an interminable wait, Clara was relieved to see Nash's Range Rover pull to a halt in the market square, closely followed by an unmarked car in which Viv Pearce was acting as chauffeur to Adil Hassan.

Nash greeted Clara and asked for an update.

'CSI are on their way, but it could be a while before they get here. It's been a busy night.'

Nash turned to the shop's owner, who was hovering nearby, clearly agitated by the event, and by the apparent lack of action by the police officers present. 'Mr Bell?' Nash showed his warrant card. 'Can I assume you have CCTV inside the shop?'

Bell nodded and took his mobile phone from his pocket. 'It's all on here, Inspector. I have an app so I can monitor the store at any time I wish, night or day.' Mr Bell seemed quite happy he had the system in place, and Nash was concerned he was going to go into great depth to explain the benefits to him.

'Yes, Mr Bell, that's extremely helpful. Now let me pass you over to one of our technical people who can deal with this.' He called Viv over and asked him to assist.

Nash, the technophobe, turned to Clara, who he could see was biting her lip in an effort not to laugh. 'Not one word, Mrs Sutton, not one word,' he said, before issuing Hassan with another set of instructions.

'Adil, get on to Control. Get them to check the town's CCTV system and see what they can find. Then I want you to take a walk around the market square and see if you can spot any external CCTV cameras on any of the businesses, note their locations, and advise Control. Tell them we need the keyholders to those premises here ASAP. We're looking for any images of the intruders we can get, particularly ones showing their activities following the break-in. If we can find out how they made their getaway, we might be in with a chance of nabbing them.'

Clara had been looking round and a road sign caught her interest. 'Mike, what about the car park alongside the ring road at the back of the market? They might have left their vehicle in that open space. There's easy access through the ginnels, and I'll bet there's a CCTV camera somewhere overlooking that area.'

'Good idea, Clara. Have a look, will you, and take one of the officers with you. They're probably long gone, but I'm not taking any chances. I'll wait here for Viv to report and CSI to arrive.'

* * *

Twenty minutes later, Pearce, with Mr Bell alongside him, approached Nash. Both men looked disappointed, and when Viv showed Nash the images he'd downloaded onto his mobile, Nash understood why.

The stolen Range Rover crashed through the shop window, and as it came to a halt, a man emerged from the driver's seat. He was followed by three more men who had clearly been waiting outside. As they entered the shop, to the accompaniment of the wailing alarm siren, Nash could see they were all clad in balaclavas and wearing gloves.

Each of them was brandishing a sledgehammer and carrying shopping bags bearing the name of a multi-national supermarket chain.

Once they had squeezed their way past the vehicle, the four men separated and began the systematic destruction of the glass-fronted wall cabinets and serving counters. As he watched this, Nash turned to Bell and asked him about the contents.

Pointing to the first of the cabinets, the shopkeeper told him, 'That one contained rings and bracelets, mostly with diamonds, rubies and sapphires. The other was full of luxury watches — mainly Rolex, Longines and Omega. As for the wall cupboards, they had earrings, necklaces and pendants, plus a few more bracelets and rings.'

As Nash continued surveying the footage, which now showed the men filling their bags with the loot, he was distracted by the CSI van pulling to a halt nearby. Signalling to Pearce to put the video on hold, he walked over and instructed the team leader. 'I want you to concentrate on the vehicle, there might be fingerprints or DNA inside. When you're in the shop, keep an eye out for possible bloodstains. The amount of glass these thugs smashed, they might well have cut themselves.'

He'd barely finished speaking when his mobile rang. The caller was Clara, and it was clear by her tone of voice that she had big news to impart. 'I'm with a Mr Carson, who owns a flat overlooking the car park. He was woken by his dog barking and couldn't get back to sleep because of the noise of the shop alarm. Mr Carson has CCTV installed, and I've just been through the footage with him. It clearly shows three men carrying big Aldi shopping bags as they cross the road from the car park in the direction of the ginnel. Later, it shows four men returning, and this time they're running. Seconds later, a car with multiple occupants drives away, heading across town. Luckily, one frame shows a distinct image of the number plate. I've updated Control so they can do a vehicle check, plus informing all officers on patrol and entering it into the ANPR system.'

'Brilliant news. That's excellent work, Clara. Please convey our thanks to Mr Carson and ask him if it's OK for Viv Pearce to come and download that footage so we have a copy.'

* * *

It was over two and a half hours later, when the team, grateful Clara had the key to the police station with her, gathered in the Helmsdale CID suite. They received an exciting update. Nash listened as Control advised him of the development, then walked into the general office to share the news.

'Northumbria police have just apprehended the suspects on the outskirts of Newcastle. Their vehicle crashed following a police chase. The driver and one of the passengers were trapped inside the car, but the other two tried to do a runner, only to come off the worse for wear. One of them fell as he tried to jump a wall and broke his arm, while the other one has also been taken to hospital to be treated for multiple bites after he tried to mix it with a police dog, a German Shepherd. All four suspects will be transferred to Netherdale tomorrow.

'When it's daylight and a more reasonable hour, I'll phone Mr Bell and tell him the good news. Northumbria reported it appears that all the items stolen from his shop have been recovered, but we'll have to check them over to ensure we've got everything. It looks as if Mr Bell's got away lightly, with only the cost of the damage to his shop, but the insurance should cover that.' Nash grinned. 'However, I think he'll be in for a shock when he gets the revised premiums on his policy next year. That's beside the point — well done, everyone. This has been an excellent team effort. Now, go home and see if you can catch up on some sleep.'

Nash waited until Pearce and Hassan had left, and then told Clara, 'All told, it's been one heck of a night, but you've nailed some villains and ensured they pay for their crimes, which is what we're here for.'

'True, but can I go home to bed now?'

CHAPTER THIRTY-FOUR

It was early afternoon, far too early for the club to open. The door was not the one used by club goers — party animals had to use the main entrance and pass the scrutiny of some tough-looking bouncers. This discreet access was near the rear of the building, where staff members could come and go without encountering their clientele.

Entry could only be achieved by banging on the door to attract the attention of someone inside. Having done this, the man had to wait until he had been scrutinized by the CCTV camera above the entrance, before the door opened.

'What do you want?'

'I'm looking for Barney. Tell him I'm here for an old friend. He'll know who I mean if you mention the name Carl Granger.'

'Wait there.' The door slammed shut.

Before he headed for the club, Mr Nobody had been told, 'Only two people know what happened to Carl Granger: me and Barney. If he proves obstructive, you can tell him you know where the body is.'

Having given him the details, his employer added, 'So now that makes three of us who know the truth.'

It was a measure of the trust placed in him, but the task was not without danger.

Later, having been given the information he'd been sent to obtain, he left the premises. That was part one of his mission complete, and it was far easier than the next element of the task.

Now he had the requisite information. He smiled to himself as he thought it through — Vincent Brown, hired killer, was posing as a legitimate businessman, albeit one with a very lucrative sideline. Real name Richard Petersen, ostensibly the owner of an online retail company, was living the life of luxury in an expensive area of the city.

* * *

Having obtained the location of his target, he reached Alwoodley, on the outskirts of Leeds, the next day. Although Barney hadn't been able to pinpoint exactly where Vincent lived other than it was an executive apartment, Ningun did a little research and decided to take a drive and take a look at a likely property. As soon as he was within range of the premises, he saw an immediate problem. Two gaudily coloured police cars were parked in the grounds in front of the large detached building. Added to that, two uniformed officers were standing like sentinels on either side of the gate to the drive. Was this connected to Vincent? Or was it something entirely unrelated? Either way, it would put his plans to discover what had happened to the missing man on hold.

After an hour spent watching the activity in and around the apartments, he eventually saw an older gentleman emerge. As Ningun watched him walking briskly along the road, he realized the man was not involved in whatever was going on inside. He decided to follow him in the hope he might get chance to engage him in conversation. That way, he might be able to discover what the police presence was about.

He was in luck, for the man soon entered a paper shop that doubled as a sub-post office.

Following him into the store, he noticed the man's purchase, a newspaper specializing in the sport of horseracing. To provide a valid reason for being in the shop, Ningun also picked a couple of national dailies. As the man turned to leave, he bumped into Ningun, who had positioned himself deliberately to bring about the encounter. After a jumbled mass of apologies on both sides, Ningun said, 'Didn't I see you earlier near those apartments round the corner? I wonder what the police are doing there. I thought it might be something to do with drugs. I heard rumours there were a couple of dealers round here.'

The man eyed him for a long moment before replying, 'I don't think dealers would attempt to trade around here, young man. Not with the security we pay for. No, it isn't to do with drugs — it's actually something worse. The guy who owns one of the apartments has died. Police have been knocking on all our doors asking a load of questions. One of the officers told me he'd been found dead on a canal boat somewhere up in North Yorkshire.'

'That sounds bad. Did you know the man?'

Once again there was a pause as his informant looked at him. 'I think he was called Richard something-or-other, but I only saw him to nod to.'

'Phew, that all sounds very dramatic.' He shrugged. 'Anyway, I'd better go pay for my papers.'

Leaving the shop, Ningun's mind was full of the facts he'd learned. He was too distracted to notice that the man he'd been talking to was walking back along the road with his mobile phone in one hand.

* * *

Mike Nash had just taken a bite of his lunchtime sandwich when his mobile rang. He muttered something impolite about people with no sense of timing, hastily chewing the mouthful before answering the call. He listened to what his informant was telling him, barely noticing that DS Mironova's lunch had also been interrupted by a phone call.

Several minutes later, he thanked the caller, and asked for his gratitude to be passed to the person who had provided what could be useful information. He was about to go into the general office to share this news when Clara walked in. She was smiling, and Nash soon learned why she seemed so cheerful.

'I've just had a chat with Lisa. I think she's enjoying motherhood, but she did admit she's missing us all. Apparently, the baby's thriving, and Alan's decided they should have a week's holiday, so he's taking them away somewhere quiet.'

'It isn't quiet enough living in the middle of a forest, then?'

Clara laughed and shrugged.

'Good for them. I've also had what might be useful news, courtesy of West Yorkshire Police, but let's finish our sandwiches and then I'll tell the others.'

* * *

Fifteen minutes later, Nash walked through to the outer office, his arrival coinciding with the whirring sound of the printer as it disgorged a single A4 sheet of paper. He collected this before he addressed DC Pearce. 'Viv, this is a copy of a photo I've just been sent by West Riding police. I've forwarded the image to your computer. I'd like you to do that facial recognition thing you're so good at and see if you get a match on the PNC. The subject is a man who has been snooping around the apartment block where Richard Petersen lived. He chatted up one of the other residents, clearly fishing for information. Luckily for us, the man he chose is a retired police officer, and was suspicious enough to take a surreptitious photo. Let's see if we know the inquisitive character. Of course, it could simply be a local nosey parker, but that wasn't the impression the officer got.'

Later that afternoon, Nash and his colleagues stared at the paperwork Pearce had distributed. Comparing the image of the man seen near Petersen's flat with the headshot taken after his latest conviction, Clara said, 'That's definitely the same person.'

The others agreed, and Nash came up with further contributory factors. 'I think it's highly significant that his last known address, apart from Frankland Prison, is near here, in Netherdale. I also think his name is important, in an ironical sort of way.'

'Why is the name Timothy Gunn important?' Adil wanted to know.

'If you shorten the first name, the result is "Tim Gunn", which sounds very similar to "Ningun", so either Roy Proctor's hearing is defective, or that has to be the worst alias of all time.'

'It wasn't Roy Proctor's hearing,' Clara corrected him. 'Roy told us all the texts he received were signed "Ningun".'

'Good point, Clara. The question is, where do we go from here? We could put Gunn under surveillance, or alternatively go in mob-handed and detain him, but as things stand, we've a shortage of evidence with which to justify an arrest. If he lives up to his reputation, it shouldn't be long before he does something that will give us the perfect excuse for bringing him in. When we do, I know the first thing I'm going to ask him.'

'What's that?'

'*Hablas Español?*'

'What does that mean?' Viv asked.

'It means "do you speak Spanish?". Because if he doesn't, I want to know who gave him that alias.'

Their mention of Roy Proctor gave Nash another idea, which he ran past his colleagues. 'I think one of us ought to visit Roy Proctor and show him this photograph. Now he's aware that his brother died as a result of actions we believe were instigated by this man, he'll be anxious to see he gets his just desserts. Now, who's going to volunteer to go to prison?'

CHAPTER THIRTY-FIVE

When Nash received an update on the search of Richard Petersen's home, the results were disappointing, to say the least. 'The only thing we found that we could link to his criminal activities was a stack of new burner phones in a cupboard. However, there was one item I think you'll find interesting, but I'll explain about that later. One of the neighbours told us he had a Porsche, but it wasn't in the underground car park. On a bunch of keys we found, one was engraved with the name of a company supplying lock-up storage facilities, and a separate pair which we suspected were the keys to a gun cabinet. Sure enough, when we inspected the lock-up, we found a gun cabinet which contained a variety of firearms and ammunition, along with a selection of knives. There was also a wardrobe containing various sets of clothing, along with neoprene gloves, coveralls, masks and balaclavas.'

The detective sergeant paused before relating their other discovery. 'One of the other keys appears to be for a safe deposit box. Our next problem is to discover which bank it's from, and that could prove tricky. However, I'll keep you posted when we get a result.'

'What was the other thing you were going to tell me?'

'Ah, yes. I take it you know this apartment was not cheap?'

'Yes.'

'Well, not only was it furnished accordingly, but it would appear he was quite the connoisseur — of art.'

'Sorry, you've lost me.' Nash was confused.

'Artwork, Inspector Nash, works of art.' The officer laughed. 'He had a collection of paintings, which I suspect are prints.'

'And your point is?'

'Van Gogh.'

'You mean' — Nash burst out laughing — 'Vincent?'

'Exactly. He called himself after his idol.'

* * *

Nash thanked his Leeds colleague and went to let the other team members know, before he returned to his office to look at the overnight reports. He spotted something, picked up his phone and rang Traffic Division. 'This is DI Nash, can I speak to Inspector Grant, please?'

'Speaking, and what can I do for you, Mike?'

'Just check this for me, will you? It's a report of a Porsche found abandoned. I assume someone is checking the owner.'

'Yes, I've just got the info. It's registered in the name of Petersen, address in Leeds. Probably joyriders.'

Nash sighed. 'Where was it found?'

'Trading estate in Netherdale. Been there a while, apparently.'

'I don't suppose it was anywhere near Carline Hire Company, was it?'

'Yes, dumped in the car park two streets away. How did you guess?'

'Never mind, Paul.' Nash shook his head. 'I just wish it had been found sooner. It would have saved a hell of a lot of work.'

'Really?'

'Does the name Richard Petersen ring any bells?'

'Shit!'

196

'Exactly!' Nash put the phone down.

Within the hour, he had the promised update from West Yorkshire. 'We've managed to trace that safe deposit key to the branch of a bank in Leeds.'

'That was quick.'

'We don't mess about. We're in the process of applying for a warrant to search the box. Once we've got that, I'll let you know the result.'

It was frustrating, but that tallied with everything surrounding this case, Nash thought.

* * *

The Keeper wasn't happy. 'Vincent's dead.'

'What?'

'I've just had word from Mr Nobody. Apparently, he got Vincent's address and real ID via Barney, but when he went there the place was crawling with cops. He chatted up one of the locals, who told him Vincent's body had been found on a "canal boat somewhere in North Yorkshire", so Nobody did some digging, and discovered the location, the name of the boat, and the owner.'

'If we've lost Vincent, that's really bad news.'

'Wait though, it gets worse, far worse.'

'How can it be far worse?'

'The owner of the canal boat is somebody called Graham Lawson, and the boat's name is *Angela*. If you put all that together, plus the knowledge this so-called Lawson character was involved with the Fawcett woman, who do you think Graham Lawson really is?'

'I've no idea.'

'OK, think back to the Skipton job all those years ago. The woman who got wasted back then was called Angela Lister. There's one connection. Her husband was a reporter by the name of Geoffrey Lister, who started asking some very awkward questions. But he mysteriously disappeared when we went after him, and was later presumed dead. Note the initials, and add the fact that his uncle, whose house we robbed, was called Eddie Lawson.'

'So you think this Graham Lawson is actually Geoffrey Lister, and that Lister is still alive?'

'I'm bloody sure of it. What worries me even more is the article in the *Netherdale Gazette* mentioned that the police were anxious to trace the boat's owner, plus, and I quote, "anybody else who might have been aboard". To me, that sounds as if Lister has someone helping him, but who that someone is, I've absolutely no idea. I don't like the way this is going. I don't like it at all.'

'So what do we do from here? Are you planning to try and do away with Lister?'

'How can I? For one thing, we've no idea where he is, and if he's got protection, it could be dangerous. Maybe that's how Vincent got killed. Apart from that, now Vincent's gone, we've only Mr Nobody to do the work for us, and he's pretty busy. I think we'll just have to sit tight until things die down, and then we can make a run for it. We've enough in the bank to retire on, and I'm starting to feel uncomfortable the way things are progressing. We've already lost several good sources of income, so let's get out while we've got chance. At least nobody knows who we are, so there's no way they can pin anything on us. Let's quit before it gets too hot.'

'OK, but where shall we go?'

'I don't know. But I think we ought to discount Spain, for obvious reasons. Let's think about it.'

'No, I don't need to think. We can go back to Spain to the hacienda in the hills. The villagers don't know who we are, only the doctor who treated your burns. He won't give us away, not after the threats and the amount of money you paid him.'

CHAPTER THIRTY-SIX

Three days into the surveillance of Tim Gunn's residence, their efforts finally paid dividends. When deploying their assets, Nash had insisted either Adil or Viv be available at all times, and that they should have a drone on hand, should this be deemed necessary. In the event, this proved to be a wise decision, and the drone once again proved its value.

Footage shot by DC Hassan during the late evening showed a visitor to the detached house, who had managed to avoid the officers on stakeout by crossing the adjacent railway line, making his way through the allotments, scaling the wooden fence enclosing Gunn's back garden, and moving swiftly to the back door.

He was obviously expected, because the door opened without him having to knock. What interested the detectives watching the footage most was the large rucksack the visitor was carrying. He had either brought this to deliver something, or he was badly absent-minded, because when he left twenty minutes later, retracing his steps across the railway line, he was no longer carrying the bag.

'There can't be an innocent reason for him to take such extreme measures to avoid being seen,' Pearce remarked. 'It's almost as if he suspected we'd be watching the property.'

'I think we can discount that, Viv,' Clara told him. 'Given Gunn's previous record, my guess is that rucksack contained Class A drugs, and if they even had a whiff of suspicion that we were carrying out surveillance, they wouldn't have gone near the place, not for all the tea in China.'

'Clara's right, so I think the time has come to strike. We've got sufficient, albeit presumptive, evidence of illegal activity via the drone footage, so I suggest we go ahead and take Gunn down.'

* * *

The raid yielded good results, some of which were unexpected. Ignoring the protocol of knocking, Nash, warrant in hand, instructed the armed response unit to use the big red key to gain entry.

The door enforcer did the trick, and officers swarmed through the property so quickly they actually detained Gunn as he was in the process of weighing white powder before placing it in small deal bags. Having secured the property, they recovered large quantities of what they suspected to be heroin, cocaine, and amphetamines. By contrast, the cannabis they seized was instantly identifiable, both by the appearance and the smell. Gunn was cautioned for the crime of PWITS, possession with intent to supply, before being placed in the back of a police van for transfer to Netherdale custody, where he would be interviewed.

True to his word, Nash waited for Clara to complete the opening announcement, before greeting Gunn. Glancing at the clock, and seeing it was shortly after 2 p.m., Nash said, *'Buenas tardes, Señor Gunn, hablas Español?'*

Gunn stared at him, his lack of comprehension apparent. Eventually, aware the officers were awaiting a reply, he muttered, 'I don't understand.'

'Really? Now, that is interesting. So tell me, Tim, whose idea was it to corrupt your name from Tim Gunn to Ningun? Please don't try to deny it, because we've already got confirmation that you were the driving force behind the Hanoi burglaries. If we throw that into the mix, plus conspiracy to murder and the drugs supply charges, you're probably looking at a lifetime behind bars.'

'No comment.'

Nash waited a few seconds and then told the prisoner, 'If I was you, I'd reconsider and make a full and frank confession, otherwise you're going to take the rap for everything the people who employ you have done. Of course, you might be worried they will try and silence you, but I doubt that's going to happen. Keeping quiet didn't help some of the other people who worked for them in the past. Added to that, their tame hitman is no longer available, as you well know. I'm willing to bet they asked you to find out what had happened to Vincent, or should I say Richard Petersen, which is why you were snooping around the area where he lived. You should be more careful who you speak to. The guy you pumped for information is a retired police officer who took your photo and sent it to us.'

'No comment.'

'OK, in that case, this interview is suspended, but I'd advise you to think over what I've said very carefully, because you'll soon run out of options.'

A few hours later, CSI officers, overseen by DC Hassan, revealed that inside Gunn's house they had recovered items stolen during two of the Hanoi burglaries. This added further ammunition for when Nash re-interviewed him.

However, the real game changer came with another discovery Hassan reported on his return to CID. 'CSI lifted the lid of Gunn's toilet cistern and found a parcel sealed in polythene to keep it dry. Inside was a handgun complete with silencer, so it looks like Gunn might also be a gunman.'

Clara groaned. 'Mike and Viv's jokes are bad enough, Adil, without you joining in.'

Hassan grinned sheepishly, before telling them, 'CSI are testing it for fingerprints and DNA, then sending it to ballistics.'

* * *

The day after Gunn's arrest, Nash was seated in his office pondering the developments in the case. He felt frustrated, both by the fact they seemed no closer to identifying the Keeper, and that they had been unable to discover where Geoff Lister was hiding, or even if he was safe and well.

His reverie was interrupted when his mobile rang. He glanced at the caller's name on screen and smiled. 'Hello, darling, is everything OK?'

'Yes, it's fine, Mike,' Alondra reassured him 'I know you're busy, but I just wanted to ask if you'll be able do a bit of shopping for me. Lucy's asleep with Teal on guard duty, while I get on with a landscape I've been meaning to tackle for ages.'

Nash smiled at the picture he'd conjured up of Teal lying alongside the pram, watching the surroundings with one eye open. 'OK, I'll see what I can do. What do you need?'

Alondra gave him a list of vegetables, the amount of which surprised Nash. 'Sounds as if you're planning to feed a large group. Have you arranged a party I don't know about?' he asked.

'No.' Alondra laughed. 'I want to do some batch cooking, so I can put basic ingredients into the freezer and pull them out as required.'

'OK, I'll go to Bishop's Cross and collect this lot sometime later today.'

'If you're going there, give Jessica my regards.'

'I will.' Nash was never certain what prompted his final question. 'Has there been any post?'

'Only the mobile phone bill.'

Nash paused. 'Of course! I should have thought of that before.'

'What do you mean?'

'Oh sorry, something you said gave me an idea I need to follow up on.'

Minutes later, he summoned DC Hassan into his office. 'Adil, have a look through the canal boat file, will you? I want a copy of the CSI report — in particular, the section dealing with the items recovered from the boat.'

When Hassan brought the file through, Nash scanned the contents and then reached for his phone. He pressed the short code for their CSI team leader and waited. It was a few seconds before the man answered and Nash was able to explain what he wanted.

'I can't deal with it myself,' the man said. 'I'm still busy with the contents of that house you raided yesterday, but I'll call the office and get one of the clerical officers to dig the details out and pass them to you.'

CHAPTER THIRTY-SEVEN

Nash signalled for Mironova to join him. 'I'm about to make a phone call,' he told her. 'It's one I could have made ages ago, if I hadn't been so dense. Let's hope it works.'

He was entering the number from the email on his screen when his landline rang. It was Steve Meadows, who told Nash, 'I've got Graham Lawson on the line — the owner of the canal boat where that guy was clobbered.'

'OK, Steve, put him through.'

Seconds later, he heard a voice say, 'Hello?' Nash grinned at the wary tone.

'Hello, Geoff, it's Mike Nash. I was just about to ring to ask if you're OK, and if the bullet wound has healed, but you beat me to it.'

There was a long silence before Geoff Lister stammered, 'How did you know? And how did you find my phone number?'

'The identity was easy, although it came as a huge shock. It was your DNA, which was on file after what happened to Angela and your Uncle Eddie. As for the phone number, I should have worked it out long ago, because among your personal possessions at the canal boat was your mobile phone bill, which naturally has the number on it. That's beside the point. Are you OK?'

'Yes, I'm fine — it was only a flesh wound.'

'I think we're going to need a statement, both from you and Joanne. I take it Joanne's still with you. We're fairly certain we know exactly what happened on the boat, but we need it in writing.'

There was another prolonged silence, and Nash could hear the shock in Lister's voice as he eventually asked, 'How do you know about Joanne?'

'Her DNA was present, along with yours, but it came up as Jolene Fraser, not Joanne Fawcett. However, when I saw her photo, I recognized her as Artie's daughter. Now, whereabouts are you, so I can come and talk to you, along with DS Mironova?'

Lister told him, and was startled when Nash burst out laughing. 'That is the weirdest coincidence of all time. My wife's given me a shopping list — I was planning on going there today. OK, we'll see you later.'

When he ended the call, Clara said, 'You don't believe in coincidences.'

'I don't as a rule, but there are exceptions. Come on, we're going to drive to Bishop's Cross Market Garden. Geoff and Joanne are staying in one of the holiday chalets there. You'd better prepare yourself for a shock, though, when you meet the owners.'

'Why will I be shocked?'

'Put it this way, do you remember when you thought you'd seen a ghost along the road near Mile Marina?'

'Yes, what about it?'

'That wasn't a ghost. It was exactly who you thought it was.'

Clara's face was a picture. 'Really? Are you joking?'

Nash grinned as he shook his head.

They had just reached Steve Meadows on reception, and as they explained where they were going, Nash suddenly turned and dashed back upstairs. He returned a few seconds later, brandishing a single sheet of paper. 'The shopping list Alondra asked me to get,' he explained. 'I'd get my head in my hands if I forgot it.'

Clara smiled. She still wasn't totally accustomed to Nash's domesticity.

* * *

As they drove towards Bishop's Cross, Clara asked him how he knew about 'the ghost'.

'Do you remember when I had to go undercover and needed a mobile home? I remembered that Jessica North had one which she'd got from Steve Hirst before he was reportedly killed in Afghanistan. So I went to see Jessica to ask if she'd lend me the camper van, and there was Steve, sitting at the kitchen table, nursing their baby daughter. They already had a little boy, Stevie, who's a teenager now.'

'So who actually got killed in Afghanistan?'

'It was that villain Tony Smith, who was planning to murder Steve. The other guy was a local Taliban chief. After he'd killed them, Steve set fire to the armoured car and then had to walk for miles before he was safe. He surrendered himself to his old army unit. British Intelligence made him promise not to go public with what he knew — which suited him fine. Apparently, there was a major clean-up operation following on from what Steve revealed, and a few "civil servants" had to take early retirement without the benefit of a pension because of what he knew.'

'By "civil servants", I take it you mean spooks?'

'Not only those involved in espionage. There was a sizeable undercurrent of people developing chemical weapons and the like, and I understand much of that operation has been disbanded.'

* * *

On entering the shop, Clara immediately recognized the young woman behind the counter. The detectives waited until she had finished serving a customer, and as they did so, Clara watched a boy she guessed to be in his mid-teens. He was filling the display shelves with a mixture of green and red peppers, tomatoes, aubergines, and courgettes.

Once the customer had left, Nash greeted the woman, 'Good afternoon, Jessica. I take it you remember DS Mironova?'

'I do indeed. It's nice to see you again, Clara.'

As the women shook hands, Nash said, 'I understand you have a couple of guests in one of your chalets we need to speak with.'

'That's right, Mike.' Turning to the teenager, Jessica said, 'Stevie, go tell your father that Mike and Clara have arrived. He'll probably be in one of the greenhouses, tickling tomatoes or watering watermelons.'

Once the boy had gone, Jessica smiled at Clara. 'I guess this has come as a bit of a surprise.'

'It certainly has. I could hardly believe it when Mike told me.'

Jessica chuckled. 'Like everyone else, I believed the newspaper reports and thought he was dead. Later, I went on a camper van holiday to the Lake District along with Sonya Williams and her kids. We'd booked into a campsite there, and I almost fainted when I walked into the clubhouse and saw Steve behind the bar drying glasses.' Jessica laughed. 'Mind you, I wasn't the only one who got a shock that day, because then I was able to introduce Steve to his son, who he didn't know existed. The rest, as they say, is history. We have official sanction, but we've promised not to reveal our past to all and sundry.'

A few minutes later, when Steve Hirst entered the shop alongside his son, Clara was able to spot the likeness immediately. Having congratulated him on his survival, she went on to say how pleased she was to hear about the new life that he and Jessica had created.

'Yes, it's all been good, but it wouldn't have happened if Geoff Lister hadn't intervened. But for Geoff I'd be dead, so when he contacted me to ask for our help and somewhere safe to stay, along with Joanne, we were more than happy to help.'

Even Nash was unaware of this part of the story, and asked, 'How did Geoff help you?'

'He'd been sent to Kabul to cover a breaking news story. I'm not quite sure how, but he got wind of the plot to have me killed. He sought me out and told me, so I was able to turn the tables on the plotters, who were led by that evil bastard, Tony Smith.'

Hirst paused before switching topics. 'That all took place well before Geoff's wife and uncle were murdered, and later, when I read that he too had died, I felt so sad, but in a way it seemed rather unreal, almost as if it had been staged. That was why I wasn't totally shocked when Geoff contacted me. He came here to prove it really was him, and to ask for our assistance should it ever be needed. In the end, all we did was get them away from the canal boat, and give them a place to stay where we could keep watch for any intruders. Mind you, I got a heck of a surprise when we were driving back from the canal and I spotted DS Mironova.'

'Not half as big a shock as she did,' Nash told him. 'Clara thought she'd seen a ghost.'

Hirst was still chuckling when he told the detectives, 'Let me take you to their chalet and I'll stand guard outside.'

Nash turned to Jessica and handed her a piece of paper. 'Before we go, Alondra sends her regards and she's asked me to do some shopping.'

CHAPTER THIRTY-EIGHT

Steve Hirst gave a pre-arranged knock on the chalet door and assured those inside it was safe to let their visitors in. Nash and Mironova entered the small log cabin.

'Geoff, it's so good to see you alive and well.' Nash shook Geoff's hand, then introduced Clara, before turning to the other occupant. 'You must be Joanne Fawcett. It's a pleasure to meet you.'

There was one thing troubling Joanne, apart from the danger she and Geoff shared, and she came straight to the point. 'Am I in trouble, Inspector Nash? I didn't intend to kill that man on the boat. All I was doing was trying to stop him shooting Geoff. I don't want to go back to prison.'

Nash laughed. 'I think you're more likely to be awarded a medal for bravery than face prosecution. What you did has to be classed as self-defence, especially as he'd already tried to murder you up at the holiday cottage.' Seeing her and Geoff's surprise, he told them, 'Yes, we know about that, and when Clara inspected the dummy you'd set up, and later looked at your photo, she recognized the blouse. Putting that along with the evidence from the boat, plus your real identity, gave us the full story.'

Nash added further reassurance. 'We now have ballistics results from the gun we retrieved from the boat. They not only matched those at the cottage, but also enabled us to identify the man you killed, whose name was Richard Petersen, as the assassin responsible for a considerable number of previously unsolved murders. From memory, I think there were nine in total, all committed using that weapon. We also suspect he was involved in other killings, ones which didn't involve the use of that firearm. Like I said, disposing of him was more like a public service than an offence.'

Turning to Geoff, Nash asked, 'Am I right in thinking you faked your death on that Indian expedition? Enabling you to continue trying to discover the identity of the man responsible for your wife and uncle's murders? And more recently, you included Joanne's stepfather in the equation? I assume that was the reason you and Joanne got together.'

'Yes, we're both determined to make every effort to ensure the vermin who has caused untold misery to so many people is brought to justice. He has ruined so many lives, purely for his own greed.'

'Do you have any clue as to his identity?' Nash asked the couple. 'Like you, we've been hunting him for a while, but so far, we haven't been able to come up with anything remotely positive.'

'Neither have we, although for a long time, both of us believed that Gabriel Welham was the head honcho.'

'Was it one of you who set up a surveillance camera outside the grounds of Kirk Bolton Lodge, where Welham and Thelma Daley lived?'

'That was my doing, Inspector Nash,' Joanne told him. 'I sent you the flash drive after Welham and his mistress were killed.'

Geoff took a flash drive from his pocket. 'And this contains a video of the incident at the holiday cottage, plus a copy of all Joanne's surveillance footage from Welham's house.'

'You did us a great favour, Joanne, because the images enabled us to rule out Terry Palmer, who up to that point had been our prime suspect. Your video clearly showed Welham's killer to be far taller than Palmer. In fact, ballistics now proves the man you clobbered with a boathook was Richard Petersen, the same hitman who shot Welham and Thelma. By the way,' Nash added, 'please drop the "Inspector Nash" bit, just call me Mike.'

'So what you're telling us is, you're no further forward than us in solving the mystery of who is behind all this.' Geoff sounded downhearted. 'Which means both Joanne and I are still at risk and alone in the world, having lost everyone we love.'

'Except we do have each other,' Joanne corrected him. 'At least one good thing has come out of this to counteract all the evil.'

'It means you'll have to remain in hiding for a bit longer, I'm afraid. You should be safe here.'

It was a while before something Lister had said enabled Nash to introduce a different topic, although he was by no means certain how Lister would react to the news.

'Actually, Geoff, you were wrong when you said there was nobody left who cared about you. There is one person, someone who has loved you since the day you were born, and probably even before then.'

Geoff looked confused.

Nash tried to explain. 'I only discovered this person's identity recently. I met with her, but I didn't tell her I suspected you were still alive. That would have been too risky, and I needed your permission to do so.'

Geoff was clearly baffled by Nash's statement. 'Who is this person?'

'Let me tell you the whole story. Your birth father was called Colin Lister. He was a young and talented journalist who worked for a regional newspaper. There, he met and fell in love with a colleague. Soon, Colin's undoubted ability brought him to the attention of a television news producer. He travelled to London to attend an interview which would have landed him a job for one of the major channels. Sadly, following his interview, Colin was killed by a drunk driver.'

Nash paused to allow this sad news to sink in, before continuing, 'Colin died before his colleague was able to tell him she was pregnant. She was a junior reporter at the time. She couldn't afford child minders and the other expenses involved in bringing up a little one. She hadn't a hope of being able to care for their son. Nor could she risk losing her job — her only source of income. Then Colin's family came to the rescue by volunteering to take care of her baby. Rather than go through the formal adoption process, your father's cousins gave you a new home, and later, Eddie and Agatha took over caring for you.

'That didn't mean your birth mother forgot you. She was kept up to date with everything you did, all the ups and downs of your life. Up to the time he was killed, Eddie used to write long letters to her, the only topic being you. She rejoiced at your happiness when you and Angela married, and was devastated on your behalf when she heard Eddie and Angela had been murdered. She then hired a private investigator to check on you, as she no longer had anyone else. The sadness she felt over your suffering, and the torment it caused her became a hundred times worse, when, along with everyone else, she believed you had died. She was unable to bear such awful news. By then she had become highly successful, but she was so traumatized by your death she quit her job. She has been grieving ever since, living a solitary, lonely exist-ence, merely going through the motions, in the belief she had lost everything precious to her, and that her life was without meaning or purpose.'

Geoff stared at Nash, shaking his head trying to dispel the emotions the information had aroused. Nash watched as he shuddered, trying to regain control, his hand rubbing across his face.

'You're telling me you know who my mother is. And she's alive?'

Nash nodded, watching as Joanne held him close.

Geoff sighed. 'I wish I'd known. If I had, I might have tried to do things differently. I certainly don't despise her. I'm only sorry I caused her so much distress. I have one question, though, or maybe two. Who is this woman, and would she want to meet me? I certainly want to touch base with the woman who gave me life.'

'This is where it gets really spooky. Your father and mother were both reporters, and you also became a very successful journalist. If ever there was a case of genetic inheritance, this has to be it. After your mother switched to television work, her career really took off. In her case, the expression "a household name" is no exaggeration. Even my wife, who was brought up in Spain, knew of her before they met.' Nash paused. 'Geoff, your birth mother is Sylvia Cross, former TV presenter of *Current Affairs*.'

There was a stunned silence as Geoff and Joanne absorbed the knowledge that his mother had become so famous, the programme she hosted being a peak viewing sensation. Eventually, Joanne said, 'I think that shows how much she cared about you, Geoff. To abandon her career and retire because she thought you had died proves she loved you. I think you should meet her as soon as it's safe to do so.'

* * *

Before the detectives left, Nash promised he would speak to Sylvia Cross and try to explain the situation. 'It's not going to be easy telling her you're alive after all these years. There is one stipulation, and I think it's a sensible precaution, I certainly won't be telling her where you are. I believe it would be wise to defer any contact until we are absolutely certain the danger surrounding both of you, and anyone close to you, is well and truly over.'

Seeing the doubt on Geoff's face, Clara backed up Nash's suggestion by adding, 'We already have ample evidence of the way this evil monster disposes of anyone he perceives as a threat — both to people who have been working alongside

213

him, and to their friends and relatives. It's an extremely potent threat.'

Geoff accepted this, albeit reluctantly, at which point Nash told him, 'Don't ask me why, but I have a feeling we will soon be able to release you from this embargo, and equally from the fear that has gripped you both for so long.'

* * *

Having collected Nash's shopping and said goodbye to Steve and Jessica, the detectives headed back to Helmsdale. Clara's final comment before leaving made Jessica smile. 'Now I know you own this place, I'll be coming here for all my fruit and veg in future.'

On the journey, Clara returned to Nash's final statement to Geoff. 'Do you really believe all this will soon be over, or were you just saying that to bolster Geoff's spirits?'

'That was part of the reason. But strangely, even as I was saying it, I had the feeling that we're due a break. I'm hoping before long there will be a significant development, one that will finally enable us to put this saga of evil and sadness to bed.'

'Speaking of beds, I got the distinct impression that even when this is all over, Geoff and Joanne will continue sharing the same one. What's happening between them is far more serious than a brief fling, or turning to one another for mutual consolation.'

'Yes, I got the same feeling, and after everything they've had to endure, I think they're overdue a little happiness, don't you?'

CHAPTER THIRTY-NINE

Nash's prognostication about the development of their investigation began to be proved correct.

He arrived at Helmsdale station to be greeted by Steve Meadows. 'The Forensic chief wants you to ring him when you've got a minute.'

When Clara arrived, she noticed Nash was on the phone. She saw him look up and waved, and in return, received an unmistakable gesture. She smiled as she removed her coat and headed for the coffee machine.

She returned bearing two mugs, one of which she placed on Nash's desk. He nodded and gestured for her to sit down. Eventually, he thanked the person he'd been talking to and replaced the receiver.

Clara noticed his faraway expression and remained silent rather than risk disturbing his train of thought. She knew Nash often looked miles away when he was seeking a solution to a problem. After a while, he smiled at her as he picked up his mug. 'Thanks for this. I have to make a couple of phone calls, following which we may have to visit someone. Before that, can you bring me the file on the cottage hospital murders? I need to check a couple of facts.'

Clara puzzled over his request. What was it he needed to know about that case? Ballistics had already proved the victims had been killed by Richard Petersen, so surely that was the end of the matter.

Nash rang down to reception. 'Steve, you remember that call I took from the mysterious lady?'

'Yes. An old flame?'

'Don't you start.' Nash sighed. 'I assume you logged the call.'

'You checking up on me?'

'I just need the number.'

'Hang on.'

Nash could hear paper rustling before Steve relayed the details.

Clara returned with the file as Nash was replacing the receiver. 'Are you going to tell me what's going on?'

'Some interesting facts regarding DNA have come to light.' He ignored Clara's quizzical expression and pointed at the phone. 'I'd neglected to take Sylvia Cross's phone number. We're going visiting. Hopefully, you'll soon be able to meet a TV celebrity.'

'You want me to come with you?'

'When I tell her Geoff is alive, I think she may need a female with her. And I need to talk to Sylvia, she's the only person I can think of who can supply the information.'

The phone conversation with Sylvia Cross was short and productive. 'I need some information from you. Would it be OK if I came to see you this morning, along with Clara, my second in command? If that's in order, I need your address.'

Seconds later, he replaced the receiver and told Clara, 'We're going to Rose Cottage in Drovers Halt. While we're on the way, I'll explain what this is all about.'

* * *

Rose Cottage certainly lived up to its name, Clara thought. Not only was the path to the front door flanked by an array of standard roses, yet to bloom, but the archway that acted as a porch-cum-pergola framing the entrance was home to climbing plants.

'I bet this place looks magnificent in the summer,' she remarked.

Nash had obviously also been struck by the appearance of the property's exterior, because when Sylvia opened the front door to greet them, he asked who tended her garden.

'Actually, I do it all myself.' Sylvia smiled with more than a trace of sadness. 'I use it as a distraction to fill in my empty days and take my mind off all the heartbreak I've suffered. Why don't you come inside and I'll make you a drink. Tea or coffee?'

Her mention of the suffering she had undergone gave Nash the ideal opportunity to pass on their news. When they were seated in the comfortable lounge with their coffee and a slice of homemade cake, Nash told her, 'I think I can put an end to your heartbreak, because I've some extremely good news for you. Please, remain calm while I try and explain.'

'OK, I'll try.' Sylvia smiled and nodded.

'During the course of our investigations, several facts have come to light.' He glanced at Clara before he said, 'Your son Geoffrey is alive and well.'

Sylvia's eyes widened. 'What did you say?'

'It's true, Sylvia, Geoffrey is alive. He's been in hiding for his own safety,' Clara added.

She looked from Nash to Clara. 'My boy . . . my boy is alive?' The tears flowed unchecked down her cheeks as Clara put a reassuring arm around her shoulders. 'Are you sure?'

Nash nodded. 'I've spoken to him.'

Sylvia pointed to a decanter alongside crystal tumblers on the sideboard. 'Brandy.'

Nash poured a drink and handed it to her, while Clara supplied tissues from a box on the coffee table.

'Is this really true?' She looked to each of them in turn.

They both nodded, giving her time to compose herself.

Knowing how little he could reveal, Nash phrased his wording very carefully. 'Geoff was investigating a series of serious crimes, and was being hunted by the villains because he knew too much. They'd already tried to kill him once. Believing he had no family to worry about him, faking his death seemed the safest thing he could do.'

Sylvia nodded her understanding and dabbed her eyes. Thanking Clara for her help, she visibly pulled herself together, sitting straighter and raising her head, her professional persona taking over. 'Please, tell me more.'

Nash continued, 'When you came to visit me, I had my suspicions, but no proof. However, we met up with Geoff a couple of days ago. He, along with a lovely young woman called Joanne, is still in hiding because the danger they both face isn't over yet. We were able to tell Geoff about his past, about you and his father. Geoff certainly doesn't resent you for having him adopted, he understands your reasons. More than that, once he'd got over the shock as to your identity, he told us how proud he is knowing he's your son. He's really looking forward to meeting you.'

He held up his hand as Sylvia was about to speak. 'However, for everyone's safety that will have to wait. I cannot stress strongly enough how what I've told you cannot become public. Not only his and Joanne's safety are at risk, but if any connection to you was made, then so would be yours.'

Sylvia nodded. 'I understand, Inspector Nash. I wouldn't want to cause any more problems. And, after all this time, I can wait a bit longer.'

Sylvia smiled at last.

Nash explained the other reason for their visit. 'Hopefully the situation will change soon, but first, I need some information from you. We need to know everything you can tell us about Colin's family.'

'May I ask why?'

'Not at this time, I'm afraid. In particular, I am referring to any males who are still alive, or were still alive around eight years ago.'

'That's a bit difficult to answer. Let me explain . . .'

* * *

When they left, half an hour later, Clara's impression of that meeting was of a woman whose situation had been transformed from despair to unalloyed happiness, and who now had a new purpose in life. However, both detectives knew that Sylvia's information had set them an apparently unsolvable problem.

As they drove to Helmsdale, Clara voiced their dilemma. 'I thought Sylvia was going to present us with a definitive answer to our problem, but it seems she's created an even bigger one. To be honest, I can't see a way round it.' Neither could Nash at that moment, but Clara's follow-up comment sparked what she referred to as his wildest idea yet when she said, 'Apart from the logistics about the family members, what she told us about them seems to portray them as decent, respectable people, far different to the type we're looking for.'

That triggered a memory of the previous time Nash had met with Sylvia, and a remark she'd made about one family member. She'd told him they were all nice, but with one exception. Could that stray comment have any bearing on what they needed to find out, or would it turn out to be another dead end? Why, he puzzled, does everything seem to keep coming back to Spain?

Before giving voice to his theory, Nash decided to do a little research, or rather, to get Viv Pearce to do some for him.

* * *

Nash called Pearce into his office and issued his instructions. Before Viv left, Nash told him, 'On no account mention this to Clara. If I've got it wrong, I'd never hear the end of it. One more thing, don't bother trying one of those online translation tools. I know someone who can do the job far better.'

While he waited, Nash called Geoff Lister and told him he had spoken to his mother. 'I told her you are alive and well, enhanced by the fact that you were with Joanne.'

'How did she take it?'

'She was shocked, as you would expect, but she gave me a message to pass on to you. She hopes you will forgive her for abandoning you, but it was the only way she could ensure you had a good start in life. The decision to give you up had been heart-wrenching, but it was her only choice. She hopes you would like to meet her, both you and Joanne, but appreciates that will have to wait until we've sorted out this case.' Before he ended the call, Nash passed on Sylvia's phone number.

Later, having received a sheaf of paperwork from Pearce, Nash created a new folder. 'I'm leaving,' he told his colleagues. 'But if anyone asks, I'll be working from home. Don't forget what I said, Viv — mum's the word.' Turning to Mironova, he told her, 'I might want you to go to HQ tomorrow first thing, to meet up with me. Then we can tell the chief constable and Jackie Fleming about this development.'

Clara was puzzled, but something about Nash's air of excitement told her that what he was hoping to achieve might be momentous. Despite her best efforts to extract information from Pearce, methods that included bribery, blackmail, and offers to babysit, she failed to get a positive result.

* * *

On reaching home, Nash asked Alondra to join him in the study. She arrived, carrying Lucy in her arms. 'I've got a little job for you,' Nash told her, gesturing to a sheaf of papers on his desk. 'I wondered if you might translate these for me.'

One glance at the top sheet of paper, which was headed *El Pais*, was enough for Alondra to realize these were all copied from Spanish newspapers. 'I'll certainly do that, providing you look after Madame while I'm busy.'

She handed Lucy to her father, who cuddled her, tickling the infant and making her giggle. An hour later, her work complete, Alondra handed Nash the translations, which had all been pinned to the corresponding newspaper article. 'Now, are you going to tell me what this is about?' she asked.

'I think everything written there is a work of fiction, although the reporters weren't to know that.' Nash explained, and with it came the realization that if his theory was correct, this had to be one of the wickedest crimes Alondra had ever heard of.

After studying her copies, Nash picked up his mobile and called Mironova. 'We're on for tomorrow morning. I've just contacted Jackie and the chief to ensure they're available. Before we meet, let me explain what I've got in mind.'

CHAPTER FORTY

The detectives walked into the chief constable's office and she greeted them with a question. 'You told us there has been a major development. Does that mean it's significant enough for an imminent arrest?'

'I wouldn't go that far,' Nash responded. 'What we've learned recently appears to have thrown up more questions than answers. Let me explain, and then you'll understand the problem.'

He paused, assembling the jumble of thoughts. 'This all started when Geoff Lister's birth mother got in touch. She'd seen the press reports about the canal boat and told me it belonged to her son. When I met her, she told me about Geoff's father and his family. Geoff was adopted because his father had died, and she was unable to support the child and hold down a job. She later became famous, but has never been in contact with Geoff. Her name is Sylvia Cross.

'That all seemed of little relevance until I got a phone call yesterday from CSI. Because of the pressure of work on more urgent cases, they have only just got round to the forensic examination of items removed from the house occupied by the directors of Dale Investments.'

Jackie Fleming looked confused.

'The bodies found shot to death in the old cottage hospital,' he added.

She nodded. 'There are so many.'

Nash continued, 'We now know via ballistics that Richard Petersen, the hired assassin, killed them — but we still don't know who paid him. Among the paperwork taken from the directors' house was the Memorandum and Articles of Association for Dale Investments Ltd. That's the document issued when a company is incorporated, and it lists all shareholders and any guarantors for the new company.

'The "Memarts", as they are known colloquially, yielded DNA from the bodies, and also a source that wasn't a match. However, when CSI ran the profile through the PNC database, it threw up a faint familial match. A male, distantly related to a person on the PNC.'

'Who is the person?' Jackie interrupted. 'Is it a known criminal?'

'No. Quite the opposite. The person whose DNA was on the company document is a distant cousin to Geoffrey Lister.'

'So if Geoffrey Lister's distant cousin handled those documents, are you suggesting he might be involved in their crimes? Might even be the Keeper?' Ruth Edwards asked.

'That was our initial thought, but, unfortunately, it isn't that simple. As Sylvia Cross knew each member of Geoff's paternal family, we asked her for information. From her, we learned that Geoff's father, Colin Lister, had a cousin, Amanda, who also had a son, Dean Abbott. He was the only male who fits the bill.'

'If this Dean Abbott is the one whose DNA is on the document, shouldn't we bring him in for questioning? Get a positive match?'

'Questioning him would be rather difficult, Jackie, unless we use an Ouija Board. You'll note I said "was".'

Both senior officers looked completely baffled.

* * *

'According to what Sylvia said, Dean Abbott was killed in a car crash in Spain years ago, along with his female passenger.'

He let the information sink in.

'To obtain the details, I got Viv to download reports from the Spanish newspapers at the time. And to ensure complete accuracy, I asked Alondra to translate them. Apparently, Abbott and his companion were travelling along a narrow, winding mountain road, having just attended a cocktail party. Both of them had been drinking. The car went off the road and plunged headfirst down a steep gorge and burst into flames, incinerating the occupants. The accident — if it was an accident — took place in a very remote area, so the remains of the car and its occupants weren't discovered until a week later.'

'There must be some mistake, surely. Perhaps CSI got it wrong, or the father of this Dean Abbott had a child by another woman.'

'Sorry, that won't work. If his father had sired another child, there would have been no genetic connection to Geoff Lister. The family line is via Dean's mother, Amanda Abbott, née Lister, and she died in childbirth. Dean Abbott was her only child.'

'So that means we're left with two possibilities,' Jackie suggested. 'Either CSI got it wrong, as Ruth mentioned, or this Dean character handled that paperwork before his death.'

'We can discount the latter of those ideas,' Nash told Jackie. 'The date of incorporation on those documents for Dale Investments was eight years ago, long after Abbot's supposed death. However, there is a third possibility, which nobody has mentioned yet.'

Knowing what was coming, Clara wondered how the senior officers would handle such a seismic shock.

'Go on then, Mike. Tell us the third possibility.' Ruth Edwards rolled her eyes and folded her arms.

'What if the man killed in the car crash wasn't Dean Abbott?'

'Do you really believe that's a possibility?' She sounded sceptical.

'I do, because of other things Sylvia Cross told us. She was a journalist at that time and the story made the news headlines. Apparently, Dean Abbott got married very young, but Sylvia didn't think the marriage was happy. Around a couple of months before the fatal accident, Dean's wife allegedly eloped with her lover, a married man. They both sent letters to their partners, stating they were beginning a new life together in Brazil. Sylvia also told us the woman who died alongside Dean in that car inferno was the spurned wife of the absconding lover.'

'It sounds as if Dean and that woman turned to each other for consolation, but with a tragic outcome.'

'That's probably true, Jackie, except I'd take issue with the last part of what you said. Remember how long ago this was. Dean and the woman had been attending a party and were seen driving away in his car. Because of that, the post-mortem would have been a formality. Apparently, the car was quite a distinctive model, so anything such as DNA testing wasn't conducted, had it been available. Identification would probably have been via nothing more than jewellery or watches.'

Nash paused. 'What I don't know, and can only guess at, is if there has been any sight or sound of the couple who supposedly fled to Brazil? Are they alive and well in South America? Or have they been lying in Spanish graves for years, having been burned to death in that car?'

'This is all speculation,' Jackie said. 'You haven't a shred of evidence. Do you really believe Dean Abbott murdered his wife and this other man, then went on a crime spree that has made him such a notorious and evil character?'

'I do, and I'm prepared to have a small bet that I'm right.'

'It's just as Jackie suggested, and you haven't a single piece of evidence to back your wild theory,' the chief added.

Nash shook his head in mock sorrow. 'You seem to have mislaid your detection skills, both of you. You've failed to ask the most pertinent questions of all about Dean Abbott.'

Clara turned her head away so neither of the senior officers could see the smile as she anticipated the shock they were about to receive.

'And what pertinent questions did we fail to ask?' Jackie demanded angrily.

'You didn't ask what Dean Abbott was doing in Spain.'

'I assumed he must have been on holiday. That's why most Brits visit Spain, isn't it?'

'Far from it. Dean Abbott lived and worked in Spain. He'd moved there when he got a new job.'

Clara realized Nash was teasing his seniors, stringing the revelation out as he continued, 'Now you should ask the second pertinent question, which is, what was his line of work?'

'Go on then, tell us.' Jackie shook her head in frustration.

'Dean Abbott was a professional footballer. Now, would either of you care to guess what position he played?'

Revelation came at last as Jackie and Ruth chorused, 'Goalkeeper?'

'Yes, he was *the keeper*. My bet is Dean's wife and her alleged lover never reached Brazil, never left Spain, and were possibly killed before being incinerated in that car crash. This would allow Dean to set up home with his mistress and continue his life of crime.'

'You said "continue", does that mean he'd already started?'

'I believe so, ma'am, but this is purely hearsay. Even so, my guess is the rumours were accurate. According to what Sylvia told us, Dean was let go by the English club he'd played for. He was suspected of taking bribes to fix games, and the same thing was about to happen with the Spanish club. We've been very fortunate, because Sylvia Cross has been a mine of information. It's not surprising she became such a successful journalist.'

'Is there anything else we should know?'

'I can't think of anything we've missed, and like you said earlier, much of this is pure speculation. As there are no other contenders for the role of the Keeper, certainly ones with the correct DNA profile, I think we've taken a giant stride forward. However, although we've solved one part of the problem, a major stumbling block still remains. We have absolutely no idea of the Keeper's new persona, or his whereabouts.'

* * *

As they drove back to Helmsdale, Clara expressed the frustration she felt, one shared by Nash, their senior officers, and colleagues. 'It seems that every time we get one step forward, we get knocked two paces back. Solving the murders of Welham, his mistress and the Dale Investments directors in the cottage hospital seemed like great news, but then we had all this new stuff to deal with. Now we've finally got identification of the man we believe to be the Keeper, which is what we've been seeking for such a long time. However, we still don't know who he's posing as nowadays, what he looks like, or anything about him.'

Nash agreed. 'There is one other aspect of what you just said that raises a separate concern.'

'What else is bothering you?'

'Accepting that we know the probable identity of the Keeper, I was thinking about his activities over the years. Whenever someone seemed to have outlived their usefulness, or if he perceived them to be a threat, he simply had them disposed of.'

'Yes, I accept that, but why is it raising a concern now?'

'I was wondering about the woman we believe assisted Abbott in his deadly scheme in Spain. The one who supposedly died in the car fire. Has she continued to consort with Abbott all this time, or is she also lying dead somewhere?'

Despite her knowledge of the Keeper's catalogue of crimes, Clara felt a shiver of horror at this possibility. Along with it was the knowledge that, although their resolve to bring the Keeper to justice was stronger than ever, they had no idea how to achieve their objective.

CHAPTER FORTY-ONE

Over the weekend, partly to distract himself from endlessly mulling over the case that was vexing him, Nash applied himself to a necessary task — one which he'd delayed for several weeks. His passport was due to expire soon, and he needed a new photograph. Rather than employ a professional, Nash decided to ask Daniel to assist. He drove with Alondra and Lucy for a visit to Daniel's school, where he had recently become enthusiastic about a new pastime.

'I need you to get that fancy camera I paid the earth for and take a photograph of me, so I can send it away with my passport renewal document. It'll make a change for you from the multitude of shots of squirrels, pheasants, deer, and badgers you've bored us with.'

'I'll have a go, Pa, and hope it doesn't break the camera,' Daniel retorted. 'I might even keep a spare copy and include it in my album of local wildlife.'

Nash, together with Alondra, viewed the results of Daniel's efforts, with the photographer hovering anxiously nearby. Lucy decided the process was too boring and had fallen asleep on her mother's lap. After inspecting the half-dozen photos on the camera, Alondra delivered her opinion. 'I think you should discard those two.' She pointed to the relevant images. 'They make you look much older than you really are. What do you think, Mike?'

Getting no response, she glanced at her husband. Noticing the faraway expression on his face, she put one finger to her lips, signalling Daniel to remain silent.

After several seconds, Nash appeared to resume concentration, and replied, 'Whatever you say. I'm not going to argue with an expert.'

Once they had selected the image Alondra described as the most accurate, Daniel promised to have a copy matching the Passport Office's stringent requirements ready later that evening, and would email it to him. 'Now, do I get my afternoon tea? Or is this just a business meeting?' Daniel laughed.

As they drove to the tea room, Alondra asked Nash what had happened to him during the viewing. 'I thought you'd gone into a trance,' she joked.

He smiled. 'No, it was nothing like that, but something you said sparked an idea to do with work. It'll have to wait until Monday morning before I can find out if it's going to be feasible or not.'

'I'm glad about that. Perhaps you'll be able to devote the rest of the weekend to your family.'

* * *

On Monday morning, as soon as DS Mironova entered the CID suite, she was summoned into Nash's office. Having explained the circumstances surrounding what he described as a light bulb moment, Nash presented the idea that had occurred to him.

'I agree, it's definitely worth pursuing,' Clara responded. 'But we'll have to run it past Viv and Adil first. They're the only ones who can tell us whether it's practical, or a non-starter.'

'OK, as soon as they're here, put it to them. If it is workable, they can get on with it immediately.'

Pearce and Hassan listened to Clara's suggestion and their response was both immediate and positive, with one huge reservation. 'You want us to get hold of a photo of Dean Abbott from back in the day and use computer technology to age it, so we'll know what he looks like nowadays, is that right?'

'That's the idea, but will it work?'

Pearce glanced at Hassan, saw him nod.

'Technically speaking,' Viv said. 'I can't see a problem, but there is one snag which might rule it out. When I downloaded all the available info on Abbott, there were no photos of him.'

Nash heard the conversation and joined them. 'I appreciate that, so I thought of a way to get hold of one, by going down a different route. I'm no great expert, but I believe football clubs at all levels of the game regularly produce team photos. If we could locate one from when Abbott was playing in England, or in Spain, he would be shown along with his team mates. I thought we — or rather you two — might be able to isolate his image, enhance it, and work the ageing process from there. What do you think?'

'It might work,' Pearce agreed grudgingly. 'But I wouldn't put money on it. Still, it's definitely worth a go, we've nothing to lose.'

'Let's hope we get lucky and locate a team photo with Abbott in it,' Hassan agreed. 'That's going to be our first challenge.'

'Would DVLA or the Passport Office be any help?' Clara asked.

'We can try,' Adil replied.

They set about it, leaving Nash and Mironova to revisit the Keeper files.

* * *

It was late afternoon when Pearce brought them their first piece of good news. 'The passport picture was bad, a typical representation — nothing like the owner. Adil's working on a team photo we found. It's been a heck of a job finding one. It's just unfortunate Abbott didn't play for one of the bigger clubs. They do a lot more press coverage.'

Clara had one reservation regarding the potential outcome of their efforts. Once Pearce and Hassan were out of earshot, she voiced her concern. 'Even if they isolate an image of Abbott and age it, how are we going to know if it's a good resemblance to what he looks like nowadays?'

'That's a question I've been pondering most of the day. I've come up with a possible solution. Always providing the people I'm thinking of are both willing and able to cooperate.'

'Who? I thought everyone surrounding the Keeper was dead?'

'My first candidate is Tim Gunn, but he might be too scared to play ball. The other person I have in mind is Terry Palmer.'

Clara gasped with surprise. She remembered Palmer, the only surviving member of the Country House Bandits, who had been taken prisoner by the Keeper shortly after being released from jail. Palmer had been tortured, and fed an almost lethal cocktail of hallucinogenic drugs.

'I'd forgotten about Palmer,' she admitted. 'Do you think he'll be able to recall anything, given the ordeal he endured?'

'There's only one way to find out. We'll ask him.'

'Do you know where Palmer is?'

'I believe he's living on Carthill estate, providing things worked out OK. You might recall, following what they'd done to him, Palmer went voluntarily into a psychiatric unit for treatment, until he was no longer a danger to himself or others. After his release, he went to live with Norma Walsh — Norma's brother was Joe Lambert,' Nash reminded her. 'He was another of the Country House Bandits, the one who was stabbed to death in an alleyway after he was released from prison. Norma and Terry had been an item when they were teenagers, so it seemed a nice ending when

I discovered they'd got back together. I just hope it worked out for them.'

'How did you get to know all this?'

Nash grinned. 'You could put it down to top-class detective work, but actually, I bumped into them on the high street a few months ago. They were strolling along, hand-in-hand. I intended to tell you, but you were away, and by the time you returned, I'd forgotten.'

* * *

Eventually, Pearce and Hassan were able to present an image they had created using a photograph of Abbott taken when he was nineteen years old. Nash and Mironova examined the finished product, and after a close scrutiny, Nash asked a further favour from their technicians.

'Would it be possible to create two further images, using this as a base? One with a beard, and another with both beard and sunglasses.'

Pearce glanced at Hassan, who nodded, and they returned to their computers.

'I suppose that makes sense, given the description Roy Proctor gave us when we saw him in Felling. The man he saw talking to Tim Gunn,' Clara said.

'Yes, and Proctor's a third person we could show the photo to,' Nash agreed. He paused and added, 'The description Roy gave us tallies with the much older version that we got from Corey Davies, who ran the drugs. However, that was a long time ago, when they were in full swing.'

Nash thought for a moment. 'The beard and sunglasses make sense for quite a different reason. Although Abbott had been playing in Spain for a while, there was an outside chance someone would have recognized him following his return to England. Although he was by no means as famous as a Premier League player, if he encountered someone who was a fan of his club, it'd be game over.'

Clara groaned. 'You're not going to start making football puns, I hope. Things are bad enough without that torment.'

Curious as to his real meaning, she asked, 'Why would it have been "game over" for him?'

Nash smiled at her protest, but explained, 'Abbot supposedly died in that car crash. He would have to assume a completely new identity, hence the beard and the shades. That would be sufficient to throw anyone who was suspicious off the scent.'

'I'm beginning to appreciate how he managed to stay clear of the law for such a long time. Everything he's done involves a huge amount of meticulous planning.'

'That's one side of it. The other, far grimmer way he's avoided justice is by disposing of everyone he considers to be a threat. That's the most ruthless way of covering your tracks I've ever encountered.'

* * *

It didn't take Pearce and Hassan long to deliver the new images, and after inspecting them, Nash said, 'Thanks, but I've just realized these won't work.'

'Why, what's wrong with them?' Viv was confused.

'I've just remembered that every description we've been given of the person known as the Keeper, said he not only wore dark glasses, but he was muffled up.'

'One minute,' Adil said, as he hurried back to his computer. Moments later, he returned bearing another picture, same as the other, but with half the face hidden by a dark scarf. 'How's that?'

'Not out!' said Viv, ignoring the frowns from the others. He stared at them. 'Well, if we're doing football puns, I thought we could include cricket too.'

There was a communal sigh.

Nash told Clara, 'I think we should visit Gunn at the remand centre and ask him to take a look at these. If he won't do so, or if he's unwilling to confirm their accuracy, we'll have to resort to Plan B, which I'm reluctant to do.'

'By Plan B, I assume you mean Terry Palmer. Why are you reluctant to do that?'

'I'm concerned that if these images are accurate, seeing the person who caused him so much anguish might be a retrograde step in his recovery. If it wasn't vitally important, I wouldn't even consider it.'

Twenty-four hours later, they received information that provided another reason to re-interview Gunn. Nash reported this to Clara as they were en route. 'Ballistics confirms the weapon found in Gunn's house is the one used in the Transit van murders at the quarry, so we need to add that to his charge sheet.'

Much as Nash had predicted, the visit to the remand centre proved fruitless, or so Clara thought. When she expressed her disappointment to Nash, she was surprised by his reply. 'I don't think it was a totally wasted effort. It might have seemed futile, because Gunn failed to identify the Keeper. However, his body language seemed to indicate the images were reasonably accurate. Did you notice he barely glanced at them, then looked away? He didn't look at the pictures again, nor did he look at us. He kept his gaze averted until we left. Having said that, as we haven't obtained confirmation from Gunn, I'm afraid we'll have to risk involving Terry Palmer. With luck, he might turn out to be our whistle-blower.'

'Mike, I did warn you, no more football puns, please.' Clara paused. 'At least we got one positive result — nailing Gunn for the quarry murders.'

'There wasn't much chance of him avoiding that!'

CHAPTER FORTY-TWO

Nash's first task was to phone Norma Walsh. He explained the reason for showing Terry Palmer the photos, emphasizing the importance of obtaining confirmation of their accuracy. 'We need to identify this man, but I was reluctant to involve Terry, because it might be detrimental to his state of mind. Would you ask him if he's prepared to do this, and also reassure him that he isn't in trouble? In fact, Terry's cooperation will be most helpful, and could prove pivotal in bringing this monster to justice.'

'Terry's gone shopping, but I'll have a word with him when he returns, then call you back. I think he'll be eager to help, in view of the suffering that beast caused him — and many others.'

Having been given the green light, Nash and Clara drove to the Carthill estate. Clara was surprised by Norma's appearance. When she'd last seen her, Norma had been suffering the double grief of her husband's death from cancer, plus the murder of her brother. At that time, she had appeared to be on the verge of middle age, belying her date of birth.

Now, Norma seemed to have shed years. She looked well, happy, and vivacious, much more like a young woman who hadn't yet celebrated her thirtieth birthday. The detectives followed her inside to the lounge. Terry was seated, totally at ease in an armchair, as he sipped tea from a mug Clara thought was approaching the size of a goldfish bowl.

It wasn't only Norma whose appearance had improved dramatically. When they'd interviewed Palmer following his ordeal, Clara had wondered if he would survive. If the trauma might take its toll on either his wasted body or his mind, scrambled by the drugs he had been force fed.

She barely recognized the contented young man who greeted them with a warm, happy smile. Seeing the loving glance that passed between Terry and Norma, Clara accurately identified the source of his high spirits.

Nash remarked on how well he looked, and Norma replied on his behalf. 'Terry's much better since he came to live with me. He's even managed to get a job. He starts next week. Actually, I think it's just an excuse to get out of the decorating I'm planning.'

'Are you sure you're going to be OK doing this, Terry? I don't want it to set off the nightmares you had.'

'I haven't suffered them for a while.' Palmer smiled. 'I'm happy to help if I can.'

'Terry did have a few nightmares at first,' Norma told the detectives, 'but I soon found a way of distracting him which he seemed to enjoy. So much so, that he actually woke me up several times because he said he felt a nightmare coming on, and wanted me to help him. I think that's the best excuse I've ever heard.'

Having obtained Palmer's confirmation that one of the images was a faithful representation of the figure in his admittedly blurred memory, Nash ended the meeting. As they were leaving, Nash assured the couple that he would inform them as soon as they'd brought the case to a successful conclusion. He added his delight at their obvious happiness and wished them well for the future, sentiments Clara was pleased to endorse.

'Now we know we're on the right track, all we have to do is find someone else, someone who knows Dean Abbott's new identity, and moreover can confirm it via these photos.' Nash added a sobering afterthought. 'How we're going to do so, I have absolutely no idea.'

* * *

Nash convened what he referred to as a brainstorming session. In doing so, he had little or no hope of a positive result, but in this instance, he was totally wrong. Furthermore, the spark of inspiration came from the most unlikely source.

Nash had invited the chief constable and Superintendent Fleming to attend, both to view the images for the first time, and also to contribute their ideas as to how to tackle what seemed an insurmountable problem.

'OK, now we know who he is — or was, before he assumed a new identity — and potentially what he looks like nowadays. But what else do we know about the Keeper?'

There was a short silence as they pondered Nash's question, before Clara responded, 'He's totally ruthless, will go to any lengths to obtain money, committing multifarious crimes, and will stop at nothing to prevent exposure.'

Pearce joined in. 'We also know he's been involved in high-end burglary, people trafficking, prostitution, internet fraud, vehicle theft and drug dealing. Add to that his liking for fancy cars, and I don't think we'll find him on the Westlea council estate. He's more likely to be holed up in some posh mansion out in the countryside.'

'The other thing we should consider, now he's lost his drugs empire, is he'll probably be looking for new ways to maintain his affluent lifestyle,' Jackie Fleming commented.

The gloomy silence was eventually broken by the newest member of the team. DC Hassan had been dwelling on something Viv Pearce had said. 'What about dealers? They might provide us with a name.'

'That won't work, Adil. The Keeper lost his drugs network when the Albanians muscled in, remember?'

Hassan grinned. 'Sorry, you got me wrong. I wasn't referring to drug dealers. Viv mentioned the Keeper's love of fancy motors, principally Mercedes, so I thought if we show that image around Mercedes dealerships, they might recognize him as one of their clients.'

Nash's reaction was immediate. 'Adil, that is sheer brilliance. The only minor drawback is, we don't know which dealership he uses. I suggest we start with the nearest and work outward from there.'

Clara added another useful suggestion. 'We could also mention that the person we're looking for might have been accompanied by a dark-haired woman with a Spanish accent.'

'Good idea,' Nash said. 'We could even mention the name Estela Moreno, which might be a key factor.'

'Who is Estela Moreno?' Ruth Edwards asked.

'That's the woman who allegedly died alongside Abbott in that car crash.'

'Surely she would also have changed her name.'

'Not necessarily. Nobody in UK would have reason to recognize her, she's Spanish. I believe those are both fairly common names in Spain. Apparently, "Moreno" means someone with dark hair, which seems appropriate. Luckily, I'm married to a walking Spanish dictionary.'

Ruth Edwards added an amendment to their plans to contact motor dealers. 'I think only our officers should conduct the visits. I realize this might mean a heavy workload, but if we keep it within our own force, it will lessen the chance of what we're doing reaching the wrong ears.'

* * *

The team didn't have to wait long before they had a result. DC Hassan had been charged with visiting the Mercedes dealership based in Netherdale.

As he watched the sales manager, Adil knew from the man's expression that he'd struck gold. 'Yes, I think this man is one of our customers, although there are some marked differences.'

'What might they be?'

'This photo doesn't show the terrible scar that runs all the way down his face from his scalp.'

'That difference poses a bit of a problem. Perhaps it would be as well if you gave me your customer's details. We can check him out discreetly. I wouldn't want anyone to get concerned without reason.'

'What's this all about? If you want, I could ring him and save you the bother.'

'No, please don't do that on any account. This is a highly sensitive issue, which must be treated in complete confidence. If word of our request got out, it wouldn't reflect well on your company's reputation in the local community — especially if that's not the man I'm looking for.'

'OK, I'll get you the details.' As he was handing them to the detective, he added, 'There is one other aspect of that man's appearance which doesn't show on a head-and-shoulders shot. He has a deformity to his left hand, so the cars he buys have to be specially adapted.'

Having reiterated the need for discretion, and obtained the dealer's assurance on that score, Adil headed to Helmsdale, reporting his success to Clara en route.

'Well done, Adil. Mike's on the phone at the moment, but I'll tell him as soon as he's free.' Clara did so, before gesturing to Nash's phone as she asked, 'What did West Yorkshire want to tell you?'

'They examined bank statements retrieved from Richard Petersen's safe deposit box. These show several very large payments received from a company by the name of Seaman and Banks Ltd. I think the fact that David Seaman and Gordon Banks were two of the most renowned and talented English goalkeepers in the last fifty or sixty years suggests that the name is a cover-up for the Keeper's activities, don't you? Get Viv to do a Companies House search and see who the directors of this outfit are. With luck, one of them might tally with the name Adil's got for us.'

* * *

When Hassan arrived back in CID, he needed no encouragement to reveal what the motor dealer had told him. 'The sales manager believes the man in the photo is one of their customers, but he mentioned two big differences. Their customer has a very bad scar running from his scalp down as far as his chin. He's also got a deformed left hand. Their customer is called David Gordon, and he lives at Ghyll Bank Hall.'

'That's brilliant, Adil, and it tallies with what we've just learned from West Yorkshire. Richard Petersen's bank statements show he received a fair number of five-figure sums from a company. That company's directors are David and Olivia Gordon, of Ghyll Bank Hall.' Nash gestured to Pearce, and added, 'Viv also discovered that Seaman and Banks own a scrapyard in Middlesbrough where we suspect the stolen cars ended up.'

'After all these years of secrecy, he's got complacent, hasn't he?'

'You may be right, Clara. But now, I'm going to phone Jackie Fleming so she can arrange for a search warrant. I'm also going to ask for an ARU team and backup to be on site when we go to make the arrests. I'm not taking any chances, given that we know how dangerous this couple are. In the meantime, Adil, I want you and Viv to exercise your aviation talents.

'I want you to take the drones to Stark Ghyll and fly them from somewhere near the summit over a wide area. Don't restrict the operation to the target property and nearby. That would appear suspicious. If by any chance someone asks why you're doing it, tell them it's a new toy, or you're providing footage for Google Maps — anything!'

* * *

Two days later, the afternoon was spent watching the drone footage. Present were Superintendent Fleming and Chief Constable Edwards, plus the leader of the Armed Response Unit tasked with leading the raid.

The chief constable had stressed that nothing should be left to chance. 'These are two of the most violent and ruthless criminals we have had to deal with. A list of the people they murdered or paid to have slaughtered would take ages to recite. And we don't know how many people are in the property. Take every precaution, and whatever happens, please return safely.'

CHAPTER FORTY-THREE

Shortly after 7 a.m. the team was in position outside Ghyll Bank Hall. The ARU leader confirmed the house was surrounded and all his men were in place. Nash had similar assurances from Pearce and Hassan, whose drones were now hovering above the property and surrounding area.

Carrying a megaphone, he approached the door and pressed the doorbell. There was a prolonged silence. He tried again. Silence.

In the large dining kitchen to the rear of the property the blinds were closed hastily, as the armed officers were seen taking up their positions. The man known for years only as the Keeper looked at his mistress. It was clear from her horrified expression that being found had shocked her as much as it had him. All their careful planning had failed. Their problems were immense, and there was only one possible ending.

They listened to the doorbell, not once, but twice. Then a voice came over a megaphone. 'Dean Abbott, Estela Moreno — this house is surrounded by armed police officers. Resistance would be futile. Exit the building via the front door with your hands raised above your head, and lie face down. Do not carry any objects. Officers have instructions to use their firearms if necessary. Do it now!'

The Keeper reached out and took the woman in his arms. 'This is it, the end,' he told her. 'We'll go together, as we agreed?'

She ran her fingers along his scarred face and smiled. 'Yes, let's go together.'

* * *

Nash repeated his instructions. Tension mounted during the prolonged silence, before the officers recoiled at the loud sound of a gunshot, followed seconds later by another.

'Shots fired, shots fired!' the ARU leader bellowed into his radio. 'Anyone injured?' Having received reassurance, he continued, 'Shields up at all times. Wait for my word.' When Pearce and Hassan reported no sign of anyone at the windows, he signalled to the officer carrying the door enforcer to move forward and watched as he swung the big red key.

'Entry team in now!' the ARU leader ordered.

Meeting with no resistance, the armed officers stormed the building. It was several minutes, which seemed like hours to those waiting outside, before they declared the house to be secure.

'House is clear. There are two occupants, one male, one female, both deceased. COD in each case is a single gunshot wound to the head. The weapon is nearby. It looks like a classic M and S scene.'

Clara looked baffled by the apparent reference to Marks and Spencer, the retail giant. Seeing her bewilderment, Nash told her, 'That's ARU slang for murder and suicide.'

Once they had donned protective clothing, they entered the house and headed for the kitchen, following directions given by an armed officer. As they stared at the two corpses, Nash was struck by the accuracy of the images produced by Pearce and Hassan to the man lying on the floor. They had only missed his disfigurement.

'I wonder what caused all that?' Clara gestured to the vivid scars on his face and arm.

Nash had been looking at the large patches of pale skin. Those blotches provided a clue. 'Fire damage, I guess.'

'What do you mean?'

'We need Mexican Pete to confirm. I'm guessing those injuries were caused when Dean Abbott torched the car containing his wife and Estela's husband. Maybe he got too close to the point of ignition. Perhaps there was a sudden gust of wind. Whatever the cause, those injuries provide another explanation for Abbott's reluctance to appear without his face hidden.'

Having reported the outcome to Jackie Fleming, Nash told her, 'We need Mexican Pete and a forensic team here ASAP. The crime scene is restricted to the kitchen, so the rest should be plain sailing, although the size of the property will probably mean they'll be here for a fortnight.'

* * *

The pathologist was in a serious mood, as Clara could tell by his failure to try and wind Nash up. His early examination when kneeling by the bodies, led to a suggestion that surprised the detectives. 'I'll need the post-mortem plus forensic examination before stating categorically, but I believe this was a twin suicide, rather than murder suicide. The angle of the wounds is more consistent with them being self-inflicted — as indicated by that second gun under the table.'

Nash nodded acceptance before turning the site over to CSI. 'We're going to look through the rest of the house, because there might be pertinent evidence elsewhere,' Nash told them.

During their search, one of their finds was the discovery of a bookshelf containing a series of diaries, which turned out to have been compiled by Estela Moreno since the beginning of her affair with Dean Abbott. One of the earlier entries confirmed the accuracy of Nash's speculations regarding the cause of Abbott's injuries. The description of the murders, and the staged car accident, made horrific reading.

Far more revealing were the segments charting the couple's criminal escapades. From these, the detectives learned that Estela Moreno was far more than simply a willing participant. She was as much a leader as Abbott. Even the murders they had commissioned were described, some of them in gruesome detail.

'The matter-of-fact tone of the entries makes them appear like items on a shopping list,' Clara commented.

The diaries also revealed the motive behind some of the murders. The shooting of the directors of Dale Investments followed the discovery that they had falsely understated the return from their online scams when remitting the percentage owed to the Keeper. Likewise, Josh Proctor and his companion had been killed as punishment for exceeding their remit when confronted by the homeowner, Raymond Watkins, during the Hanoi burglary.

Reading these and other entries, Nash agreed with Clara's comments. Even the most brutal crimes seemed, to the writer, to be nothing more than everyday events. When he had completed his first examination of the journals, Nash came up with an idea, but deferred mentioning it, preferring to concentrate on more immediate tasks.

* * *

'We should call Geoff Lister, Joanne Fawcett, and Terry Palmer, to inform them their nightmare is finally over,' Nash suggested, as he and Clara were leaving the house.

'Yes, I was thinking along those lines, but it's a shame we'll not be able to put those evil swine on trial for the horrific things they've done. If we'd done that, the rest of the world would learn what monsters they were. Not only that, but there must be quite a number of people still living in terror. We'll be unable to contact them and ease their fears.'

Clara's thoughts tallied with his to such an extent that Nash was determined to pursue his plan, but he would need official sanction for something that was outside the bounds of normal procedure. To begin the process, he told Clara, 'As soon as CSI has finished with their forensic investigation into those diaries, we'll take them to Netherdale and let Jackie and the chief constable read them.'

'Why is that so important?'

'I believe there's a possible way to make everything those two vermin did public, and provide reassurance to many people still afraid of the Keeper.' He explained what he had in mind, and Clara saw the logic in his reasoning.

* * *

Having received a phone call from Nash telling them their troubles were over, Geoff and Joanne began discussing their future, the first time they had dared to do so.

'First of all, you should phone your mother, introduce yourself, tell her you're now safe, and arrange to meet up,' Joanne told him.

'I'll certainly do that, and I'd like her to meet you. I was also wondering where we should settle down. I don't want to stay on the canal boat forever, although it does hold some precious memories for me — especially the thunderstorms.'

'I agree, but I wouldn't want you to sell the boat, because it has similar memories for me too. Maybe we should keep it and use it as a holiday retreat, maybe taking it on some of those canal journeys they show on TV. We'd have to make one or two minor alterations, though.'

'What sort of alterations?'

'I was thinking we could convert the smaller cabin by removing the bed. That would leave ample room for a cot and a playpen.'

It took a moment for Geoff to catch on. Joanne's slightly nervous smile gave him a clue. 'Does that mean what I think?'

'Absolutely, and it's hardly surprising after the past few weeks.'

* * *

The press conference was noisy — journalists and all sections of the media filled the local sports hall. The chief constable stood in front of the microphone. On either side stood Nash and Superintendent Fleming.

'Ladies and gentlemen, good afternoon.' She raised her hand for quiet and looked round the room as cameras flashed. 'I can report that the body found on the canal boat at Mile Marina has been identified and no further action will be necessary.'

The cameras flashed again, along with shouts for more information.

The chief waited for silence. 'I also want to inform the public that in the past twenty-four hours my detective team, led by DI Nash, have managed to solve a large number of serious crimes which have been committed over a long number of years. A gang, named the Country House Bandits by the media, committed high-value burglaries over many years, and were also involved in various other nefarious activities. Their leader was a figure known only as the Keeper. I can confirm this man to be Dean Abbott, a former footballer.'

There was a gasp around the room.

Again, she waited for silence.

'I should add that yesterday, in the process of serving an arrest warrant at the property, before my officers could gain entry the offender and his partner took their own lives.' The chief paused and looked round the room. 'I have reported this matter to the IOPC as a matter of course.'

Cameras flashed again and questions came from around the hall.

She raised her hand. 'Dean Abbott was also wanted in Spain for questioning about the murder of his wife, Cynthia Abbott, and Carlos Moreno, his current partner's husband, some years ago.'

There was stunned silence as the press waited like hungry lions for more.

'He was also wanted on charges of conspiracy to murder Byron Morris and Audrey Morris, whose bodies were found in the old cottage hospital.'

The chief paused, took a deep breath and began to read from her list very slowly. 'And also Frank Watson, Jo Lambert, Peter Swallow, Lauren Watson, Cindy Swallow, George Briggs, Arthur Fawcett, Gabriel Welham, Thelma Daley, Joshua Proctor, Derek Bates and Nicholas Balderstone. And also, the attempted murders of Corey Davies, Tamsin Charlton, Geoffrey Lister, Joanne Fawcett and Terence Palmer.'

She stopped reading and raised her eyes from the paper, folding it in half. 'Those are the ones we are aware of — there may be others. There will be no questions today. Thank you for coming.' She turned and walked towards the door.

As they left the hall, Nash remarked to Jackie, 'The chief was right.'

'About what?'

'It did take her ages to recite the list.'

* * *

Some weeks later, having received the chief constable's blessing, Nash put forward his idea to Geoff Lister, who was now living on the canal boat with Joanne.

'We need someone to tell the victims' stories, because without a trial there could be many more people continuing to live with the fear you and Joanne have had to endure. That must end, and we believe you're the man to do it. As I recall, you used to be quite good at writing.' He grinned. 'I've even had sanction to reveal parts of the story that would otherwise remain hidden.'

Having received Geoff's wholehearted approval, all Nash and his colleagues could do was sit and await the outcome.

* * *

When Edward Michael Lister was born, Nash was proud to stand sponsor as the child's godfather. His pride, though, was outdone by that of the boy's parents, and even more so by the child's grandmother, Sylvia Cross.

248

Twelve months down the line, there was a double cause for celebration in the Lister household. Not only was it Edward Michael's first birthday, but the event coincided with the news that Geoff Lister's true crime thriller, *Dead or Alive*, had become a worldwide number-one bestseller.

THE END

ACKNOWLEDGEMENTS

My grateful thanks to the entire team at Joffe Books for their help with what has been a difficult project. Working with Laura, my editor Jodi, Kate, Matthew and Elane, has helped enormously. I just hope *Dead or Alive* resolves some previously unanswered questions for my readers, whose satisfaction is important to me.

My own knowledge of Spanish was also very helpful.

As always, I should thank my in-house editor, Val, who has helped so much, and of course my reader, Wendy McPhee. They both enjoy pointing out the error of my ways.

THE JOFFE BOOKS STORY

We began in 2014 when Jasper agreed to publish his mum's much-rejected romance novel and it became a bestseller.

Since then we've grown into the largest independent publisher in the UK. We're extremely proud to publish some of the very best writers in the world, including Joy Ellis, Faith Martin, Caro Ramsay, Helen Forrester, Simon Brett and Robert Goddard. Everyone at Joffe Books loves reading and we never forget that it all begins with the magic of an author telling a story.

We are proud to publish talented first-time authors, as well as established writers whose books we love introducing to a new generation of readers.

We won Trade Publisher of the Year at the Independent Publishing Awards in 2023 and Best Publisher Award in 2024 at the People's Book Prize. We have been shortlisted for Independent Publisher of the Year at the British Book Awards for the last five years, and were shortlisted for the Diversity and Inclusivity Award at the 2022 Independent Publishing Awards. In 2023 we were shortlisted for Publisher of the Year at the RNA Industry Awards, and in 2024 we were shortlisted at the CWA Daggers for the Best Crime and Mystery Publisher.

We built this company with your help, and we love to hear from you, so please email us about absolutely anything bookish at feedback@joffebooks.com.

If you want to receive free books every Friday and hear about all our new releases, join our mailing list here: www.joffebooks. com/freebooks.

And when you tell your friends about us, just remember: it's pronounced Joffe as in coffee or toffee!

9 781805 730965